4-F BLUES

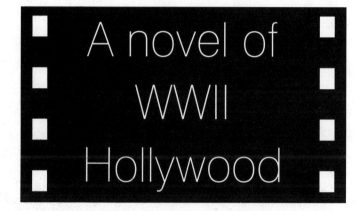

A novel of
WWII
Hollywood

CHARLES RUBIN

NEW
CENTURY
PUBLISHERS
Petaluma, California

Library of Congress-in-Publishing Data

Rubin, Charles
4-F blues: a novel of WWll Hollywood
Charles Rubin
p. cm
LCCN 00-91038
ISBN 0-9679790-0-5

1. World War, 1939-1945--Fiction. 2. Motion
Picture Industry--California--Los Angeles--
Fiction. 3. Hollywood (Los Angeles, Calif.)--
Fiction. 4. Sabotage--Fiction. 1. Title

PS3568.U19F68 2001   813' .6
QB100-901064

Cover Design and type formatting: Estera Alvarez
Editorial Consultant: Verna Shaheen
Photography: Bonnie Hansen-Perdue

Printed in the United States of America
First Edition
1 2 3 4 5 6 7 8 9 10

A portion of the proceeds from this book will go to the
WWll Memorial in Washington, D.C.

NewCentury Publishers
P.O. Box 751434,
Petaluma, CA 94975
tel. (707) 769 9808
Email: editor@newcenturypublishers.com
www.NewCenturyPublishers.com

Alfred S. Los Banos, U.S. Army
Kenny Ruth, U.S. Navy
Don Schneider, U.S. Army
Frances Langford, singer
Doris Miller, Steward and Hero, U.S. Navy
Jerry Blank, U.S. Marine Corps
Hattie M. Stone, Norma Edwards, and
Rita Jacobson, WAVES
Howard K. Petschel, U.S. Army Air Corps
Bobbie Omoth, WACS
Cheryl Walker, Actress
Earl Holger Sorensen, U.S. Navy,
The U.S.S. Arizona Navy Band

For all the guys who wanted to serve but were
classified as 4-F* for medical reasons

And for my dear father,
Harry Rubin

*4-F: A classification during the Second World War for young men not fit for
military service. Those men, in many cases, had to endure their own private
disappointments along with public ridicule.

Acknowlegements

Thanks for your encouragement and support:
Melinda Young
Tom Driskill
Frances Hogan
Carol Bianco
Pam and Grainger Brown
Diana, Lady Avebury
Janie Booth
Marlena and Dr. Mark Fahey
Sonni Scher-Wengert
Winni Lum
Sabine Stetson
JD Warrick
Estera Alvarez
Dorothy Sikorski
John and Annette Nicolls
Bonnie Hansen-Perdue
Izumi Motai
Jaclyn Grace
Mark Prusinowski
Daedalus Howell
Jack Rubin
Marion Hayes
Irene Levy,
and my wonderful wife, Betty

Other books by Charles Rubin

Hard Sell, a novel

Don't Let Your Kids Kill You: A Guide
For Parents of Drug and Alcohol Addicted Children

4-F BLUES

A novel of
WWII
Hollywood

Part I

Day 1

Chapter 1

The lone dive bomber broke through a mass of cloud into a Technicolor blue sky and zoomed overhead. It was a SBD Dauntless of the type deployed by the Navy and Marine Corps in the battle for Guadalcanal. At the controls, a young Navy pilot, on his way back to his carrier from a reconnaissance mission, spotted the elusive Japanese battleship, *Shigato*. There it was on the silvery waters below, the ship responsible for having sunk more Allied tonnage than any other in the Japanese fleet. It was a killer on the prowl that always, as if by magic, managed to escape the wrath of its enemies. But it wouldn't escape this time.

The pilot let out a cry of joy. This was a prize catch for him, one that he vowed to send straight to the bottom of the ocean. Without as much as a moment's hesitation, he dove in a perfect arc toward his target, dodging the sudden and fierce barrage of the ship's gunfire.

"This one's for Pearl Harbor," the pilot shouted as he released a 500 pound bomb. It pierced the *Shigato*'s upper three decks, detonating the massive magazine stores below. The ship, mortally wounded, lifted almost completely out of the water in much the same way the doomed U.S.S. *Arizona* had risen and then sunk during the Japanese raid on Pearl Harbor.

"And here's a little something for Bataan," he again shouted, releasing another bomb. This one hit the bridge squarely, leaving it a tangle of twisted, red-hot metal.

As he watched, the *Shigato* stopped steaming. The bow turned aimlessly north, then south. The rudder wouldn't answer. Amidst the fire and smoke, there was complete pandemonium: compartments filling rapidly with water, sailors panicking, officers shouting orders. The eerie sound of sirens was soon silenced by the all-engulfing sea. The last vision of the *Shigato* was that of its vertical plunge to the ocean floor.

Wearing a happy grin now that it was all over, the pilot winked at a photo he kept taped to the controls panel. It was of his girl, a lovely young woman with her hair in an elaborate pompadour only slightly higher than his own stiffly pomaded version.

She looked like the all-American girl and with his blond hair, blue eyes and dazzling smile, he looked like the all-American boy. He also had a rich baritone which he used to belt out a rousing *Fighting To Keep America Free* while homeward bound. But his singing suddenly trailed off. Coming after him was what appeared to be Hirohito's entire air force, guns blazing orange death.

The pilot quickly assessed the situation and realized there was no way he'd be able to return to his carrier. Not now, not ever. If he did head back, he'd be leading the enemy right to his ship, his shipmates. No, he knew what he'd have to do. He'd have to face down the enemy and perhaps die for it. But hadn't many others like him done just that for America? Not only in this war, but in all the wars dating back to the Revolutionary War? He asked all these questions aloud and he decided, again aloud, that if they could do it, so could he.

But there was another story within this story. The young

man had come from a wealthy family and hadn't been accepted by his fellow pilots as one of them. His arrogant attitude had branded him as a rich kid who didn't care about anyone. Certainly not for the Navy or his country. But now, today, his concern for his shipmates and this selfless act would reverse what everyone thought of him. They would see that he was a good guy after all.

Japanese bullets were now making contact with his tail assembly. In a moment or two they might hit the fuel tank. The pilot grabbed his girl's photograph and pushed back his canopy to bail out. A bullet tore through his arm though he expressed none of the excruciating pain he was feeling. He climbed out of the crippled plane's cockpit and jumped.

He wasn't a good target until his parachute opened, and then the Japanese converged, firing like mad, their bullets miraculously missing him.

"Okay, you rats," the pilot roared, "Maybe it's guys like me who have to pay the price for freedom, but I'm not going down without taking a few of you with me."

With his good hand, he drew his pistol and fired, getting one of the enemy right between the eyes. The dead pilot's head jerked back and a trickle of blood emerged from his mouth as his plane dove straight into the water below and exploded upon contact.

The pilot, with every hair in place and a white scarf draped rakishly around his neck, hit two more planes in their gas tanks, causing them to collide and disintegrate midair.

"I didn't qualify as an expert at the rifle range for nothing," he announced.

From his left came a Zero, abruptly cut off as he coolly pumped some bullets into the prop mechanism. The plane simply stalled and fell.

The enemy had flown so close that it was possible to tell his rank of first lieutenant.

"C'mon, you lily-livered cowards. Come and get it," the pilot bellowed while reloading his pistol single-handedly.

One by one he knocked the Zeros out of the sky until there weren't any left.

And then he was alone, a tiny figure drifting toward the choppy waters off Guadalcanal.

Chapter 2

Sitting in front of a viewing screen in one of Grove Pictures editing rooms, Tom Driscoll. a Hollywood stuntman, watched himself drifting not toward the choppy waters off Guadalcanal, but what were, in actuality, the choppy waters off Santa Monica, California.

He was watching the rough cut of a projected biggie for Grove, slated for an early '43 release. It was a picture that would certainly enhance the reputation and he-man image of its highly popular, highly publicized, and not to mention highly profitable star, Vance Varley, who'd portrayed the young Navy pilot.

"So what do you think of it?" the editor, Erne Parkin, asked as he flicked on the lights.

"It's a piece of shit," Tom answered. He was the only one in the editing room besides Erne, his long-standing buddy.

The movie was being called *Dive-Bomber Rendezvous* and in it Tom had been assigned to do what Vance Varley had been too squeamish to do, and in fact what most of Hollywood's 1942 crop of so-called rugged males were too squeamish to do: their own stunts.

This wasn't the same Hollywood that Tom knew when he first hit the place back in '37. In those days, stars like Clark Gable, Jimmy Stewart, and Douglas Fairbanks, Jr. didn't mind how difficult or dangerous a task was. As far as they were concerned, no mere stuntman was going to do their jobs for them, not if they had anything to say about it.

"I don't ask a stuntman to kiss the leading lady for me and I don't ask him to risk his life for me, either," Gable was reputed to have once boasted.

But now Gable was a private in the Army, Stewart was serving under General Jimmy Doolittle in the Army Air Corps, and Fairbanks was a Navy officer fighting the Nazis in the North Atlantic. Even Ty Power was off in the Marines.

Which left Vance Varley in the position of being one of the last male stars left, a position he was sure to hold onto for the duration of the war. He was the ultimate hero figure for teenage boys while also being the heart throb dream fantasy of females of all ages. His movies portrayed him as consistently, and single-handedly, destroying the enemy: A battalion of Germans in *Berlin Bombardier* and half the Japanese navy and air force in the soon-to-be-released tale of selfless heroism and undying patriotism in *Dive-Bomber Rendezvous*.

Besides these kinds of movies, he'd also been teamed with Maggie Graym, Hollywood's top female box office draw, in a series of mindless popular musicals in which he sang and danced, neither very well.

"What do you mean, a piece of shit?" Erne Parkin asked, as if he had just heard Tom's reply. He was concentrating on his work, splicing endless lengths of film in the process of either adding or deleting scenes and/or bits of scenes.

Erne was what was considered an "old timer" by Hollywood standards, having arrived out west more than thirty years before, straight from the fabled studios of Astoria, Long Island where Mary Pickford and Rudolph Valentino had made their first films. He'd grown up with the film industry and had witnessed all of it. The silent era, the scandals, the emergence of the big studios and the big studio bosses who now ran Hollywood with an iron fist.

And he'd paid his dues. He'd moved up through the studio system from editorial apprentice to assistant editor to editor to his present job, at age fifty-nine, as one of the senior editors at Grove.

Erne was good. With his talent for knowing where to make the precise cut, and his practiced eye for detail, he could have been one of the big shot editors in the film business. But he never went out of his way to promote himself or to make alliances with those in power. Instead, he took his luck as it came and shirked both studio politicians and filmland phonies.

This was something he had in common with his friend, Tom Driscoll: an annoyance of things pretentious in a town that couldn't be labeled anything but.

It had been this dislike of Hollywood glitter that had helped form the friendship between Tom and Erne. Shunning the croquet mallets and martinis crowd, Erne preferred tossing back boilermakers with his old cronies. These were the gaffers and electricians and lighting technicians and sound men and camera men. In other words, the people who did all the work in getting movies made. They'd meet regularly over at Jimmy's Tropical Bar and Grill off Melrose. Hollywood, being a place where everyone was always looking for the big break, it was nice to do your drinking at Jimmy's with guys who couldn't care less.

Tom was one of those guys. After a few conversations between him and Erne, they became good pals, though Tom was thirty years younger. Many a weekend would find them fishing at Lake Arrowhead or taking in the races at Santa Anita. And Tom's small rented house in the Hollywood Hills was always a safe haven for Erne when he was in trouble with his latest wife, which had been often. At the moment he was between wives and was liking it that way.

"Well, we made old Vance look pretty convincing," Erne said, holding some footage over the lightbox. "From what I hear, the guy never got more than four feet off the ground and the producers even had to get down on their knees and beg him to go up as far as that."

Erne was referring to the fact that Vance, known to be terrified of heights, had done all his combat scenes in a stationary cockpit in the studio. As for his courageous parachute jump, he'd been fitted into a cleverly designed rig that elevated him four feet off the ground while previously shot scenes of aerial warfare and actual newsreel footage were being run off on a curved screen behind, above and below him.

The special effects that were added—along with the long shots of Tom leaping from an actual plane—attempted to give the film as much realism as possible, which isn't saying much. It was like the scene in the *Sun Valley Serenade* with Sonia Henie carrying on a conversation with John Payne while hurtling down one of the most dangerous ski slopes in Idaho, if not the world. If audiences believed that was possible, they would believe anything.

"You're the only one who took any risks making this picture," Erne continued. "Okay, okay, so that's what they pay you to do, that's your job, but ten fucking times outta the plane? I mean, what the hell is going on with that director? What's his name? Bradford? Don't he know that film stock is getting damned scarce around here? I got no less than ten takes of you jumping out that plane. Each and every one of them good. Each and every one of them identical. You know they continue to let all them idiots and morons who think they know something about how to make a movie use up all our film supply and guess what? There ain't gonna be no more film supply and I'll tell you something else. There ain't gonna be no more Hollywood."

Erne's never-ending stream of verbal diarrhea continued as he put *Dive-Bomber Rendezvous* back on the projector to review the credits which listed, amongst others, the lovely, fragile, Jane Allen who had played the young pilot's girlfriend.

"Well," Erne said, "one thing this picture's got, if nothing else, is Jane Allen. Ain't she a beauty? I ain't seen an actress that sweet and pretty and pure since Lillian Gish was a girl. She's got a big future ahead of her in this town, that's for sure. In fact, I wouldn't be surprised if she was lent out to Selznick for The *Song of Bernadette*, that movie they're making about the French girl who said she saw a vision of the Virgin Mary."

"It'll never happen," Tom said when Erne was finally finished conjecturing.

"Oh, yeah?" Erne challenged. "How can you be so sure?"

"Because they've already cast someone called Jennifer Jones in the part. I read it in the trade paper."

"Well, they shoulda cast Jane," Erne said. "You only have to take one look at her to know she couldn't be anything but a virgin. This girl is so innocent-looking she makes Shirley Temple look like a madam."

Tom had been hearing a lot about this Jane Allen recently. Grove Pictures was giving her an enormous buildup. She was clearly being groomed as the most stainless, chaste, and unsullied of all Hollywood's leading ladies and it had been announced recently that she would star in *Nine Nuns in a Jeep*, with the production to begin early in the new year. This bit of news was something else Tom had caught in the trades.

"Hey, I gotta get going," Tom said, suddenly noticing the time.

"Who you got a date with tonight?" Erne asked.

"Betty Grable, Dorothy Lamour and Lana Turner. Only thing is I'll have to share them with a couple of thousand soldiers, sailors, and marines."

"Oh, the canteen again, huh?" Erne was referring to the Hollywood Canteen that had recently opened. Tom was helping out on a regular basis, doing whatever jobs had to be done.

"Yeah. They need all the help they can get these days." Like its counterpart in New York, the Stage Door Canteen, the Hollywood Canteen relied heavily on volunteers. There were, at present, 42 unions and guilds offering the services of its caterers, painters, carpenters, electricians, actors, and actresses for the duration of the war.

"Lemme buy you a beer before you head over there," Erne said, looking through a mile of film for a particular section. "I just have to insert a little more of the Japanese battleship sinking and a little more of the Jap pilot getting it between the eyes. That's what the public likes, you know."

"You mean that's what the recruiting officers like," Tom replied sarcastically. "Do you know how many guys are going to join up when they see that movie?"

"Plenty," Erne said, focusing his attention on what he was doing. "And you're pissed off as hell because you can't be one of them."

Erne heard the words that came out of his mouth at the same time that Tom did and stopped short. He glanced at Tom to see what his reaction had been. For what seemed an eternity, there was that awkward silence that takes place when one person has said something to another person for which he is instantly sorry.

"Me and my big mouth," Erne said.

"Forget it," Tom said, knowing that Erne, who didn't have a mean bone in his body, hadn't meant anything. But he couldn't help thinking back, with some degree of bitterness, to December 8, 1941, the day after Japan's sneak attack on Pearl Harbor.

Tom had arrived at dawn outside the U.S. Army recruitment station off La Brea along with about two hundred other young men eager to go off and fight the Japanese whose bombing of the American fleet had incensed all Americans.

Inside, the medics had put Tom through the usual tests and had discovered him to have an irregular heartbeat. And even though Tom, with the build of Johnny Weissmuller, was in otherwise top condition, he was written off their books.

Tom couldn't believe it. Here they were, the United States fighting the greatest war in history, and he'd been kept out of it because of something he didn't even know he had. He thought they must have made a mistake, mixed up his records with someone else's, or had just got it wrong in the first place. The whole thing was totally nuts as far as he was concerned.

"That heart problem of yours could flare up on you without any warning," the Army medic had told him. "And we don't want you in the middle of some big battle when it does. Not only would you be endangering the lives of your fellow soldiers, but you might seriously get in the way of the operation, botching it up for our side."

"Listen," Tom had replied, "I'm not volunteering for the job of five-star general, you know. I just want to be an ordinary soldier, just like the next guy."

"Sorry, fella," the medic had said while stamping his papers with the classification of those turned down for military service: 4-F.

Not to be able to join in the fighting had been, and still was, hell for Tom. In the months since the war began, he tried the Navy, the Marines, the Army Air Corps, the Coast Guard, the Seabees, the Merchant Marine, and even the Royal Canadian Air Force and had been rejected by all of them.

Recently, he'd been considering going down to Mexico or South America to get into some outfit there. He thought there had to be an army or a navy somewhere that would welcome a big, strong guy like him and overlook this dumb ailment that didn't bother him, had never bothered him, and as far as he could determine, would never bother him.

The amazing thing was that he was already risking his life on a daily basis while stunting for those idiotic Vance Varley war movies. With all his experience, there was no telling how valuable he could be to the Armed Forces. If only the Armed Forces would give him the chance to prove it.

"Listen," Erne was saying, "I'll gladly put my tongue in the splicing machine if you want."

Tom looked at his chubby, nearly bald, big-mouthed friend, his best friend in the world, and laughed.

"Finish up that fucker," Tom said, referring to the Dive-bomber movie, "and let's grab that beer."

Chapter 3

Veronica Lake tilted her head so that her trademark peek-a-boo bang fell seductively over one eye. She stood onstage at the newly-opened Hollywood Canteen which was located at 1451 Cahuenga Boulevard, about a half block off Sunset. The place was filled to capacity tonight with hundreds of liberty-happy servicemen, the girls who came to dance with them, the stars of stage and screen who came to entertain them, the musicians who came to play for them, the caterers who came to feed them, and the large contingent of civilian volunteers who came to do "their bit."

The band started to play, and at first the applause was so loud that it drowned out the opening strains. The bandleader, none other than Tommy Dorsey, led his orchestra, the members of which were all wearing white dinner jackets. They began a mellow rendition of *I'll Be Seeing You*. The lights dimmed slowly except for the one beaming down on Veronica who just stood there in shimmering silver, taking in every word of the lyrics being sung by Dorsey's male vocalist, a skinny guy named Sinatra.

The couples floated dreamily across the darkened dance floor, totally removed from the reality of war and the fact that so many of these men would be shipping out soon, some of them as early as the following morning, bound for the mosquito-laden jungles of various enemy-held islands in the South Pacific, or for the flat fenlands of Norfolk in England where the big American warbirds took off on their bombing missions over Germany.

At this point in the war, the Americans were taking advantage of the stunning and unexpected victory they'd achieved over the Japanese at a far-off place called Midway, part of the Hawaiian Island chain some 1300 miles northwest of Honolulu. It was during this battle the previous June that the Americans had sunk four of Japan's largest warships and had forever changed the course of the war, not to mention history. It was now pretty evident that Japan could never invade the west coast of America, although a great many of the people living in the area were still jittery.

Meanwhile, in North Africa, Rommel's army was still on the loose having fought a series of battles against the Allied Forces, including one at El Alamein.

There was still a lot of work to be done in order to win the war. All America was united in the quest for total victory, but tonight, at the canteen, it seemed as if the war didn't really exist. The young couples, men in their uniforms and girls in pretty dresses, held onto one another. For a little while, at least, life was a fox-trot under a few dim lights.

Finally the song ended, and Veronica Lake stepped down off the stage to mingle with the crowd. She was instantly surrounded by soldiers, sailors, and marines, all of them wanting her autograph or at least a closeup of her smile.

"Where are you from, soldier?" Veronica asked a young infantryman.

"Indiana, ma'am," he answered nervously while blushing a deep red.

"Is this your first time at the Hollywood Canteen?"

"Yes, ma'am," the soldier answered. "This is my first time

anywhere, other than Indiana, that is."

Veronica moved closer to the soldier. "Indiana," she said huskily, "is one of my very favorite states. Would you like to dance?"

"I'd like to, ma'am," he said, "but I've promised the next one to Miss Hayworth."

"And the dance after that?"

"To Miss Darnell," he admitted.

Throwing back her beautiful head of soft blond hair and laughing, Veronica peered around the room. All around her were servicemen dancing with the canteen girls.

"I guess I'll just have to dance with the dishwasher," she joked.

Across the dance floor, adjacent to the snackbar, Tom Driscoll stood with his arms up to the elbows in soapsuds as he washed dishes. Wearing a little canteen apron that barely covered his large frame, he handed each dripping plate over to Humphrey Bogart whose job it was to dry it. A cigarette hung from Bogart's lips as he conscientiously went to work on each plate.

Dorsey's band continued to play the soft, romantic ballads the servicemen seemed to like best, and the canteen was as quiet as it had been that night.

In the quietness Bogart dropped a plate, making a shattering noise.

"Shit," he said. "Ain't this just some way to fight the fucking war?" Tom looked at Bogart and knew exactly what he meant.

A moment later, they both heard a familiar voice approaching. With a tray piled high with dirty dishes balanced precariously on his shoulder, Bing Crosby was asking people to please step aside so that he could get by.

"Whew," he said, putting the tray down. "This is the first real work I've done in years, but it's worth it for those fine, brave lads of ours."

Bogart looked at Crosby and grinned. "That's the spirit, Bing," he said, ribbing his friend. "Every tray you carry brings us that much closer to victory. The Allies are counting on you. Hey, what's all that commotion on the dance floor?"

"Maggie Graym just walked in," Bing replied. "Happens every time she shows up at the canteen. She walks in and that's it for the rest of the girls. See what I mean?"

On the dance floor, the servicemen were abandoning their partners and were forming a line in order to have a dance with the most popular star in Hollywood.

With her long red hair and her million-dollar legs, she was just as beautiful and sexy-looking this evening as she'd been when she'd posed for the alluring bathtub photo that had been responsible for her becoming the number one pinup of the armed forces.

"She's doing more for the war effort than a battalion of Marines," Crosby said.

"Who'd want to dance with a battalion of Marines?" Bogart returned.

"She's a nice kid, too," Crosby said, ignoring Bogart. "I just did a USO tour with her and I can vouch that she's a sweet, down-to-earth girl. And gorgeous, too."

"You sound like you're head over heels in love with her," Bogart said.

"Aren't you?" Crosby asked.

Bogart took a slow drag on his cigarette. "Well, yeah," he said thoughtfully. "Now that you mention it, I guess I am."

Every man in the room had his eyes on Maggie. Every man, with the exception of Tom Driscoll. Tom regarded her as just another Hollywood redhead. Scrape away some of that paint and there was no telling what you'd find underneath.

As far as he could determine, there weren't any natural women in Hollywood. Women with normal goals and expectations for marriage and motherhood. It seemed to him that the women here were always acting as if a talent scout from 20th Century Fox or MGM or Grove Pictures was going to jump out from somewhere and immediately sign them to a seven-year contract.

Tom had dated woman after woman with this fantasy including waitresses, carhops, starlets, actresses, secretaries, extras, hairdressers, department store clerks, singers, dancers, bank tellers, Rosie the Riveters, telephone operators and script girls, all inspired by Lana Turner having supposedly been discovered sitting in Schwab's Drugstore sipping a soda.

It would be nice, Tom thought, just for once, to date someone who simply wanted to be ordinary.

Under the dim lights, Maggie was now dancing cheek to cheek with a rugged-looking Army sergeant. Maggie was careful to allot each dancing partner exactly two minutes and would then go on to the next serviceman waiting in line. But the sergeant that Maggie was presently dancing with didn't seem to think two minutes was long enough. He was holding her tighter than she wanted to be held. She struggled to get free of him, but his massive arms, encircling her body and pinning her to him, were impossible to break away from.

"Hey, what's your problem, baby," the sergeant snickered. "You know you like it."

Maggie finally managed to remove his arm from around her waist and attempted to walk away from him, but her freedom was short-lived. The sergeant, getting rough, grabbed her and pulled her back to him.

Bogart, spotting what was happening, threw down his dish towel and went to Maggie's rescue.

"Okay, Mac," Bogart said. "Let go of the lady."

"Who's gonna make me?" the sergeant sneered.

The answer came immediately in the form of six strapping Marines.

"Okay, okay," the sergeant said. "I know when I'm outnumbered. I was just leaving this dump."

The Marines took his arms and escorted him, none too gently, to the door.

"Thanks, Bogie," Maggie said.

"Don't think anything of it, kid," Bogart said and went back to drying the dishes.

After a few minutes, Maggie was dancing with a Coast Guardsman, and it seemed as if the incident with the Army sergeant had never happened.

On the stage, the Andrew sisters sang an energetic "boop boop, dittum dittum, wattum chew".

Chapter 4

Four hours later, the roar of the crowd had been replaced by the roar of vacuum cleaners and floor waxers, as well as the sound of mops banging against pails.

The cleanup crew, civilian workers like Tom, were in the process of getting the canteen in top shape so that its doors could reopen to the horde of servicemen and women who were certain to appear the following afternoon. Operating in three shifts, the canteen entertained 25,000 people in uniform weekly.

Tonight, there were a few soldiers who were cutting it close to the wire in heading back to camp. They were lingering awhile just outside the canteen doors talking to the girls they'd spent the evening dancing and chatting and laughing with, and would probably never see again.

It wasn't rare for a soldier to propose marriage to a girl he'd met just a few hours earlier, and it sometimes turned out that the girl would accept, basing her decision on his natty looks or his smooth line or his ability to dance a mean jitterbug—or just because she was caught up in the drama of the war and felt that this was the right thing to do.

But it was far more usual that once a guy walked out the front door, it was forever. Some of the girls would be left in tears, not because they expected anything more than a brief meeting with these smiling, joking young men, but because they knew that so many of the servicemen who passed through the Hollywood Canteen were destined to either die in battle or to be wounded or maimed in some horrendous way.

Tom understood this. On the nights he was scheduled to oversee the workers and then to lock up the canteen, he let the young people take their time saying their goodbyes.

Besides the young men saying goodbye to the canteen girls, there was also a small group of soldiers who were merely standing by the canteen entrance, waiting patiently. Tom saw them and asked if there was anything he could do for them. One of the soldiers, a youngster of about nineteen who wore the uniform of an Army Air Corps cadet, spoke up.

"We were, well, wondering if perhaps Maggie Graym was going to, well, be coming out this way soon," he said. "We'd like to tell her, well, what a big boost she, well, gives all of us guys in flying school and, well, we'd like to tell her just how much her movies and, well, her visits to see us on the base mean to me and, well, my pals Joe and Bill and Paul and Johnny here."

Tom listened to the young cadet trying to express himself and although he didn't want to disappoint him or Joe or Bill or Paul or Johnny, he had no choice.

"Sorry, fellas," he said. "But Maggie Graym has already gone home. Must have been about five, maybe ten minutes ago. She went out the back door to her car."

Maggie had, in fact, been the last of the stars to leave the canteen, slipping out the Ivar Street stage door just after midnight where her baby blue Lincoln Continental was parked. But not until every soldier, sailor, and marine had also left. Had she known that these men were waiting for her, she would have

made sure she saw them. It was a very well known fact around
Hollywood that there was no one more patriotic or willing to
donate her time and talent (and monthly pint of blood at the
Red Cross) than Maggie Graym.

And to prove it, she appeared at the canteen almost every
night dancing with the servicemen, getting to know them, listening to their stories of war and homesickness, promising to
write each and every one of them when they were out at sea
and especially when they'd reached their destinations: the
Japanese-infested jungles of Guadalcanal or the sun-parched
deserts of North Africa in hot pursuit of Rommel and his
Afrika Korps.

She'd even stayed on the job this evening though she had
been badly shaken up by the unpleasant incident concerning
the abusive Army sergeant.

Both Bette Davis and John Garfield, the founding members
of the Hollywood Canteen, had approached her just before
closing time and had thanked her.

"You were an ab-so-lute troop-er to-night," Bette had said,
taking her hand.

"Yeah, thanks a million for sticking it out," John Garfield
joined in, sounding just like the tough guy he portrayed in
most of his pictures. "We got a lotta guys here that woulda been
pretty disappointed if youda taken a powder."

Tom hung up his apron and went about his rounds. These
included supervising the work done by the clean-up people and
letting them leave after his approval. The main area for super-
vision was the kitchen which had to be ready to receive the
army of caterers arriving early each morning. It was there that

they prepared the food that would be heartily consumed the following evening by America's fighting forces. In one month alone, servicemen would consume 4,000 loaves of bread, 400 pounds of peanut butter, 1,500 pounds of coffee, 50,000 pints of milk, 30,000 gallons of fruit punch, 1,000 pounds of cheese and 150,000 pieces of cake.

Also on the list of Tom's duties was the job of turning out the many lights and a last minute check of the lounge and poolroom areas in case there were any soldiers who might have fallen asleep there. He didn't want some poor guy to suffer the consequences of accidentally going AWOL because he hadn't been awakened from a nap.

Seeing that there were no such snoozers tonight, Tom snapped out the remaining lights and left the premises by the back door, locking that one behind him.

A blast of night-blooming jasmine scent hit his nostrils. Tom loved the familiar fragrance of outdoors Los Angeles. He knew from Erne, who was always reading all those scientific magazines, that the air in Los Angeles wasn't as pure as it had once been. Like so many of Erne's pet peeves, this one really riled him up. Especially since, a few years before, several major car and gasoline companies had bought up and then closed down L.A.'s trolley line, one of the finest in the country. This was done so that people would have to buy more cars. Now, even with gas being rationed, there was still the pollution, and the experts recently coined a name for it: Smog.

Erne, genuinely concerned with the problem, predicted that Los Angeles would one day face the same pollution problems that plagued New York, London, and Pittsburgh. Tom consid-

ered this just another of Erne's alarmist routines and not to be
taken seriously. To him, the air in Los Angeles was still clean
and fresh. And always would be.

He started to walk over to his car and thought that he heard
something. A shuffle followed by a groan and then a cry cut off.
He decided it was probably one of the cats trying to get into the
tin cans of rubbish that were placed out back for early morning
collection. After hesitating for a moment, he started toward his
car and again heard the noise.

This time he identified the sound more accurately. It was
one of someone struggling.

And then he saw what was happening.

About 15 yards away from him, Maggie Graym was being
held down on the sloping trunk of a '41 Buick Roadmaster
coupe by the same sergeant who had been so aggressive with
her just a few hours earlier on the canteen dance floor. It was
obvious to Tom that the guy had snuck around the back here in
wait for Maggie. With only one thought in mind.

The only light was coming from the moon and a single light
bulb outside the door Tom had just come out of. Maggie, with
her skirt hitched high over her beautiful knees, was trying to
fight off the rapist with her fists, but she was losing the battle.
Soon, he would get from her what he'd hidden in the darkness
of the parking lot for.

Tom moved swiftly, grabbing the sergeant away from Maggie
and then landing a punch on his chin. The sergeant, instead of
falling into an unconscious heap on the ground, let Tom have a
powerful blow to the solar plexus followed by a resounding
punch to the left temple. A severe kick to the kidneys caught

Tom just as he was in the process of falling heavily on his face. With Tom down and trying to regain his breath, the sergeant took the opportunity to run. He sprinted across the canteen parking lot and down along a narrow alley that led to a busy Cahuenga Boulevard.

Tom managed to get onto his feet. Staggering at first, he went after the sergeant with Maggie not too far behind him trying to keep up. On Cahuenga, there was a huge number of servicemen still evident. In fact, the street was a sea of white with sailors off their ships looking for some late night entertainment. The sergeant had successfully lost himself somewhere in the vast crowd and was sure to get away. But Tom spotted him, a khaki figure against the brightness of the sailor uniforms, rapidly approaching a drive-in restaurant on the corner of Sunset.

Tom moved as fast as he could through a crowd that was hardly moving at all. He headed for Sunset, losing sight of the sergeant a half dozen times, but always miraculously catching a glimpse. The sergeant then tried to cross Sunset, a mistake that made him stand out even more. Tom reached Sunset and ran along the center lane, dodging cars and jeeps and finally caught up with the sergeant. He tackled him around the legs, grounding him, and then added a crippling punch to the head to keep him down. The sergeant tried to get up, but fell back, out for the count.

A moment later, two burly military policemen were moving fast toward the scene, having just witnessed some wild-looking civilian attacking a member of the United States Army, a sergeant, no less. There had been a lot of reports lately of innocent GIs having been attacked and robbed by civilians, and according to everything the MPs had been told about those attacks, this one looked exactly the same. Only this time, they had the culprit right where they wanted him.

One of the MPs was just about to bring his nightstick down upon Tom's head when Maggie came hobbling up to them, the heel having come off one of her shoes.

"Don't," Maggie screamed.

The MP with the nightstick raised over Tom's head paused a moment, stunned to see Maggie Graym, *the* Maggie Graym, his favorite movie star and the woman he dreamed about every night, running in his direction. But it was too late as far as Tom went. The other MP, not seeing or hearing Maggie, let his nightstick go into action and it landed, with a sickening thud, on Tom's skull.

Maggie was boiling mad at the MP who had clobbered Tom and who was now staring at her, astonished.

"This man just saved me from being assaulted back there, and you two want to brain him!"

The two military policemen, who were usually unusually tough, were now reduced to shame-faced, weak-kneed fools who were probably wondering what being locked up in the army stockade would be like.

"We didn't know, Miss Graym," they said in unison.

By now, Maggie was on the ground kneeling next to Tom, cradling his head in her lap. She dabbed at his wound which was bleeding slightly and when her small hanky was damp, she demanded the MP's larger one.

The MP who'd smacked Tom informed Maggie respectfully that an ambulance was on its way. When Tom finally regained consciousness and opened his eyes, he saw Maggie's concerned and anxious expression.

"Boy, are you one dumb broad," was the first thing he said, wincing at the pain coming from the top of his head.

"Dumb?" Maggie asked, shocked at his rudeness.

"Yeah. Dumb for going into the canteen parking lot alone at night."

Maggie dropped Tom's head off her lap and onto the hard tarmac of Sunset Boulevard.

"Don't you dare call me dumb."

"Okay," Tom said, "how does *stupid* suit you?"

Without either Tom or Maggie realizing it, a large crowd of onlookers had formed around them, listening to Maggie and Tom's every word and watching their every movement with a lot more than just curiosity. They were especially interested in the disheveled Maggie who looked very familiar to them.

"Oh, I don't believe it," a woman yelled. "That's Maggie Graym!"

It seemed as though everyone on Sunset Boulevard and vicinity had heard the woman and were now congregating excitedly to see what was going on.

A few press photographers materialized almost instantly and began snapping pictures, first getting all the shots they needed of the Army sergeant who was now handcuffed and being led away, and then of Maggie who was still kneeling at the prone body of Tom Driscoll. Nobody in the crowd seemed to care one way or the other about Tom Driscoll.

Maggie was clearly getting more and more upset. "Don't let them take my picture," she said, alarmed at the prospect of winding up on the front page of the Los Angeles Times, not to mention the national papers.

The two MPs walked over to the photographers and took their cameras away. They removed the film and informed the photographers that their cameras were being confiscated for the duration of the war.

"You ain't gonna do this fine lady here no harm," one of the MPs said.

"Everybody loves Maggie Graym," the second MP added.

Chapter 5

"Everybody loves Maggie Graym," the head projectionist told his assistant.

He was getting ready to run a copy of Maggie's latest Technicolor extravaganza, the one that had proved so difficult for the agents to obtain. Taking the film out of its canister, the projectionist was extremely careful in the way he handled it. He was a tall, skinny man with a receding chin, a receding hairline, and a prominent Adam's apple. He was wearing a thick, moth-eaten sweater and scarf in the projection room as there was hardly any heat up there. His nose and hands were red from the chill in the air, but the problem with his extremities was the last thing on his mind. Not two feet away from him in the crammed little room, his assistant stood ready to do whatever he could to make the showing of Maggie's movie come off without a hitch.

"I pray to God that there is no terrible botch-up this time," the projectionist said. "The last time the film broke mid-reel was nearly the end of us both. If such a thing was to happen again, and please God, don't let it, they would march us both out of here and hang us on meat hooks."

"You worry far too much, Wilhelm," the assistant said consolingly. "I've gone over the reel inch-by-inch to make sure that there are no weak spots. And I can assure you with the greatest of confidence that this film is in absolutely flawless condition, despite the fact that it has been played a number of times in that cinema in Des Moines or wherever it was confiscated from. So please take a load off your mind and rest assured when I tell you that there is absolutely nothing at all to be concerned about. Not a thing."

"Rest assured? You want me to rest assured?" the head projectionist asked, his face taking on a look of utter incredulity at the suggestion. "I would not be doing my job as head projectionist if I left the checking of this film to a mere assistant, especially one who has already almost got us killed through his incompetence. So I, also, went over this reel inch-by-inch. And for your information, it was not from Des Moines that this movie was picked up by our agents, but from Detroit."

"Des Moines, Detroit," the assistant said under his breath. "All those towns in America sound the same to me."

The two men now heard a the sound of voices and heavy boots rising from the floor below. They rushed to the little window in the projection room that looked out onto the auditorium and could see that the party they were expecting had indeed arrived.

"He's here," the head projectionist said, panicking. "Start the film. Fast."

The assistant did as he was told. The credits of the film were just starting to come onto the screen as Adolph Hitler and his legion of aides took their seats. Hitler took his usual place, the second row. He slumped down in the seat and brought his knees upward onto the back of the chair in front of him. In a few moments, Maggie Graym appeared larger than life above him. He was virtually stricken with pleasure at the sight of her as she floated down from a cloud in a sea of blue ostrich feathers. His leg twitched in time with the music. Oblivious to all those around him, he drew out of his trousers something soft and small and started rubbing it.

"Uncle Adolph's at it again," an officer out of Hitler's earshot said to several other officers.

Onscreen, there was now a closeup of Maggie going into her big number: "You're probably wondering why I'm on a cloud," she sang, "well, please excuse me for thinking out loud..."

Maggie had been walking along at a slow pace on her lovely, dimpled legs, exposed to the thighs, as she sang. She now stopped in front of a grinning Vance Varley in his white tie and tails and addressed her song to him:

"A perfect couple you'll agree, is a guy like you and a girl like me..."

In the projection room, the head projectionist who had once spent a year in Oswego, New York, learning English, wondered how such trite words and banal music had ever avoided their rightful destination: the garbage. But in the audience came the little squeals of delight issued by Hitler as Maggie and at least two or three dozen gorgeous girls who'd also floated down from the clouds began kicking their combined fabulous legs high in the air. The girls wore pink ostrich feathers in contrast to Maggie's blue.

Maggie then went into a tap solo, weaving in and out of rows of male dancers who seemed to have been born for just the purpose of being human props. Four of them picked Maggie up and passed her along through the ranks of the other men until she was in the arms of the still grinning Vance Varley once again.

It was at this very moment, when the cameras were zooming in on Maggie's face and when Hitler was at his absolute happiest that it happened, exactly what the head projectionist had been praying so desperately wouldn't.

The film broke.

It made a blubbering, drowning sound and became visually blurred in such a way as to horribly distort Maggie's otherwise uniform features. And then, skidding to a screeching halt, it snapped loudly and the big screen went blank and silent and dead.

Adolph Hitler, who had been transported for once from his usual duties of murdering innocent people and bombing cities and taking over huge territories that did not belong to him, started to shriek uncontrollably. He demanded that the person responsible for this...this...criminal act be brought before him immediately.

The head projectionist stood quaking in terror as a bunch of Gestapo men came bursting into his little room.

His assistant spoke first. "I had nothing to do with this," he said. "It was him. He's the head projectionist. I'm just an assistant. I don't know anything about film. It's all his fault. He never looks to see if the film is in good shape."

"Why, you little..." the head projectionist began to say, but instead of finishing the sentence, he found himself being dragged down the stairs to der Fuhrer. He was amazed that he was alive, that he hadn't been shot on the spot. And now he was having trouble believing his ears. Hitler, if he was hearing right, was giving him the opportunity to fix the film.

"If it isn't in perfect running order by the time I count up to sixty," Hitler screamed, "I will have the skin peeled from your scrawny body and fed to the dogs, do you understand me, you illegitimate son of a toad?"

The projectionist, his forehead wet from the spray of Hitler's spittle, scampered dizzily back to the room that would surely serve as his execution chamber if he didn't remedy the problem. His hands trembled so violently that he found it almost impossible to rewind the film, but he took two deep breaths and forced himself to calm down. That way he was able to locate the break which, fortunately for him, was almost immediately visible.

As for his erstwhile assistant, he was nowhere to be seen, having evidently snuck out of the theatre—via a small window onto the rooftops of Berlin—while der Fuhrer was yelling his head off about the interrupted filming.

No doubt he was cowering in terror somewhere, waiting for the Gestapo to pounce upon him, but to the head projectionist's way of thinking, the Gestapo's treatment of the assistant would be nothing as compared to his own. He swore to himself that if it was the last thing he ever did, he would get his hands around that little swine's neck and crush every breath out of him, rejecting all pleas for mercy.

But the pleasure of seeing his assistant dead would have to wait. Right now, he had problems that were immediate. Under the sinister gaze of the scar-faced SS guard who was holding an equally sinister- looking luger on him, he hurriedly spliced the break and, hoping that there were no others, quickly placed the reel of film onto the projector.

Meanwhile, Hitler, sitting in the theatre, asked for an up-to-date report as to what Maggie Graym was doing these days in terms of her personal life. Hitler was an ardent reader of Hedda Hopper and Louella Parsons, and he ate up all the gossip that came out of Hollywood. When he could get it.

It wasn't always possible for the agents in California to transmit a translated version of the daily Parsons/Hopper newspaper columns via radio. But even when the transmissions were available, there was no guarantee they would carry news of his beloved Maggie. Which made him even hungrier than usual for information on his very favorite movie star, the only woman who could make him forget the stress and the demands made upon him in his position as der Fuhrer.

"Is she planning any new movies?" Hitler asked. "Will she be appearing in a bathing suit again? Will it be a two-piece? Would she consider abandoning Hollywood in order to take up a career in Germany?"

He had flown into a rage over the defection of Marlene Dietrich who had once been considered a national treasure. Dietrich was now a tireless worker for the Allies, entertaining soldiers within millimeters of the battlefront. Which, to Hitler, made her a national disgrace. To have Maggie Graym in Dietrich's place would more than make up for it. If he was to send her a letter requesting her autograph, would she answer it? Would she be amenable to making films for him in the not too far-off distant future when he'd taken over Hollywood? Hitler fired off his questions one after another, eagerly awaiting the answers.

The officer he was addressing, whose sole responsibility to der Fuhrer was in organizing and arranging the viewing of Maggie Graym's films for him was, like der Fuhrer, obsessed with Hollywood and everything about it. He informed Hitler that, as far as he knew, Maggie would indeed be making lots and lots of new movies and most of them would feature her in a bathing suit, possibly a two-piece bathing suit. Which is where he should have stopped talking.

Instead, he went on to say that Maggie was getting more and more popular in the United States, not only with the general movie-going public, but with the American fighting forces who, in a recent poll, had voted her their number one pinup.

An officer sitting nearby gently nudged the young officer's elbow in an attempt to warn him not to follow along these lines, but the young officer didn't understand the warning, nor did he especially notice the maniacal expression beginning to creep across Hitler's face.

"As a matter of fact," he continued, "Maggie Graym is proving to be a major asset to the Allies. From the most recent reports we've received from our sources in Hollywood, it appears that she lends greatly to the morale of American GIs. Our sources also report that she is untiringly dedicated to promoting the kind of spirit and fervor amongst these troops that is aimed at bringing about the eventual annihilation of the Third Reich and, more specifically, your trial and execution by the Allied forces and furthermore..."

"Stop!" Adolph Hitler screamed, his eyes bulging out of his head. At the news given to him by the young officer, he became hysterical and accused the man of being a filthy liar and a disgusting traitor.

The young officer, finally realizing the kind of mess he'd got himself into now tried to get himself out of it again. "I was only repeating what our contacts in Los Angeles have said, I..."

"Shoot him!" Hitler shrieked. Within seconds of this command, a contingent of soldiers entered the theatre to remove

the stunned officer. The sound of rifles being discharged outside the building a few moments later told Hitler what he
wanted to know: that this vicious snake in the grass and his
despicable lies about the glorious Maggie Graym were forever
blotted out.

In the rear of the theatre an officer whispered into the ear of
the man sitting next to him, a somewhat flabby colonel, softened by his cushy job in administration. "I have repeatedly told
young Gerhardt: young Gerhardt, you must never, ever say anything critical or even remotely incautious to Adolph about his
precious Maggie, that he was madly infatuated with the
woman. Why in hell didn't the schmuck listen to what I was
telling him?"

"Even more tragic than that," replied the colonel, "is the fact
that Adolph simply won't accept what anyone has to say about
this movie star who is so incredibly valuable to the Allied front.
Now we're doomed to these inane movies that she makes for as
long as der Fuhrer lives."

"Which is probably the most important reason to kill der
Fuhrer," the other officer replied.

"I know what you mean," sighed the colonel. "But until
someone comes along willing to undertake such a task, I've
decided to request a transfer to the Russian front just so I don't
have to sit through the torture of another *boy like you, girl like
me* routine."

A few moments later, the lights dimmed and the film began
to roll. Once again Adolph Hitler was returned to his former
reverie, raving over the Aryan beauty of Maggie Graym.

Outside the theatre, the "executed" young officer checked

himself for bullet wounds. There weren't any. The fact was that he hadn't really been executed.

Somewhat perplexed, he watched the officer in charge walk up to him. He wondered what exactly was going on here. Der Fuhrer had ordered him executed, and the order had obviously been disobeyed. He couldn't figure it. out.

"Blanks," the officer in charge said.

"Blanks?" asked the supposedly condemned man.

"Blanks," the officer repeated with a chuckle. "If we were to go around executing all the clerks and secretaries and chauffeurs and servants and junior officers like yourself who'd annoyed der Fuhrer, we'd have no bullets left for the enemy. What's your name, anyway?"

"Gerhardt Vanderschloffer," Gerhardt answered, still amazed he was alive. And also aware of the risk this officer had taken in saving his life.

"Yeah, well, listen, Gerhardt. Do me a favor. Just stay out of der Fuhrer's way for a few days and he'll forget that he ever had you killed."

Gerhardt watched the officer walk back to the rest of the firing squad sharpshooters who were now casually standing around taking a smoking break.

"Hey, thanks," Gerhardt called after him. "Uh, thanks for the blanks."

Without looking back, the officer flashed him the victory sign, and strode off. Gerhardt knew the officer was taking a chance on him because in this Germany where sons turned in their fathers and brothers betrayed brothers, there was no such thing as gratitude or loyalty. There were a number of fanatical officers who would have, had they been condemned to die as had Gerhardt, reported the officer for not carrying out Hitler's orders.

Gerhardt stood there a moment longer and then headed back to the barracks. Passing a theatre window he heard the sound of joyful squealing escaping Adolph Hitler due to the almost paralytic pleasure he was deriving from Maggie Graym.

Day 2

Chapter 6

Maggie Graym puffed nervously on her Lucky Strike and kept crossing and recrossing her legs as she sat in the spacious reception area that was decorated in the sickly sweet tones of pale pink and even sicklier pea green. It was mid-morning and she'd already been sitting there for over an hour according to the kitsch porcelain cupid that sat on a table nearby with a clock fashioned in its belly. To kill time, Maggie had been counting the endless array of cupids that seemed to adorn just about everything in the room from lamps and mirror frames to the design of the wallpaper and the weave of the carpet.

Lighting her fifth cigarette since she'd arrived, she resigned herself to an even longer wait when an impatient buzzing sound came over the intercom on the secretary's desk.

In an alcove across from the reception area, the secretary stopped what she was doing, listened to the voice coming from the little box, and then motioned to Maggie.

"Hitler will see you now," she said, Hitler being the name she used when referring to her boss, Emerson Waldie, who was the head of Grove Pictures.

"What does he want this time, Harriet?" Maggie asked, hoping that she wasn't going to have to go through another of Waldie's crazy sessions. There had been so many of them since she had come to the studio, and they always left her feeling drained.

"I haven't got a clue, Maggie," Harriet said, looking up from her typing. "But I wouldn't plan on it being very pleasant if I were you. I have yet to meet even one person, yours truly included, who ever thought of a meeting with Emerson Waldie as anything but a grueling, horrifying and extremely degrading experience."

Maggie wondered if she was going to be chastised for having been at the center of the Sunset Boulevard brawl the night before. But she realized Waldie couldn't have heard about it. Because if he had, he wouldn't have waited until now to pounce. He would have had her on the carpet the minute she walked in at 6 a.m. that morning.

"Well, I may as well get this over with," Maggie said, taking one last drag on her cigarette and then mashing it out in one of the ashtrays. She noticed that even the ashtrays were designed around a cupid motif. Emerson Waldie, crazy about cupids, often referred to himself as "The Hollywood Cupid" because he'd brought so many famous screen couples together, most of whom acted lovey-dovey in public but, unbeknownst to their adoring public, loathed one another in private.

Having to be romantically involved in front of the camera with someone picked out by Waldie was one thing, but having to be seen at such public spots as the Trocadero or the Brown Derby with someone picked out by Waldie was quite another. Maggie didn't like it. And yet, being seen in glamorous places with one's leading man was what the public expected. Movie magazines such as *Screen World* and *Film Land* were full of stories and photos that created an illusion of romance and excitement for the ordinary reader. As a professional, Maggie had no choice but to comply with Grove Pictures publicity stunts, some of them quite awful, most of them created by Emerson Waldie himself.

Maggie walked across the room to the dreaded door and opened it. Waldie was sitting at an enormous mahogany desk working on something or other and it was only after a full minute and a half that he looked up and acknowledged, if that's what it could be called, Maggie's presence in his office.

"Sit down," he said bluntly, pointing to a chair across from his desk that was at least a half foot lower than his own and one which left the person sitting there feeling like he or she was in a hole looking upward toward his or her master. Which was exactly the way Waldie wanted the person to feel.

Waldie, an extremely short but powerfully built squat figure, returned to the work he was supposedly concentrating on. It was only after another ten or so minutes, that he looked up at Maggie. Or down, as was the case.

The expression on Waldie's face, which usually spelled doom for whomever was unfortunate enough to be sitting opposite him, was somehow different today. As Maggie sat and wondered what the difference was, Waldie did something extremely unnerving. Something he never usually did.

He smiled.

His face wasn't used to smiling and he was having a little trouble getting the various unused muscles to work.

"I have some news for you," Waldie announced, still trying to get his face to do what he wanted it to do. "It has to do with Vance Varley."

"Vance?"

"That's right. I want you to be the first to know that he's finally going to take the plunge. He's finally going to get married."

Maggie was surprised due to the fact that Vance was known in Hollywood to hate women. She was also surprised that Waldie had called her into his office to tell her about Vance's plans.

"So what does Vance's getting married have to do with me?"

"Everything," Waldie said.

"You want me to be one of the bridesmaids," Maggie ventured.

"Close, but no bouquet." Waldie's smile was more of a grimace below deadly earnest eyes. "You, Maggie, are going to be the bride."

Maggie let what Waldie had just said sink in before answering. "Oh, I get it. You mean in Vance's and my new picture, right?"

Waldie said nothing.

Maggie continued. "Well, considering that I've already married Vance in *Aloha Honeymoon* and *Coney Island Conga* and *Music in The Stars* I don't think this is going to be a big problem. After all, it's what the public expects from screen teams. I mean, just look at Astaire and Rogers, Loy and Powell, Hepburn and Grant, Mickey and Minnie..."

"You're not reading me, honey," Waldie interrupted. "This time, it's for real. In a real church. With a real minister. With a real ring. Followed by a real honeymoon. This time, when you and Vance walk down the aisle, it's going to be legal. You'll not only be man and wife on the screen, but you'll be man and wife off the screen. "You'll be happy. I'll be happy. All of America will be happy."

Maggie looked at the face across from her, the features now set in grim determination.

"Wait a minute," Maggie broke in. "If you mean what I think you mean..."

"Listen, Vance has to get married," Waldie said in a sudden conspiratorial tone. "There are rumors circulating all over town that he likes the boys, and that means people might stop going to his pictures. Most of which are your pictures. All of which are my pictures. So you can look upon this marriage as an investment in all our futures."

"Hold it, hold it, hold it," Maggie said, getting up out of her chair. "If you think I'm going to marry some guy just to save a few lousy pictures, you're out of your mind."

"I don't think you have much choice in the matter," Waldie said.

"Oh yeah?" Maggie answered. "Well, just don't hold your breath to see if I show up at the church."

Waldie looked at Maggie and wished he'd never pulled her out of the chorus back in 1939 to groom her for the enormous stardom that was hers today. Even though he knew that it was only because of her that the studio still existed in the first place. What Waldie couldn't bear was that Grove Pictures would have disappeared without a trace without Maggie. Her movies were loved by people of all ages, and they grossed millions around the world. And it looked like there was no end in sight.

All this was great as far as the studio went, but the truth was that Maggie's popularity irked Waldie. He had meant to create her merely as a vehicle with which to increase his riches. And she had done that for him, he had to admit. But at the same time, she had become the most important person at Grove in the eyes of movie-goers as well as Hollywood's upper echelons. When people talked about Grove, they were talking about Maggie Graym in the same breath, not Waldie. And it was driving Waldie crazy.

There had been many a night when he lay awake plotting Maggie's professional demise. And many a day when he sat at his desk thinking of nothing else. It had become his obsession. But he never acted on his feelings because he knew that in hurting Maggie, he would destroy himself.

As for Maggie, she was pretty much unaware, or uncaring, of any power she might have had outside of her screen stardom. To her, being in pictures meant nothing but hard work, long hours, hot lights, sore feet, dumb scripts, difficult leading men, little time off and worst of all, having Emerson Waldie for a boss.

She'd been tapping her tap shoes around Hollywood since '36, and before that she'd tapped them around Broadway. Neither location had done much for her until she'd received a casting call to appear in a Grove Pictures production with the title *Dance, Cowgirl, Dance*. It was about a bunch of vaudevillians stranded on a Texas ranch after their bus broke down.

She and ninety other girls had reported to the soundstage to begin rehearsals and there was this loudmouthed guy with the big torso and short legs and the obnoxious manner who was watching them as they went through their routines. He'd turned out to be Emerson Waldie, Hollywood tycoon and tyrant.

"Hey you, the redhead with the nice ass, yeah you, I'm talking to you, step out of the crowd." Waldie had ordered. No less than a dozen redheads with nice asses had immediately stepped forward, but it was Maggie, the redhead that hadn't stepped forward, to whom Waldie was referring.

And that had been the start of it. Waldie had been on the lookout for a curvaceous, redheaded star and she more than looked the part. From that moment on, Maggie's career took a brand new turn. She went from one picture to another gaining the attention of audiences all across the country in a way that no other actress, or actor for that matter, ever had before.

In less than three years and seventeen pictures she'd become the top box-office attraction in Hollywood and the highest paid actress in the history of motion pictures. And there was no getting away from it, she owed it all to Emerson Waldie: the fame, the success, the vast financial rewards.

Waldie now sat behind his desk trying his best to look reasonable, to look "sincere".

"You won't even have to live in the same house as Vance, except for the publicity shots. In a year or two, three at the most, after you've had the baby, you can go to Reno and get a quickie divorce."

"The baby!" Maggie exploded. "You don't just want me to marry a man who beats his dogs, you want me to have a baby by him. No thank you."

"Who says he beats his dogs?"

"Louella Parsons. That's who."

"To hell with Louella. That woman will print anything in that damned column of hers just to destroy me. She's like everybody else in this town. Out to get me. To see me ruined and this whole studio that I built up from nothing put out of business."

Maggie could see that Waldie was heading in a completely different direction, his usual paranoid one. She hoped that he would just stick with that for awhile, raving about all the people against him. So that he might forget all about her marrying Vance. But no such luck.

"And you're just like all the rest of them," Waldie said, pointing a finger at Maggie. "Willing to take, take, take and give nothing in return."

"I don't care what you say, Emerson," Maggie said firmly. "There's no way that I'm going to marry Vance Varley or anybody else you have in mind, except on celluloid."

"You'll do what I damn well tell you to do," Waldie said, now standing. "This is my studio and you're nothing more than another employee. I made you and I can break you. And besides anything else, it's about time you got married. You're getting a bit long in the tooth. Pretty soon I'm gonna have to cast you in spinster parts."

"Okay, so I'm an old maid of twenty-six. Ten million servicemen don't seem to mind."

Waldie could see that Maggie wasn't going to be swayed by his usual tactics of threats and abuse. He would have to think of something else.

"Look," he said, lowering his eyes and putting the pathetic, puppydog look on his face that always seemed to work when all else failed. "I wouldn't do anything to make you unhappy, Maggie, you know that. Why, I've been like a father to you, looking out for your interests, giving you the best treatment and privileges of any actress on the lot. The only thing I'm asking for is a little cooperation in return for all the help I've given you over the years. I'm just asking for you to do this one eeny, teeny little publicity stunt for the sake of the studio, nothing more."

"Fine," Maggie said. "I suggest that you get a stuntwoman to marry Vance."

Waldie knew when he was beaten. There was only one last thing to do in this situation. Throw a tremendous fit. Maybe that would scare Maggie into submission.

"I'm gonna put you in lousy movies," he yelled loudly enough for the film crew working two streets away to hear.

"Anything would be better than having to sing that *boy like you and girl like me* crap," Maggie countered.

"And furthermore, I'm going to find someone to replace you here at Grove Pictures. You're not the only dyed redhead in Hollywood, you know."

"Nothing lasts forever," Maggie said coolly.

Exasperated almost to the point of cardiac arrest, Waldie stormed around his office yelling wildly, threatening to team her up with Vance Varley for her next fifteen pictures.

"Try walking out on that," he bellowed.

"Fifteen more pictures like the ones we're been making and I won't have to walk out," Maggie said as she got up from her chair. "Every audience in America will do it for me."

Chapter 7

"And on your left," the voice announced, "is the compound where the head of Grove Pictures, Emerson Waldie, has his offices and if you look out of your windows, you'll see none other than your favorite Hollywood star and mine, the beauteous, the glamorous, the talented Miss Maggie Graym. There she is coming out of the main door."

The voice belonged to the driver of the Hollywood Tours Comfortliner which passed, eight times daily, the huge sculptured hedge surrounding Emerson Waldie's ornate pink and yellow twelve room *chateau* on the Grove Pictures lot.

Judging from the way the passengers were now frantically craning their necks to catch a glimpse of Maggie Graym, who'd disappeared into a powder blue convertible with the top up, it was apparent to the driver of the tour bus that his usual spiel would fall upon deaf ears.

He moved past the chateau with its inescapable adornment of concrete cupids, and then turned down a street lined with sleazy tenement buildings. These were the tenements of Stage A, built by Waldie in the mid-1930s when the studio had tried to romanticize the poverty and hopelessness of ghetto life. And had succeeded in doing so.

If anybody had known what ghetto life had been like, it was Emerson Waldie. He'd come from the real tenements of New York's lower east side. To avoid eye-contact with this dismal reminder of his youth, he'd had a huge hedge grown outside his windows, blotting it out. Just because he had exploited an American tragedy for all it was worth in terms of box office receipts didn't mean that he had to stare at it from his window.

But now that the studio focus was on making war movies and musicals—these two forms of entertainment being the most profitable to the studio—the tenement set wasn't used quite as often as it had been during prewar days. Not that it was totally deserted. Waldie, as a sort of monument to himself and his own humble beginnings, insisted that Grove Pictures produce at least one tenement picture a year.

Which was the reason why Tom Driscoll was now standing on the roof of one of the tenements, poised for the scene in this new production called *Born In The Bowery*, in which he was to rescue a little boy from a raging sixth floor fire. Tom had been called in at the last minute after the previous stuntman assigned to the picture had walked off the set in a huff about something.

The action called for Tom, doubling for yet another of Hollywood's so called he-men, Whitney Paris, to inch his way, hand over hand, along a rope leading from one decrepit building to another, where he was to harness the boy onto his back and then carry him back to safety. The boy, a stand-in for the cute little child star, Bunkie Milligan, was looking pretty annoyed by the time Tom reached the perch he was standing on.

"Do you realize this is the fifth fucking take this morning?" the child asked.

"Hey, partner," Tom said gently, "don't you know that kids your age shouldn't use swear words?"

"So who the fuck is a kid?" the stand-in said. "I'm twenty-fucking-seven years old. You think I like standing in for some pimply-faced little actor? If I'd grown to my full height, I would have been a tail gunner on one of those big flying fortresses over Germany or I would have been navigating a PT boat out in the Pacific. I would have been taking on those fucking nips and krauts, that's for damned sure. But here I am, a 4-F dwarf working for these crackpot second-unit directors like the guy they put on this flick who makes you do take after fucking take on the same fucking shot. That's why the stuntman before you took a powder."

Tom harnessed the agitated dwarf onto his back for the hand over hand trip back to the other tenement building, taking note of the fact that this, indeed, was no lightweight child, but a rather heavy short adult with a corpulent stomach and long, ape-like arms.

The stand-in was silent for a minute or two until about a quarter of the way back when Tom was asked the inevitable question, the same question he was asked day in and day out by either gas station attendants or air raid wardens or people on the street he'd never seen before or bartenders or kids or grandmothers or grocery clerks or barbers or newspaper vendors or traffic cops or waitresses or studio personnel:

"Say, why the hell ain't you in an Army or Navy uniform doing your bit to win this war?" the dwarf asked vehemently. "What're you, afraid of getting hurt or something? What're you, yella, fella?"

Tom said nothing as he continued slowly toward the other tenement, but he wondered how the dwarf he was carrying on his back would enjoy bouncing off the safety net 60 feet below. "It makes me want to puke every time I see guys like you avoiding your duty as Americans," the dwarf continued. "And believe me, buddy, if I had anything to say about all this, I'd line the whole bunch of you lily-livered cowards up against the nearest wall and shoot you."

Having experienced this kind of verbal abuse as often as he had, Tom just let his passenger have his say and proceeded along. As he was nearing the other tenement he heard an announcement from below. It was coming over a loud speaker and it was the call to break for lunch.

"Well, that's the best fucking thing I've heard all day," the dwarf said. Half a minute later Tom reached the building and gladly unsaddled the dwarf who scrambled like a monkey down off the tenement rig. Tom followed and once on the ground, headed for the exit, certain that he wouldn't be needed for any more shooting on this particular scene, there now being five takes, more than enough. But Bradford, the second-unit director, beckoned him back.

"Okay, we're all gonna report back here in an hour for a reshoot, got that?" Bradford said.

He was a tall, gaunt, humorless man who was considered the reigning second-unit director at Grove, a second-unit director being the person who shoots all the scenes in a movie that the main director doesn't have time for or simply can't be bothered with: long shots, secondary angles, extreme closeups, scenes in which the actors don't have to be directed, and all of the lesser important shots such as the tenement rescue scene.

Until working with the guy on *Dive-Bomber Rendezvous*,

nobody had ever heard of Bradford, certainly Tom hadn't. He'd just sort of popped up all of a sudden in the position he was in. The grapevine had it that he'd been installed in the job through the influence of Marcus Wood.

Wood wasn't just one of the most powerful producers and businessmen in the film industry, but was thought of as a *personage* in the sense that he was highly respected in all the right circles, a friend of Warner, Meyer, Cohn, Goldwyn, Zanuck and other studio moguls as well as the official advisor on Hollywood matters to the President of the United States, Franklin Delano Roosevelt.

Tom stood at the exit for a moment wondering whether or not to make a comment to Bradford about the reshoot. After all, there had to be more than enough film in the can to cover the scene which would eventually appear on the screen for no more than three or four seconds tops. The closeup scenes of the child's rescue had already been shot with the actual stars of the film. The work that Tom and the previous stuntman and the stand-in had done was merely a long shot filler. Tom approached Bradford.

"Got a problem, stuntman?" Bradford asked, not completely looking up from his paperwork.

"No problem," Tom answered, "but maybe you can tell me what's wrong with the last five takes?"

"I don't like them," Bradford said. "That's what's wrong with them."

Tom considered for a long moment what Bradford had said. "Okay," he said, "but is there anything you'd like us to do that we're not already doing?"

"Nah. Just keep doing what you and the little guy are doing. We'll get the shot I'm looking for in two, maybe three more takes."

Tom was doing his best to be helpful. "Yes, but if you can point out exactly what it is you want, maybe we can get the shot you're looking for in less. Tom paused and then remembered what Erne had said. He echoed Erne's words: "Film's scarce these days."

Bradford regarded Tom icily before speaking. Tom could almost tell what was coming.

"So since when are *you* directing this segment?" Bradford asked sharply.

"I'm only trying to understand what you'd like us to do in order to get this production wrapped up," Tom said, unable to figure Wilson. "I mean, why would you want to go on shooting the same thing over and over again when you know the results aren't going to be any different than what you already have in the can?"

Tom waited for an answer from Bradford, but none was forthcoming. He continued talking: "The audience isn't going to see anything but a couple of small figures in the far distance for just a few seconds. This is just like the situation we had on *Dive-Bomber Rendezvous* when you had me jumping out of that plane a dozen times for no apparent reason."

"Keep it up, wiseguy," Bradford said, his face rapidly flushing a deep, angry red. "Just keep mouthing off and not only will you be off this picture, but you'll be off this lot so fast you won't know what hit you. I don't have to take this kind of crap from some dumb stuntman who doesn't know how to mind his own business."

Tom let it pass just as he'd let what the dwarf stand-in had said pass. He'd worked on all kinds of pictures with all kinds of directors in all kinds of difficult situations, but he couldn't recall this kind of thing ever happening before. Most directors Tom had worked with had just wanted to get the shot in the can and go home. At least the second-unit directors had. And as a stunt-man, he usually kept his comments to himself. Even if he was being told to do something fairly stupid. As was the case here.

It was now starting to occur to Tom that maybe he was a little out of line. After all, Bradford was the guy in charge and that was that. If Bradford wanted him to do a hundred takes, he'd do a hundred takes. It was up to Bradford to decide.

"Okay," Tom said, "have it your way."

Leaving the sound stage, he thought he'd grab a sandwich at the studio commissary, but he didn't feel hungry. Underneath it all, the abuse that the dwarf had hurled at him had seeped in. No matter how many times he heard it, he couldn't get used to practically everybody he came into contact with thinking he was a coward.

And if he really wanted to get himself depressed, he only had to consider that he'd probably have to put up with this until the war was over.

He felt like going over to Jimmy's Tropical Bar and Grille and having a few. Except that the place would be empty this time of day and there'd be nobody to have a few with.

Tom walked over to where his car was parked. It was a shiny black 1941 Packard Clipper Deluxe, a beauty of a machine with its fenders flowing gracefully into the door panels, its innova-tive lack of running boards, and its sleek vertical grill.

Getting into the car, he noticed three or four of Bradford's men standing nearby watching him. They didn't look anything like film guys. They looked more like ordinary street thugs. They weren't in the Army or the Navy, either. And it flashed through Tom's brain just why. From the sneers on their faces and the deadliness in their eyes, he realized that they weren't the kind of guys the Army or Navy would want. Even in an all-out war like the one being fought right now. Stories of prisons emptying out the cells so that the Armed Forces could have more manpower were just that. Stories. As Tom well knew, the services were pretty damned fussy.

So these were the kind of people he got to sit the war out with: undesirables, rejects, petty thieves, ex-cons, punks.

He started up the engine and moved out of his space. The clock on his dashboard told him he had about forty minutes before having to report back to work, and he was trying to decide where to spend them. He decided to spend them over at Erne's.

Chapter 8

While the block of tenements on the Grove Pictures lot was just a film set, the rundown, brown shingled building with the sagging verandahs and the drooping drainpipes that housed the studio's film editors was a reality.

Located about a quarter mile from Emerson Waldie's compound, this was one of Los Angeles' oldest surviving structures, dating back to the time when L.A. was a rural, agricultural community isolated from the rest of the country by the San Gabriel mountain range that surrounded it on the northeast.

Everything about the editor's building squeaked. From the floor boards to the mice that lived under them. And as for such 20th century amenities as proper plumbing and air conditioning, they didn't exist. On a really hot day, when the temperatures climbed to over one hundred degrees, even the film broke out in a sweat.

But even with all the building's drawbacks, to Erne Parkin, this was home. He preferred to stay where he was rather than to take up the offer of moving to Grove's executive office building, an eight floor, Art Deco structure on the other side of the lot. This was where all the stuffy, and in Erne's opinion, useless, executives had their offices. If there was ever a Hollywood specimen Erne had absolutely no use for, it was the studio exec.

"They wouldn't know a good movie if it crawled between their legs," Erne had said when he'd been ordered to completely re-edit the only good movie the studio had made in years. It was called *End Of A Rhapsody*, the story of a concert pianist who loses the use of his hands.

The top execs at Grove had strongly opposed the director's cut and the way Erne had originally put it together. The director, a man who never strayed too far afield of his master's wishes, then had Erne start all over again with the emphasis now being on the weepy scenes.

Head office had dictated that a great movie was measured not by what the critics thought of it, nor by how many academy awards it received, but by the number of handkerchiefs a movie-goer was apt to go through during one sitting.

It was this kind of thinking on the studio's part that so mightily pissed Erne off. But in separating himself from Grove's executive class and the entire way of life that went with it—the dinner parties, the golf course scene, the martini lunches—Erne found himself unable to complain about the conditions of his present workplace. Which was pure torture for a man who spent his life complaining.

When Tom arrived at the badly-decaying building, he found Erne busily sorting out the various takes on four different features he was editing simultaneously.

To make sure he didn't mix up the stock, he had strips of film hanging from special hooks into what looked like oversized laundry baskets.

Erne rummaged through the bottom of one of the baskets and came up with what he'd been looking for: an unopened bottle of Jim Beam, not always possible to get during wartime.

He poured a generous glass for Tom and another for himself. "To Maggie Graym," he said, winking at Tom and downing his drink in one.

"How did you find out about that?" Tom asked, referring to his rescue of Maggie in the parking lot of the Hollywood Canteen.

"I have my sources," Erne said with a grin on his face as he poured them both another. "Seen her since?"

"Didn't you know? We went dancing at the Trocadero last night."

Erne looked at Tom to see if he was serious. "Old man Waldie would drop dead if that was true," he said. "His very own creation, the beautiful and highly marketable Maggie Graym. And a mere stuntman."

Tom poured the third round. "Waldie doesn't drop dead. He hires other people to do it for him."

The two men said nothing for awhile. Tom watched with admiration as Erne sliced and spliced film with the extraordinary speed and accuracy that only a master editor possesses.

"Anyway," Tom said after a few minutes. "Maggie Graym doesn't do a thing for me."

Erne stopped what he was doing. "Well, she sure as hell does something for me," he said.

Erne poured another drink for himself and offered the bottle to Tom who declined.

"I'll pass," Tom said. "Gotta get back to the set before Bradford has a fit."

At the mention of Bradford's name, Erne's mood shifted from one of cheerful banter to one of irritation. It didn't happen all that often that Erne became serious, but he was serious now.

"I've been doing a little investigating on that guy," Erne said. "And if I ever get a break from all this work they keep shoving in my face, I'm gonna do a lot more. I wanna find out, number one, why he's wasting so much film around here, and number two, how he's getting away with it."

"What are you getting so steamed up about?" Tom asked.

"You're not the one he had doing the same dumb stunt over and over again." He tried to make a joke of it because he didn't like seeing Erne worked up like this. The guy already had a couple of ulcers as well as high blood pressure. He didn't want to see a heart attack added to the list.

"You may think it's funny. But I don't. Aside from this whole film thing, that idiot keeps entire film crews working overtime for no reason at all. If Waldie knew about it, there would be hell to pay, I can tell you that much. Waldie makes you use both sides of the studio toilet paper. Can you imagine how loud he'd scream if he knew what Bradford was trying to pull off here?"

"Hold on, buddy," Tom said, trying to calm Erne down. "We don't know that he's trying to pull anything off here. He's probably some kind of perfectionist or something, will probably turn out to be a great director someday."

"Bullshit," Erne said.

"And besides," Tom continued, "he has to get his requisitions for film stock cleared. Along with the fact he has to account for all the extra takes. He can't just do what he damn well pleases, unless somebody in head office isn't paying much attention."

"Or," Erne said, "unless somebody in head office knows all about this and is in this with Bradford."

"In *what* with Bradford?" Tom asked frustratedly.

"I don't know, I don't know," Erne shouted. "But I mean to find out."

"Hey Erne," Tom said, "I know this is Hollywood where everybody's imagination works overtime, but if you ask me, I think you've been editing too many of those *Phil and Rosemary, Junior Detective* series."

"Well, nobody asked you," Erne snapped. "And you can just think what you want to think. But I know something fishy is going on at this studio and I don't like it."

"Okay, okay. Just calm down, willya? I'll see you later and we can discuss it, alright?"

Tom left Erne muttering to himself and working on his miles of film. He was pulling away from the editor's building when a wine-colored Cadillac Fleetwood Limousine arrived. Marcus Wood, long considered Hollywood royalty, sat in the back and waited for the chauffeur to open the door for him.

Wood, in addition to his many wartime responsibilities and business interests, had, six months previously, been summoned to Washington where he had been appointed executive director of the Motion Picture Information Bureau, also known as MPIB. This was a government office established shortly after Pearl Harbor. Its main function was to make sure American movie audiences were being given Washington's version, not Hollywood's, of how the war was progressing.

According to Washington's rules for Hollywood, propaganda was encouraged, but rewriting history wasn't. That honor was reserved for Washington itself. Especially when it wasn't in Washington's best interests to let the public know what was *really* going on. Too realistic a picture of the war could create a flurry of bad publicity resulting in an enormous public outcry. It was better to do a cover-up job when mistakes were made or when promises were not kept.

A fairly recent promise not kept was to the troops during the fall of Corregidor. Instead of backing them up with reinforcements and supplies, these troops had been sacrificed to the horrors of the Bataan Death March and the infamous Japanese POW camps. But rather than blame Washington for what appeared to be a case of heartless abandonment, the American media machine focused on the self-sacrifice and suffering of the trapped soldiers. This, apparently, painted a more acceptable picture for the American civilian population to digest.

To have even *hinted* at betrayal in a feature film about Corregidor would have spelled disaster for the film studio. The same would have been true for a studio exploring a possible conspiracy theory concerning the attack on Pearl Harbor. Some critics of FDR had claimed that he'd arranged for the American warships to be left as sitting targets, thereby inviting Japan to attack. That way, America could be drawn into the war and the Great Depression would be over. It was, of course, just a theory, but a dangerous one.

Therefore, it was the job of Wood's staff to scrutinize all of the scripts from which war movies were being made. A second check at a later date would be made on the completed film to see that it conformed with the script that had been initially okayed by MPIB.

Grove Pictures, known as the studio making the most war movies these days, was also known as the studio that disregarded MPIB regulations most often. As a result, Grove Pictures was under almost constant surveillance of the MPIB.

Wearing a superbly tailored pearl gray suit and matching fedora, Wood got out of the limousine and climbed the rickety steps of the old wooden building. This was an unannounced visit as were all his visits. Wood's policy was to try and catch people in the act of doing what was strictly forbidden by MPIB. And then pounce on them.

His presence at the Editor's Building would irritate Erne Parkin quite a lot, Wood knew. Especially when he went through the MPIB stipulations as he did each visit. And even though Erne wasn't in a position to say exactly what was to go into a film and what wasn't, this being up to head office, Wood knew that his real control lay in inspecting films at random during final editing, just in case the studio was trying to sneak something through, as it did on a regular basis.

Wood would have liked nothing better than to have gotten Erne retired from the studio. Waldie, however, had been extremely stubborn on this point because Erne, despite his well-known stand-offishness, was very valuable to Grove Pictures.

Both Wood and Erne went back the same amount of time in Hollywood, the two of them having arrived from the east just as the industry was starting to grow. But whereas Erne had stayed out of the political arena, Wood had used it to his own advantage. And with great success. His charm and tact were legendary. Everyone admired him and loved him. With possibly one exception: Erne Parkin.

But he could handle Erne, and then do what he really came

to the editor's building to do today.

Which had nothing whatsoever to do with his position as head of the Motion Picture Information Bureau.

Chapter 9

The editors weren't the only ones who occupied the decrepit, barely-standing building. On the second floor to the rear were the offices and studio of Desmond Slater, Grove Pictures' official portrait photographer.

Slater, in the tradition of the great George Hurrell, was credited with having made so many of Hollywood's stars, both female and male, flawlessly glamorous looking, at least on silver gelatin.

He was able to accomplish this through his expert use of dramatic lighting which created an illusion of mystery, elegance and sexual intensity. The application of this kind of lighting also cast the shadowing that created high cheekbones and cleft chins when, in reality, these features didn't exist in most of his sitter's facial structures.

Everything was an illusion when it came to photographing the stars. The public didn't want to see the unsightly moles or the large facial pores or the furrows on the forehead or the lines around the neck or the bags under the eyes or more chins than one. The public wanted to believe that these super-beings of the silver screen were free of all the physical afflictions and imperfections that ordinary mortals experience and suffer: aging, acne, turkey necks...

Very rarely had Slater been able to achieve a look of flawlessness without the use of heavy makeup and severe retouching. Except in the case of Maggie Graym. The process by which he worked with her was just the opposite from the way he worked with his other subjects.

With the others, he'd have them slather on the makeup; with Maggie, he'd have her remove it all. That way, he could capture her luminous skin which, when not covered up, made her appear sexier and more desirable than any other female star he'd ever photographed.

He'd shot her more than a dozen times during the past few years. The most recent session had taken place about a month before when he had positioned her prone on a divan with her luxurious red hair fanning out behind her, her eyes heavy-lidded, and her mouth slightly open. The photograph accompanied an article claiming that Maggie's sheer animal magnetism left a man no choice but to submit to her will. Maggie's reaction, when reading the article, was to burst into gales of laughter. "I should only have such power," she'd said.

Working now in his darkroom, Slater was busy developing a series of shots of the young actress, Jane Allen. She was Hollywood's sweet, virginal girl-next-door who was currently being given an enormous buildup by the studio and had been assigned the part of Vance Varley's girl in *Dive-Bomber Rendezvous*.

The photos, however, showed Jane looking anything but sweet and virginal.

"Good God," Slater said aloud having developed the film he hadn't taken, but that had been passed on to him by another source. What movie-goers, the studio, and Jane's increasing number of fans in the armed forces didn't know was that before she was in clean, wholesome movies, she was in a lot of dirty ones.

These photos were stills from some of those dirty movies. And they were the key ingredient in a file on Jane's former career which initially began in a San Diego strip joint where, known as Ice-Cream Cohen, she did her nightly bumps and grinds.

The transition from Ice-Cream to Jane, orchestrated by an ex-pimp and now movie producer who'd introduced her to Waldie, had been very successful. Recently voted the "Girl I'd Most Like to Be In a Blackout With" by the U.S. Army Corps of Engineers, Jane was the perfect vehicle with which to severely humiliate her studio, the patriotic Grove Pictures, maker of anti-Axis pictures since long before the war began.

Slater was in the process of drying the Jane Allen photographs when Marcus Wood walked in.

"Are they ready?" Wood asked.

"Just about," Slater answered. "C'mon over here and have a look. You won't believe what this little girlie has been up to."

The photos of Jane, who was clad only in an ankle bracelet, showed her in a number of positions. She was seen standing, sitting, reclining on her back, and lying on her stomach. In some of the shots there was a flabby male with a lack of hair on his head and an abundance of it on his back. In one photo he was playing with Jane's breasts, and in another, he was lying on top of her in what appeared to be the sex act.

"How do you plan to distribute these photos, Marcus?" Slater asked.

"Now, now," Wood smiled, "that would be giving away trade secrets. After all, I don't ask you to name your sources and in the same way, I never divulge mine...for the very good reason that the less we know of one another's operations, the less we're able to talk in the face of interrogation, should interrogation ever become something to face."

Interrogation wasn't really something that Wood feared. He was too well respected in Hollywood to ever be suspected of perpetrating harm upon the industry. But one could never be cautious enough, especially when one's goals weren't even remotely what others perceived them to be.

Covert operations was his specialty and it was he who had arranged the placing of a lethal bomb aboard the TWA DC-3 Sky Club Airliner carrying the lovely Dorothy Ennismore. Dorothy had just completed a sensationally successful bond-selling tour and was returning to her home and husband, actor Bax McClain, when the plane exploded and crashed into a Colorado mountainside.

With her death in the fiery crash, Wood had knocked out a vital link in Hollywood's fund-raising network. That the vivacious, fun-loving Dorothy had considered Wood one of her very best pals, a man with whom she had shared so many of her feelings, secrets and victories, hadn't bothered him in the least.

Both Hedda Hopper and Louella Parsons would find this file on Jane Allen very interesting, Wood thought as he put duplicate folders containing the expose on Jane into his alligator briefcase which was, incidentally, the same briefcase that Dorothy had given him on his most recent birthday.

One of these folders would be delivered anonymously to Miss Hopper that evening at a fancy dress charity ball, given in aid of Chinese orphans.

Wood didn't suppose this expose would do nearly as much

damage as had the "supposedly accidental" death of Miss
Ennismore. But it was bound to cause a feeling of betrayal in all
of the men fighting for their country who had looked upon Jane
as someone pure, a symbol of the girl back home. And just in
case Hopper felt that this scoop had better wait until the war
was over because of the threat to the American morale, the second folder in the alligator briefcase would go to Miss Louella
Parsons whom he knew to have no such compunctions.

From there, he was prepared to let the two gossip powers of
Hollywood slug it out as to which one of them would be given
the ultimate credit for breaking the story.

Wood loathed them both and was looking forward to witnessing their extreme discomfort in having to perhaps share
mutual credit for this story on Jane Allen. Up until now, the
only thing the two ladies shared was mutual hatred for one
another.

"This is big, eh?" Slater asked Wood, referring to the Jane
Allen expose.

"Big," Wood agreed. "But not nearly as big as the next thing
I have planned. This one is going to knock the stuffing out of
America, that I can guarantee."

"And what's that?" Slater asked, knowing full well what
Wood's answer would be.

"Nice try, Desmond," Wood said. "But I couldn't possibly
discuss this matter with you for the reason I outlined before. It
would simply weaken security. But suffice to say, we will all be
pleased with the results." By "we", Wood was referring to the
small, but potent group of Axis sympathizers he'd recruited,
including Slater, born Hermann Schlatter in 1893. Schlatter and

Wood, born Marcus Wodenheim in 1892, had been a fellow students at the Halpenhofferschmidt Gymnasium in their native Dusseldorf, Germany. Now they were fellow conspirators. As a founding member of the group, Wood was one of the few who knew the identity of the leader. The two of them met often to go over strategies. Along with his penchant for covert actions, Wood was considered an invaluable strategist with ambitions that he hoped would one day grant him a high place in the "New Order".

Having been of German blood hadn't necessarily been the deciding factor in his choosing the Axis over the Allies. Had he truly believed the Allies would prevail, he would have been totally in their corner. However, in his opportunistic view, he was of the opinion that Germany would be the victor. He'd met Hitler in 1935. Never before and never since had he felt such confidence in another individual.

Slater was still fishing for the inside story. "Does your latest plan involve anyone I know?" he asked with a grin.

"Someone you know very well," Wood answered. "Someone you know very well, indeed."

Day 3

Chapter 10

Vance Varley seemed to be having a terrible problem. He came running out of his dressing room both horror stricken and hysterical. The commotion he made was so loud that it was heard all over the set. A number of personnel gathered around the bathrobe-clad star to find out what was wrong. Something had frightened him out of his wits, that was apparent. It was almost impossible for the producer of Vance's current film to calm him down.

"Here, here," the producer soothed. "Why don't you tell your old buddy here exactly what's scaring you and making you so upset? That way maybe we can do something about it and you won't be scared anymore."

When Vance finally stopped shaking he said between small sobs: "There's a daddy long legs in my sink and I'm afraid of daddy long legs."

"Oh," the producer said. "So that's it, a daddy long legs in your sink, huh? Well, no wonder you're scared. But now there's no need to worry about it anymore. You just stay right where you are and I'll go in there and take care of that big, nasty daddy long legs."

Vance sat on a folding chair holding the hand of the motherly coffee wagon lady while the producer went on his mission. A moment later he came out of Vance's dressing room and looked into Vance's big blue eyes.

"Okay, Vance, the coast is clear. That bad old daddy long legs is dead."

"Are you sure?" Vance asked, his voice still fearful.

"Sure I'm sure. Now why don't you let me help you back into your dressing room so that you can get yourself ready for your next scene, okay? The cameras are just about to roll." The film being made was about a young soldier on leave and a girl who'd fallen in love with each other during a Ferris wheel ride in an amusement park. The story line had the soldier proposing to the girl and her accepting followed by the pair's having to find someone to marry them before the soldier's departure to a far-off battleground scheduled for the very next morning.

Vance, playing the young soldier, allowed himself to be helped back to his dressing room, but was still wary of the spider.

"What if he had relatives?" Vance asked, stopping suddenly before stepping foot into the luxuriously appointed dressing room.

"He didn't," the producer said in a calm voice. "He lived alone."

It was another half hour for Vance's dresser to get him into the uniform of the soldier and a further hour for the film's director to persuade him to get into the waiting Ferris wheel car.

"It looks shaky," Vance complained.

"It's perfectly stable," the director said as patiently as he could. With all of these delays of Vance's, the production was going to cost a fortune. But he knew from bitter experience that it was absolutely pointless ordering Vance to do something that he didn't want to do. With Vance, you had to be exceedingly gentle or he might walk off the set. And he was a big enough star to get away with it.

In the Ferris wheel car, Maggie Graym waited patiently while Vance was being coaxed to sit beside her. She kept an

Agatha Christie paperback tucked into the folds of her butter-
cup yellow frock, just in case this turned out to be yet another
one of those marathon sessions with Vance being difficult.

One thing about working with this guy, Maggie recently
realized, was that she had read just about every Agatha Christie
mystery ever published. Not to mention Ellery Queen and
Dorothy Sayers.

When Vance was finally seated, the wheel started to move
slowly upward.

"Stop," Vance shrieked, practically deafening Maggie as he
did so. "You didn't tell me that this thing was going to move. I
hate heights!"

"You'll be okay, Vance," the director said, slowing the car
almost to a halt. "Just sit there next to Maggie and remember
not to look down from the top."

"I refuse to do this scene," Vance answered loudly. "I
demand you get a stuntman for it."

Tom Driscoll stood near the set having just completed yet
another whole set of stunts for Bradford on the tenement set.
Again, they were all identical, but this time, Tom just kept quiet
about it.

"It won't work to have a stuntman in this sequence,
Vance," the director was telling his highly agitated and pan-
icked star. "I want to go from closeup to longshot in one
sweeping, continuous movement. Which means that you
have to be in the car with Maggie for the whole time or it
won't come off. So you'll just have to stay seated where you
are until I get the shot I need."

Tom wondered if this director was going to pull a

"Bradford" on Vance and have him do a lot of takes. He would never stand the strain.

"I don't have to do anything. I'm a star," Vance said, starting to get up.

Maggie, usually cool toward Vance, was now beginning to feel sorry for him. He was, without a doubt, absolutely petrified. "Listen, Vance," she said, trying to comfort him, "it won't be nearly as bad as you think. I'll hold your hand the entire time and you won't even know that we're climbing."

The word "climbing" set Vance off once again and he was about to leap out of the car when the director, seizing what might be his last chance, gave the order for the wheel to move and the cameras to roll.

With the speed of the car, Vance was thrown back into his seat and he felt Maggie's arms around him in a romantic pose. Anyone witnessing the scene would have seen what appeared to be a beautiful young woman and a handsome soldier gazing deeply into each other's eyes. No one could know that through Vance's clenched teeth, he was saying: "Keep your sympathy for yourself, bitch."

The people on the ground gave a huge sigh of relief when the car was underway, but when it reached the top, they saw Vance suddenly push Maggie away from him and stand up on his seat causing the car to rock violently back and forth. Maggie did her best to get him to sit back down again, but to no avail.

Then Vance's vigorous rocking of the car turned his greatest fear to reality.

There was a heavy grinding sound like metal separating from metal and the car actually started to detach from the structure of the wheel.

Almost instantly, the car fell sharply to one side with such force as to propel Vance right out of it. With a hideous, ear-deafening scream, he plunged toward his death leaving Maggie only slightly more fortunate: clinging to the side of the dangling car for dear life.

As the spectators down below watched in horror, Vance had miraculously grabbed a crossbar on the way down and had somehow managed to swing himself into another car positioned directly below the one he'd been in with Maggie. Whereupon he promptly fainted.

The chance of Maggie swinging into another car as Vance had done was about one in a million.

Below her, the studio people gathered, shocked at the prospect that Hollywood's most beautiful and most valuable property was about to die in a tragic fall.

Emerson Waldie, just then coming onto the set, looked up at his famous star hanging some sixty feet above him.

"I don't remember that being in the script," he said to one of the producers. "How many times do I have to tell you guys to keep me informed of all script changes?"

"I hate to tell you, E.W.," the producer answered, "but this is no script change. The car just fell. All of a sudden," he tried to explain.

"Well, do something," Waldie shouted. "Climb up there. Get her down!" The look of fear on his face now reflected not so much the death of Maggie Graym, but the death of Grove Pictures.

"We've got the fire department coming," the producer said.

"If she can just hang on until they get here."

Just then the suspended car fell even further off the Ferris wheel frame and Maggie was left hanging from the side of it, her feet dangling in space. She could feel her fingers giving way. It was apparent to her that her struggle to hold on was about to come to an end.

One hand lost its grip and the other was slipping fast. And then it was impossible for her to hang on any longer.

She let go.

Chapter 11

Maggie saw it all. She saw herself at the age of six months being posed in the nude on a little fur rug by her parents. This vision was followed by her first day in kindergarten, followed by scenes of her grade school years and leading up to her graduation from high school. Next, she saw her first boyfriend, Artie Peterson, as he drove her around in his '35 Ford roadster. And then she saw herself dancing in the chorus line of a Broadway musical. And then she saw herself in Hollywood as she danced in front of the cameras. And then she felt herself being grabbed from around the waist.

Instead of that swift and fatal downward journey, she was being carried swiftly through the air as if on a vine which was propelled by the sheer force of the person who'd rescued her. It was as if she was flying, being held by these two strong arms.

They belonged to Tom Driscoll. While everyone else on the ground stood around, helpless, unable to help Maggie, he'd climbed the frame of the wheel in a matter of seconds and with the aid of some rope which he'd fastened to the very top, had swung outward to where Maggie had been hanging.

Grabbing her just in the nick of time, he had then swung back with her to the wheel's frame. Now he knew what it was like to be Johnny Weissmuller playing Tarzan.

But Maggie was in no way acting like Tarzan's Jane.

Maggie, glad as hell to be saved from being splattered all

over the set below, was mad as hell that it had been Tom Driscoll who'd saved her. Especially when he proceeded to rub it in.

'You seem to make it a habit of getting yourself into some pretty tricky situations that you can't get yourself out of again," he grinned after they'd reached the other side of the wheel. Maggie didn't answer, but climbed awkwardly into one of the cars, tumbling into it head first with her skirt falling over her head.

The wheel started to move again a few seconds later and the car in which Vance lay reached the loading platform. He was helped out of the car and led, shaken and sobbing, to his dressing room. It was obvious that this was all the filming Vance would be capable of today, and possibly all week.

His absence from the set meant a loss of many thousands of dollars, hundreds of thousands perhaps, depending upon how much time Vance would demand in order to recuperate from his harrowing ordeal.

For those people who'd wanted to see Maggie and Vance's car crash to the ground, and had gone to all lengths to see that it would, the prospect of Grove Pictures losing a substantial amount of cash was at least some sort of victory. The disappointment of seeing their big plan go awry would be softened by having caused a major financial setback for the studio.

Emerson Waldie, realizing just how close he'd come to possible ruin, exited the set fast. He didn't want to come into contact with Maggie and give her the slightest indication that he was glad she was alive. Or, more precisely, that the studio's main money-making property hadn't perished.

It was extremely galling to him that with all the years of labor he'd put into building this studio, all the work and all the sweat, the whole operation could disintegrate in a matter of minutes with the demise of this one person.

The strange twist was that to Waldie, it wasn't the threat of losing the studio that obsessed and frustrated him as much as the fact that it was Maggie Graym, and not him, who held the power that could make this happen or not. Well, he had a few ideas of his own when it came to dealing with Maggie Graym. And one of them, already underway, was to create a new star to take her place at Grove Pictures. Or, to be more specific, to create a brand new redhead with a great body and great legs who could dance a little and "sinc" (that being the phrase for actresses whose singing voices were always dubbed) a little.

This would show Maggie that she wasn't as unique as she seemed to think she was. And even more important than this, it would show her just who the boss was around here. To see her knocked off her pedestal would give him no end of satisfaction.

As Waldie reveled in these thoughts on the way back to his compound, Maggie and Tom's car was being lowered to the loading platform where it came to a halt.

It had been quite an ordeal for Maggie. As for the people crowding around her as she came down the little gangplank, they were sure she'd be grateful to the man who had just saved her from a horrible death. What they heard, however, indicated to them that Maggie was anything but grateful.

"The score is two to zero, buster. So I owe you a big favor in return," Maggie was saying to Tom. "Anytime you want that favor, just let me know. In the meanwhile, the next time I happen to be in trouble, I'd appreciate it if you'd mind your own damned business."

"Anything you say, lady," Tom returned with a big smile on his face.

Maggie turned on her heel and strode off to her dressing room, escorted by her personal maid and her hairdresser.

At the same time, Tom found himself surrounded by a bunch of his friends on the camera crew whooping it up.

"Hey, Tom," one of the guys said. "You're gonna get yourself one hell of a reputation around here if you keep rescuing Maggie Graym all the time."

They'd obviously heard about the Hollywood Canteen incident of the other night, probably from Erne Parkin. There was no doubt the number of rescues was beginning to add up. But Tom was too tired to go into any detail.

"The only thing I'm gonna get me," he said, "is a good, stiff drink." He walked past several people in the crowd who, in comparison with Tom's excited friends, were strangely quiet and whose eyes solemnly met one another's.

Chapter 12

As was the case each evening, Jimmy's Tropical Bar and Grille in North Hollywood was full of real Hollywood folk, the people behind the scenes: the lighting men, grips, gaffers, best boys (assistant gaffers), sound engineers, sound boom men, set designers, art directors, follow-up men (production coordinators), carpenters, scenery shifters, continuity people, prop handlers, and juicers (electricians).

The place was a favorite hangout every night of the week, decorated in Hawaiian bad taste that blended perfectly with an atmosphere that was homey, noisy and smoky. When the jukebox wasn't blasting out Tommy Dorsey and Frank Sinatra's *Shake Down The Stars* or Artie Shaw's *Frenesi* or Glenn Miller's *In The Mood* or the Benny Goodman/Peggy Lee rendition of *Why Don't You Do Right?* or Frances Langford's *I'm In The Mood For Love*, a live ukulele band struggled with *Lovely Hula Hands*.

Tom Driscoll walked in and made his way to the crowded bar. Jimmy Xsos, the flamboyant Greek owner of Jimmy's, and an incurable movie fan, especially when it came to Maggie Graym, greeted Tom just as he settled himself onto a barstool.

"I don't want to see you taking this man's money," Jimmy instructed the Hawaiian-shirted bartender. "Whatever he wants to drink, you give him to drink, on the house, understand?" Obviously, the news of Tom's second rescue of Maggie Graym had also reached Jimmy's ears. For a moment, Tom thought about getting off the stool and going to some other bar where nobody knew him. Anything to get some peace regarding this damned Maggie Graym business.

"This man," Jimmy announced loudly and emotionally, "has saved from certain death, Hollywood's most luscious, most adorable, most fabulous and talented star and I, as her number one fan, salute him."

"A beer," Tom told the bartender dully.

"So let me in on it," Jimmy asked conspiratorially. "What was it like to, you know, be that close to Maggie Graym, to actually hold her in your arms, to..."

"Like hugging Mussolini," Tom said.

Jimmy, thinking that Tom was joking, laughed heartily. "Oh, by the way, your buddy, Erne Parkin, called a little while ago. He said if I should see you in my joint that I should tell you to wait here for him. He said he has some important information to talk to you about. He said you should make sure and wait."

"Okay, okay," Tom said, both wondering what it was that was so urgent with Erne and wishing that Jimmy would go away so he could relax and enjoy his beer.

"You want a nice plate of corned beef and cabbage?" Jimmy asked. "Or maybe some of Jimmy's famous meatloaf?"

"No thanks, Jimmy," Tom said, knowing that all of the meat dishes on Jimmy's menu were nothing more than disguised Spam. Ingeniously prepared. But still Spam.

"How about a hamburger then? On the house."

Tom again declined and swallowed his beer. Now that Erne wanted him to wait there for him, the plan to move on to some other spot had to be abandoned.

"Well, whatever you want, you just let me know," Jimmy said, finally starting to move away. "It's all on the house. As far as I'm concerned, you're a hero."

A hero, Tom thought. He couldn't believe he was being called a hero, not just by Jimmy, but by just about everybody he'd bumped into since the Ferris wheel incident.

To Tom, rescuing a Hollywood actress was nothing for him to be called a hero over. Wiping out a nest of Japanese artillery men on some remote island somewhere—that constituted being called a hero. Or mowing down a platoon of German soldiers. Two things he wasn't going to get a chance of doing if things continued to go this way.

And then there was Maggie Graym herself. He didn't know what to make of her. Here he'd saved her from getting raped the first time and killed the second, and she never as much as said thanks. Well, what could he do? She was a star, Tom thought. She didn't have to say thanks.

By the time he was on his fourth beer, practically everybody in Jimmy's had come up to him to say something nice. This whole thing was getting to be a gigantic pain in the ass.

It really got to be too much when an apprentice wig man asked Tom for his autograph.

"Just sign it 'from the man who saved Maggie Graym' or words to that effect," the apprentice wig man said.

Until this incident blew over, Tom could see himself being referred to as *the man who saved Maggie Graym*. He was in the middle of being slapped on the back and told what a great guy he was by the man in charge of film processing at Grove when, to Tom's relief, Erne walked in.

Only he wasn't exactly walking.

It was more like he was dragging himself. Tom watched, thinking Erne was drunk or something. But then he noticed that Erne was bleeding badly.

There was quite a lot of blood and it was gushing out from several different places on Erne's body, including the stomach area that Erne was clutching.

Erne stood upright for one more moment as he tried to walk over to Tom and then, like a great big toddler, tumbled to the floor. Except for a few twangs from the ukulele band that had now ceased playing, there was total silence in the bar.

Tom rushed to Erne's side, knocking over his barstool. The older man's eyes were wide open. He tried to lift his head, tried to say something. No words emerged. He tried again, desperate to give Tom a message.

With Erne so obviously wounded, Tom shouted for someone to call an ambulance. This galvanized into action the others at the bar who had appeared mesmerized by the sight of Erne lying on the floor.

But Erne, always in a hurry, seemed to have made up his mind that he wasn't going to wait around for an ambulance. He was a man who didn't hold on to anything once it was finished, even life. Tom watched as the light in his friend's eyes dimmed and went out.

Day 4

Chapter 13

"It's murder," Emerson Waldie shouted. "I tell you it's first degree murder."

Waldie sat at his big, ornate oak desk holding his head in his hands. The cupid clock on his desk showed it was just a little after eight in the morning. On the floor where he threw it in a rage, lay an early edition of the Los Angeles Times with a picture of Jane Allen on the front page.

It wasn't a photograph of the dewy-eyed virgin of twenty-two, the pretty little thing who'd so completely captured the heartstrings of America, but a closeup of Ice-Cream Cohen in the hard makeup and the hardened expression of a seasoned star of pornographic movies.

And along with the photo were the hard facts revealing Jane's unsavory past and the story of how she'd successfully switched, with the help of Emerson Waldie, the head of Grove Pictures, to legitimate motion pictures.

The story, an alleged exclusive by Hedda Hopper, didn't so much focus on Jane's early career as it did, according to Hopper, on her betrayal of the American people who'd been so devoted to her, but more specifically, the American fighting man.

In Hopper's words, the young manhood of America was dying on foreign battlefields so as to preserve and protect the purity of the girls and women they'd left at home, and to make sure they would never fall into the hands of those heinous rapists and murderers, the Germans and the Japanese. Jane

Allen, the article pointed out, had symbolized all those girls and women, and had become the shining beacon of hope and faith that would lead our wonderful, brave American soldiers, sailors and marines home again.

"I don't know how our boys will take this terrible blow," Hedda wrote. She predicted that the exposure of Jane Allen might cause vast losses of life and limb in all theatres of war due to a radically lowered military morale. Because, and again in Hopper's words: "What will our boys feel there is left to fight for if our womanhood is so despoiled?"

Lyle Brenner, Emerson Waldie's personal assistant looked over at his boss who was practically crying. "How could they do this to Janie?" Lyle asked. "How could they purposely set out to destroy her like this?"

"To hell with her," Waldie roared. "What about me? What about me? How could they do this to me? How the hell did I know she used to make dirty movies?"

Not only was the scandal sure to kill Jane Allen's career, but as far as Waldie could tell, it was also sure to bring a ton of the worst, most devastating and ruinous publicity upon Grove Pictures.

And it wasn't the kind of publicity that was going to die down with time. The Fatty Arbuckle case was ancient history yet people in Hollywood still talked about it as if it had happened only yesterday.

"Can I get you some coffee, boss?" Lyle asked.

"With cyanide in it," Waldie answered. Lyle wore a look on his face that was, as usual, bright and friendly. Behind it he only wished he could fulfill Waldie's request.

"The sonofabitch, whoever he was, gave that vulture, Hopper, the story without even trying to sell it to me first. And I would have paid a mint for it."

"So it wasn't money that the culprits were after," Lyle deduced.

"No, it wasn't money, you pinhead," Waldie said. "They just wanted to get the studio and they just about have. Now I'll have to scrap all those new pictures that little tramp's in, including *Dive-Bomber Rendezvous* and *Nine Nuns in a Jeep*. Who'd want to see her after this? Have you got her on the phone yet?"

"I tried several times, but she's not home," Lyle replied.

"Of course she's not home," Waldie exploded. "She's at my house. Probably still in bed. Go up there and get her up. I don't want her slashing her wrists on my property. That's all I need."

Lyle didn't understand at first. "...She's at your house?"

"That's right, now get over there and fast."

"Should I phone Mrs. Waldie in advance so as not to upset her?" Lyle asked.

"Mrs. Waldie? Mrs. Waldie's in Palm Springs," Waldie said, revealing the fact that Jane Allen wasn't just a "houseguest".

"I'll get right over there," Lyle said, now understanding that the rumors *were* true, that his boss *was* screwing Little Miss Purity. This was something that would shock America even more than the exposure of Jane's sordid past, were it to be known. Lyle walked quickly to the door and then stopped as if something had suddenly occurred to him. Something *had* suddenly occurred to him. He slowly turned around again.

"Well go!" Waldie demanded. "What are you standing there for?"

"What would you like me to tell Jane?"

"What would you like me to tell Jane? What would you like me to tell Jane?" Waldie mimicked. "If she hasn't already heard the news on the radio, just show her this." He shoved the newspaper toward Lyle.

"That'll be quite a shock," Lyle said.

"What the hell do you think I've had?" Waldie shouted. "Just get that broad out of my house and out of Hollywood before noon today. Give her a couple of hundred dollars and a Greyhound bus ticket. A one-way ticket."

Lyle ventured an opinion. "Don't you think that figure is kinda low, Mr. Waldie? Jane may thumb her nose at a mere few hundred dollars, especially when she realizes that she can cash in by giving the newspapers and magazines a story on how she was living it up with Emerson Waldie in his big Beverly Hills mansion while his trusting wife was out of town."

Something in Lyle's voice and manner made Waldie look up. Lyle, usually someone Waldie used as a doormat, now had a strange grin on his face and look in his eyes.

Unless Waldie was mistaken, which he generally was not, Lyle, whom he'd bullied and overworked for the past nine years, was making him a business proposition. He was more than certain of it.

"You know, Mr. Waldie," Lyle said, walking slowly toward him, "I was just thinking. Considering all the inconvenience this is going to cause little Janie, the figure of a couple of hundred dollars should be revised to least ten grand, don't you agree?"

"Ten Grand?" Waldie growled and then stopped talking for a moment. "Oh, now I get it. Five for Jane and five for you, is that it?"

"Oh no, Mr. Waldie," Lyle said as if totally shocked by this suggestion. "About a grand for Jane and the rest for me, as well as a huge raise and an assistant of my own. And, oh yes, a change of job. I think I'd like very much to direct pictures, thank you very much."

"You must be crazy if you think I'll give you anything. You're fired. Now get out."

"Very well, Mr. Waldie," Lyle replied. "But do you want to break the news about your friend, Miss Allen, to Mrs. Waldie and the press? Or would you like me to do it?"

Chapter 14

At the same time that Lyle was exacting revenge upon Emerson Waldie for all the years of abuse, Tom was standing in the middle of Erne's living room in Silver Lake, looking at the disarray around him. Anything that had been standing upright was now upside down or lying on its side. Pillows were slashed, drawers emptied, shelves cleared.

The past ten or so hours had been a nightmare with Erne's death, the police questions and the process of accompanying Erne's body to the morgue. And then this morning, after just a few hours sleep, going to the mortuary to arrange Erne's funeral which was scheduled for later in the week. He'd also phoned all of Erne's ex-wives, informing them of Erne's death, before dropping over at Erne's place to pick up his one good suit for the burial. To find it, he'd have to burrow through a pile of clothes ripped from the closet and thrown into a heap on the floor.

You didn't have to be super-smart to figure out that Erne was killed because he found out something he wasn't supposed to find out. And that he'd probably threatened to expose what he'd learned. His last message to Tom was that he had some important information to talk to him about and that he should make sure and wait at Jimmy's. Whatever that "important information" was, his killer or killers had also wanted it. As evidenced by the state of Erne's apartment.

It was only after Tom had left Erne's apartment and had got into his car that he noticed the envelope on his front seat. It contained the personal items found on Erne's body when he was killed. They had been released to Tom by the people at the morgue. Opening the envelope, Tom took out Erne's wallet, watch, signet ring, pipe and tobacco. Gone was his little notebook into which Tom had often seen Erne jotting things down.

Tom wondered if those "things" were, as it turned out, a record of everything Erne had been complaining about, mainly the outrageous wastage of supplies such as film, and the matter of personnel that were needlessly kept overtime. Was there even more than that in the notebook? Perhaps a few names?

These and other questions started plaguing Tom, clouding his mind. Starting up the car, he drove toward Hollywood, trying to figure what Erne had been on to and why it had cost him his life. But when he reached Hollywood and Vine, he was jarred back into reality. He saw that the road ahead was almost unpassable.

Up by the traffic lights, a large crowd of people were craning their heads upward as if they had spotted a squadron of enemy aircraft in the skies above Los Angeles.

Tom pulled his car over to the side of the street and got out. Just then, a woman ran past him screaming hysterically. "It's poison gas from Japan," she yelled. Up above, a sizeable grayish mass of smoke crept slowly across the otherwise unblemished blue California sky. It had no apparent connection with a ground fire of any sort, such as a blaze in downtown L.A. or in the Hollywood Hills that had got out of control, and there was nothing to indicate that it had come from an industrial smokestack of which there were many in wartime Los Angeles.

Tom knew, or thought he knew, what had caused the smoky

looking substance. A few days before he was murdered, Erne
had read aloud a newly published article having to do with air
pollution. The article had reported that gray masses of dirty air
had been sighted over Los Angeles in recent months. Erne had
then voiced, in his own inimitable doomsday fashion, how air
pollution would eventually smother L.A., block out all traces of
sunlight, snuff out all forms of life.

And now Tom was out of his car trying to calm down the
crowd. "That smoke is from the exhaust pipes of your cars,"
Tom shouted above all the noise. He wanted to give them the
benefit of Erne's words and tell them about the accumulation of
automobile and factory fumes that were trapped in the L.A.
basin by the San Gabriel Mountains surrounding it. But the
people were in such a panic that they didn't seem to hear a
word of what he was saying.

"It's going to kill us all," a man shouted as he ran up the
road, barely missing being hit by a fast-moving car.

The car, trying to avoid hitting the man, swerved to the
opposite side of the street and sideswiped a drab, khaki painted bus. It was transporting a group of Japanese/Americans and
Japanese aliens from an assembly center at the Santa Anita race
track. They'd been kept there, in the most rudimentary conditions, for six months and were now being taken to a relocation
camp in Inyo County.

This move was in keeping with the Civilian Exclusion Act
of 1942, also known as Executive Order 1099 which had been
signed, at the insistence of west coast military authorities under
General DeWitt, by President Franklin Delano Roosevelt the
previous March. Even though a study had shown there to be *No*

'disloyalty' to the American flag by this particular segment of society, they were still being forced into "concentration" camps.

The exclusion act called for the evacuation of all people of Japanese ancestry now living in the western states of America. This meant the loss of homes, businesses, possessions, but most important, the dignity and freedom of these people, most of whom had been born in Los Angeles, San Francisco, Portland or Seattle. Word of who was on the bus spread through the crowd like wildfire.

"Let the yellow rats breathe in a little of their own poison," a formidable matron yelled, suddenly rushing the huddle of bewildered evacuees who'd been ordered to get off the crippled military bus.

"My nephew was at Pearl Harbor," the woman announced, hitting out blindly with her handbag.

"They should be strung up on telephone poles up and down Hollywood Boulevard," someone else shouted. The roaring crowd was in total agreement. Completely out of control now, and with no law enforcement in sight, the crowd advanced menacingly, someone actually wielding a length of rope.

Tom, seeing what was happening and how the situation was escalating, jumped into the crowd's path and tried to hold them off as best he could. There was no doubt that this bunch was hell-bent for revenge and wouldn't be appeased until someone was killed.

"Now hold on just a minute," Tom shouted into the crowd. "These people are Americans, most of them, and what you're doing, taking the law into your own hands, is wrong."

"Get the Jap-lover," someone shouted. The crowd surged

toward Tom who now found himself being pelted by an avalanche of fists, handbags and knees.

One of his attackers, a maddened old lady who looked like she taught Sunday School, when she wasn't trying to lynch people, attempted to kick him in the groin.

Another attacker, a fox-faced man of about fifty ran up from behind Tom and slammed him painfully in the kidneys with an auto wrench.

"Take that, you lousy draft-dodger," another person bellowed in his ear. The remark was accompanied by a sharp blow to the head, but Tom stood his ground and was now the only barrier between this ugly, out-of-control mob and the frightened evacuees, some of whom were very old.

Six or eight black and white patrol cars from the sheriff's department finally arrived and the cops, getting out of them, halfheartedly came to the rescue of those being attacked. It was obvious that some of the officers would have preferred the carnage to continue.

Fifteen or twenty minutes later, the traffic on Hollywood Boulevard was moving normally again and the evacuees were in the process of being transferred to another bus.

They boarded the bus with an air of resignation, their destination being a place called Manzanar near Lone Pine. This was an isolated spot in the Sierras, a few hundred miles south of Yosemite. But before the bus pulled away, many of its occupants had thanked Tom for what he had done for them by protecting them against the unruly and violent crowd.

Tom thought about Lone Pine. He didn't know anything about the area other than the fact that geologists spent a lot of time in that region, and also that movie companies sometimes filmed there when they needed a stark, mountainous background that was abundant in sagebrush and good for cowboy movies.

Tom stood on the side of the road watching the bus as it merged with the flow of Los Angeles traffic, the very traffic that Erne had predicted would one day turn the city into one big black cloud of gas fumes.

Well, Tom thought, at least Erne didn't have to see if his prediction was to come true or not. At least he'd been spared that much. When the bus was out of sight, Tom returned to his car and drove off. It was only after he'd driven a quarter of a mile or so that he realized that there was someone crouching on the floor right behind his seat.

Chapter 15

Without reducing the speed the Packard was traveling, Tom veered suddenly and sharply to his right and onto a narrow shoulder of the road where he abruptly put his foot on the brakes, unbalancing his passenger in the back.

"Okay," he said impatiently to the hunched-over figure on the floor behind his seat, "the game's over. Maybe you wanna tell me what you're doing back there?"

"I'm escaping from that bus taking us to the concentration camp," an anxious looking sixteen year old boy named Douglas Tanaka answered. From where Tom sat, twisting his body in order to get a better look at Douglas, his first impression was that of a delicately-built Asian teenager with a head of thick, unmanageable black hair.

"Not in my car, you're not," Tom said angrily. This was all he needed, he thought. An escaped evacuee. On top of everything else that had happened in the last 24 hours. "How did you get back there, anyway?"

"It was easy," Douglas replied. "When they told us to get off the bus after the accident, I just didn't get back on again, that's all. I just sort of snuck away and made my way up the street when nobody was looking. I didn't have a plan or anything, but when I saw this car, I got in the back here. I thought maybe I wouldn't be discovered."

"That was pretty clever," Tom said, "but you picked the wrong car, kid. And the wrong driver. I'm putting you back on that bus where you belong. He had to wait for an army convoy of trucks to pass and then he made a U-turn back onto the road and in the direction he had just come from.

"That bus isn't where I belong," Douglas said, somewhat defiantly and started to get up from where he was kneeling. Before he could get far, Tom put out a restraining hand, keeping him down.

"For Pete's sake, stay out of sight for the rest of this ride, willya?" Tom said. "I don't need another one of those nuts out there on the street banging on my car."

Douglas stayed down and didn't speak for a few minutes. He could tell from the vibrations of the car that Tom was exceeding the thirty-five mile an hour speed limit imposed by the gasoline board on all drivers.

"I saw what you did for my folks back there," he said finally. "And I want you to know everybody was grateful. Ever since this war started we haven't had anybody stand up for us like you did. Even the cops that came to break up the mob didn't do as much."

Tom didn't reply. He was leaving the center of Hollywood trying to catch up with the bus which wasn't anywhere in sight.

"Damned bus must be miles away from here by now," he muttered. "I'll just have to deliver you to the authorities and let them figure out a way to get you to your camp or wherever it is you're supposed to be going."

"I was born in Los Angeles," Douglas said angrily. "I'm just as much an American as you are. It isn't right that I should be put in prison behind barbed wire. It isn't right for the government to imprison any of us of Japanese descent."

"I'm not taking any sides here," Tom said. "It's just a matter of doing what the law says, that's all. If it was up to me there wouldn't be any of these camps, but since we're at war with Japan and since the government thinks your people might be a threat to the security of this country, it's not up to me to decide. Besides which, I'm no expert on the subject. I don't know a damned thing about these places they're putting you."

"Not too many people do," Douglas said. "What they do is crowd us into barracks that nobody wants to live in and they don't care about old people or sick people. And there's only one bathroom for about a hundred families, and the way the barracks are made there's no protection against hot weather in the summer or freezing weather in the winter."

"Sounds like you've already spent some time in one of those places," Tom replied.

"Worse," Douglas said bitterly. "They didn't have any barracks for us so they put us into horse stalls. The ones at Santa Anita Racetrack. They called that place an 'assembly center' and kept us cooped up for over six months. But we've heard through the grapevine about the conditions in the camps and the word is they're not much better than the horse stalls we lived in."

"Well, there's nothing I can do about it," Tom said resolutely. "I don't have any choice except to turn you in and let the people in charge work it out."

Not very far behind Tom, another car followed. Tom had been so busy trying to deal with the young man on the floor behind him that he hadn't noticed how closely the car was on his tail.

Then, on a long, undeveloped stretch off Lankersham with deserted lots occupied mostly by wild sagebrush, the driver of the other car gained on Tom and forced him to pull over.

"Now what?" Tom said, noticing four men getting out of their car and walking toward his.

"What can I do for you fellas?" Tom asked, opening the door and stepping out. He instantly recognized them as Bradford's boys, the ones he'd seen hanging out at the studio. The draft board rejects.

For an answer, Tom was thrown back against the car with his arms pinned by two of them. Was this some sort of scare tactic because he'd disputed Bradford the day before? Or because he had been Erne Parkin's friend?

"Where's your boss?" Tom asked.

"He couldn't come," the spokesthug said. "But he told us to give you his best. So that's what we're going to do. Give it to him, boys."

The "boys" were just about to pummel Tom when they heard a horrifying scream originating from the other side of the car. It was an eerie, unearthly sound, and like nothing Tom had ever heard before. And it was coming from Douglas Tanaka.

Douglas had leapt from the passenger side of Tom's car expelling the blood-curdling shriek. The startling effect of it caused the four men about to work Tom over to pause in amazement.

"What in the fuck?" one of them said just before Douglas executed a crippling blow to the man's head with the heel of his foot, a movement he'd achieved with all the grace and agility of a ballet dancer.

A second man pulled a knife and had it promptly kicked out of his hand.

In a matter of a few seconds, Douglas had turned from a timid- seeming young man into someone who had the power of a deadly samurai. They suddenly rushed him as a group and were felled as a group. Douglas wasn't out to kill, just stun. It was obvious that he could have put the four attackers in the hospital for a long time, but had chosen to let them learn from this lesson and live. He let out a howl of laughter as they got up and ran for their lives. It was comical how they scrambled into their car and sped off. Tom leaned against the fender of his car not believing the scene of near-carnage that he'd just witnessed.

"Are you okay?" Douglas asked, approaching Tom. In contrast to the one-man hurricane of destruction he'd just been, Douglas was now the calm young student he'd been before. There was nothing about him to indicate the act of violence he'd just moments earlier carried out. His clothes were neat and intact and there was a peaceful, almost serene look on his face.

"Fine," Tom said. "Just fine...what do you call that stuff you just did?"

"Oh that." Douglas said matter-of-factly. "It's the ancient art of self-defense known as karate. All the males in my family are expert at it. I had my black belt when I was seven years old. That's about as far as you can go."

"Karate, huh?" Tom said, still amazed. "I've heard of judo and jujitsu. The army uses them. But I've never heard of karate."

"Neither have they," Douglas laughed, pointing into the distance where the thugs car was leaving a trail of dust.

"Well, I'm kinda glad that you just happened to be in the

car," Tom said. "If you hadn't, I probably would have been a goner by now." He was somewhat confused as to what he was going to do next regarding the teenage boy in his charge.

"Who are these mugs, anyway? And why were they after you?" Douglas asked.

"That's what I'd like to know," Tom said, opening the car door to get in and inviting Douglas to do the same.

Backing away, Douglas said, "I'm not going to the camps. I'll try to make my way from here. You won't call the authorities on me, will you?"

"Are you kidding?" Tom answered, "You just saved my skin with that kicking and screaming routine. The least I can do is help you save yours.

"Thanks," Douglas said, "but I don't think there's anything much you can do."

"I don't know about that," Tom said. "Have you ever used a bayonet?"

Day 5

Chapter 16

If hanging by her fingernails from a Ferris wheel was a terrifying experience for Maggie Graym, wondering if and when Vance Varley was going to show up to do his scenes with her was a frustrating one.

It had only been one day since the incident on the big wheel but Maggie, being the true professional that she was, had reported back to work first thing.

Vance, however, was nowhere to be seen this morning, and as the minutes passed, it didn't look likely that he was going to show up. Finally, at around nine, Vance's live-in secretary, a curt young man called Adrian, phoned in saying that Mr. Varley was emotionally over-wrought due to having been tossed out of the Ferris wheel car and was currently indisposed with horrendous headaches.

So it looked like production would focus on scenes that didn't require Vance's presence. There was a big musical sequence in which Maggie would lead a group of women in a military extravaganza. Maggie had been rehearsing for this scene for the past two weeks and had even learned how to call cadence. Coaching her in drill and rifle was a tough female Marine who put her through her paces as if she was a raw recruit, but finally told Maggie she'd make a great sergeant. Maggie took this as a big compliment.

As for when the blond, blue-eyed, pug-nosed, freckle-faced boy wonder might report back to work so that they could final-

ly finish the picture, who could tell? One thing was certain:
Waldie wouldn't want it getting out to Vance's considerable
audience that their rugged, masculine hero, the man who was
winning World War ll before their very eyes, had emotional
problems. Nor did Waldie feel it prudent were Vance's female
fans, of which there were probably millions, to learn that
Adrian was more to Vance than just a live-in secretary.

Maggie considered phoning Vance herself to try and determine just how "indisposed" he really was. But then she abandoned the idea knowing she would never get through Adrian.

Instead, she headed for makeup, hair and wardrobe. She'd
already been there at six that morning getting the full glamour
treatment for the scene she was supposed to have filmed with
Vance. So she'd now have to go through the whole routine all
over again for the military musical scene.

Turning a corner, she accidentally bumped into someone
coming from the opposite direction. Stepping back to let the
person pass, she was amazed at what she saw: a woman who
was about the same age and height that she was, with the same
figure, facial features, and way of dressing. The color and style
of her hair was also identical. She was an almost perfect
look-alike.

Maggie, unable to take her eyes off her, felt as if she was staring into a mirror.

The look-alike stared back at Maggie until finally Maggie
snapped out of it.

"Hi," she said, smiling. "I'm Maggie Graym." And as she did
with all people new to the studio, she extended her hand as a
warm gesture of welcome. The look-alike regarded the out-

stretched hand in front of her as if she had just been offered a plate of dog turds.

"Emerson says that I don't have to talk to you if I don't want to. And I don't want to," the look-alike said in a rather high and unattractive voice.

After saying this, she turned her back on Maggie and walked away. Maggie stared at the young woman's back for a moment. "Well, I never..." she said, not liking the way she had just been snubbed.

"Did you see that, Johnny?" she asked the makeup man, near whose door her encounter with the haughty young look-alike had just taken place.

"Sure did, Maggie," Johnny said. "Old man Waldie sent her over. Told me to make her up so she looked just like you. I thought she was your stand-in or something."

"As far as I know," Maggie said, taking a seat in front of Johnny's big mirror, "my stand-in is the same one I've had for the last three years. Ethel McCreedy. She was even on the set doubling for me yesterday."

"Then who's this new girl?" Johnny asked, applying some powder to Maggie's cheek.

"Damned if I know," Maggie answered. "But it wouldn't surprise me if Emerson Waldie is finally doing what he's been threatening to do all these years: grooming a new Maggie Graym."

"Impossible," Johnny said. "There's only one Maggie Graym in this town and that's you."

Maggie had known Johnny ever since he'd done her face for her Grove screen test. She considered him one of her loyal friends at Grove.

"I'm not so sure about that, Johnny," she said. "That young girl I just bumped into looked more like me than I do. If you were to put the two of us together, the audience wouldn't know the difference."

"Gee, Maggie," Johnny said, "if I've done anything to hurt you or your career, it was unintentional. The order came through to give this girl the Maggie Graym treatment. You know, the works. I had my whole staff working on her. Old man Waldie even came down here and supervised. I had no idea he might be double-crossing you. Or I would never have gone along with it, job or no job."

"Don't worry about it, Johnny," Maggie said. "If Waldie wants to create a new Maggie Graym, let him. I've had a pretty good run for my money here in Hollywood and to tell you the truth, I never expected to get even half this far. I mean, I can't sing, really. I can dance a little, and that's not saying much. and when it comes to acting, I have no talent whatsoever."

"Oh, c'mon, Maggie. You're the greatest."

"The greatest what? That's the question."

"Star. Nobody in Hollywood comes close to you."

"Thanks, Johnny, but I'm getting a little sick of being Maggie Graym. I want to quit this business before the public gets sick of her, too."

"You quit and you'll break a million hearts," Johnny said, finishing up by painting Maggie's lips a glossy red. "And mine," he added, "will be number one."

Chapter 17

Not far away, on a Grove sound stage several lots down from the makeup building, Douglas Tanaka was putting on the uniform of a Japanese soldier. In his scabbard was a sharpened bayonet and the rifle that was issued to him was real.

Also issued to him were the exaggerated protruding teeth and the thick-lensed eyeglasses that were so identified with the average Japanese soldier. A current propaganda poster seen all over the United States portrayed a Japanese soldier with such teeth and glasses silently crawling into the bedroom window of a young American girl with the intention of raping and murdering her. Trying on the glasses, Douglas greatly resembled the soldier in the poster, his eyes becoming as small as pinheads. Impossible as they were to properly see through, he kept them on and walked past dozens of people who took no particular notice of him.

Douglas was on the Grove Pictures lot masquerading as one of the many extras who were also masquerading as Japanese soldiers for the making of yet another of the war films that seemed to be the mainstay of the studio.

Most of the extras were of Chinese, Korean and Indian origin, made up to look Japanese. It didn't matter that they didn't look even remotely Japanese since the general public seemed to lump all Asians in one group, not being able to discern one type from another.

Douglas fitted his false teeth in place and passed Tom who

was standing near the coffee wagon, observing the proceedings and keeping an eye open for Douglas.

"You're right," Douglas said, sideling circumspectly next to Tom. "This movie set is the safest place for me to hide out."

Tom Driscoll wasn't quite certain just how he'd managed to become the caretaker of a runaway Japanese/American evacuee, but that's the way it was. Instead of going off to war to fight a bunch of guys of Japanese extraction here he was, on a Grove Pictures movie set, looking out for one.

Sure Douglas had saved his ass back there on the road, but did that mean he had to take on the responsibility of making sure the kid wasn't picked up and hauled off to one of the camps? Apparently it did. Because making sure that Douglas wasn't picked up and hauled off to one of the camps was exactly what he was doing.

Since his encounter with Douglas the day before, he'd hidden the boy in his garage, but that was very chancy because he had the nosiest neighbors in Los Angeles. He'd seen Mrs. Foley, next door, scrutinizing him from her window as he carried some dinner out to Douglas who slept in the car. And now he was taking yet another chance, setting Doug up as a film extra. But it was working.

Like anybody in Hollywood with ears, Tom knew that there was always a war production in progress at Grove that involved the portrayal of Japanese soldiers in combat. It was just a question of finding out the particulars on the current production which Tom did by dropping in at the casting office to make a few casual inquiries. That had been the simple part. The hard part had been figuring out how to get Douglas into the uniform of a Japanese soldier. Wardrobe had done all the fittings for the two hundred or so extras the previous week. To get a uniform, Tom would have to sneak one out of the wardrobe department and that wasn't going to be easy. And then he realized that the best way of getting a uniform for Douglas was to let Douglas get it for himself.

When the coast was clear, Tom had ushered Douglas from the back seat of the Packard into the narrow corridor outside wardrobe and had instructed him on how to go about it.

"Just go in there and tell the ladies you've just been hired for the war picture on sound stage eleven and that you need a uniform fast," Tom said. "And if they give you any trouble all you have to do is mention that the director is holding up the entire production until you get there and that if they know what's good for them, they'll get on the ball quick."

"What if somebody in there says something about me looking Japanese?" Douglas asked.

"Tell them you've just come from makeup and that your name is Manuel Rodriquez." Fifteen minutes later, Douglas was on the film set blending in with the other extras. Tom waited until after the coffee break to make sure things were going smoothly, and then feeling he'd done a great job stashing Douglas, decided to take off for awhile. He glanced at his watch and saw it was nearly noon.

Tom didn't even think about the fact he hadn't had much sleep in the past few days. There hadn't been much time what with arranging Erne's funeral, the battle with the crazy mob that wanted to savage a busload of innocent people on Hollywood and Vine, and then the attack by the thugs who seemed intent on doing him some serious bodily harm.

Finally, there was the friendship that he'd struck up with Douglas, and he still didn't know what he was going to do about that. For the time being, everything looked okay, but what was he going to do with the kid later? He couldn't stash him at his place with his nosy neighbors always on the lookout. He'd have to find a safe place for the kid to hide out.

This picture being made was called *Behind Japanese Lines.* According to the shooting schedule, which had been posted for all personnel associated with the picture to observe, the cameras were set to keep rolling until at least ten in the evening and possibly midnight.

The studio was anxious to get the film finished and released as quickly as possible so as to capitalize on the progress being made by the United States Marine Corps on a remote South Pacific island nobody had ever heard of called Guadalcanal. And apparently the unions were relaxing their rules in favor of patriotism. Not to mention huge amounts of overtime for their members.

"War movies like the ones we make at Grove Pictures are what keep this great land of America and her brave Allies informed and united against tyranny," Emerson Waldie had recently sermonized at a major war bond rally in Washington.

As usual, he had played up the patriotism of his studio for all it was worth while playing down something he knew wouldn't go over well: Grove's financial gains.

Tom took one last peek on the set to see how Douglas was doing and concluded, upon seeing that Douglas was doing just fine and would be okay until later that evening, departed. He had a few things to do and one of them was to ask Bradford a bunch of questions. Such as where he was two nights earlier.

It took less than five minutes to drive over to and park near the tenement set. Strangely, there were no other cars parked there, nor was there any sign of life. Getting out of his car, Tom walked over to the sound stage door. He opened it and saw that the place was deserted. Just the other day it had been teeming with people. Second unit filming there had obviously been a wrap and Bradford was probably on his next assignment. But when Tom went to the studio's personnel office to find out where Bradford was now assigned, the clerk looked absolutely blank.

"Bradford?" she asked with just a little too much sincerity in her voice. "I don't believe we have anyone working at Grove by that name."

Chapter 18

The Art Deco executive office building that Erne Parkin had refused to acknowledge, let alone move into was, next to Emerson Waldie's chateau, the most important building on the Grove lot. That was because it housed the Grove Pictures elite: the executive producers as well as the top financial brains. It was also where Grove kept all its personnel records, both past and present.

Tom had spent the better part of the last two hours on the lot trying to trace Bradford, without luck. Some people said they knew of him, but they had no idea where he could be located. Others flatly stated they'd never heard of him, people that Tom knew had *worked* with the guy. Why would they and the personnel department deny he'd been employed at Grove?

Tom was determined to prove that Bradford did exist. If there was a file on him, this is where it would be. Not that Tom knew what he'd do with such a file if he actually found one. If anything, this exercise was simply a starting point, a search for something tangible that might lead to something else. Erne's killer, for instance. But getting the file would be tricky. He couldn't just walk in and casually ask to see it. He'd have to *take* it.

Sitting in his car under a huge chestnut tree, Tom tried to figure out how to get to the Records offices on the second floor of the building without using the front or back entrances, the stairs or the elevators. This was something he'd have to do without being seen.

And then it hit him how to do it. Of course. He'd go in through a window. He'd simply climb up the side of the building and find a suitable window to enter. He'd been scaling walls and skyscrapers and castles and sheer faces on mountains and masts of ships—*and recently, a Ferris wheel*—since his early days in Hollywood, doubling for the likes of Vance Varley and Adam Morley. Scaling this building would be a piece of cake.

Taking a length of rope from the trunk of the car, Tom moved stealthily by foot to an alcove on the side of the building where he wouldn't be seen climbing. He swung the rope onto one of the art deco gargoyles that jutted out above the first floor

The gargoyle held as he quickly walked/climbed up the exterior of the building and managed to negotiate a foothold on a ledge. Several people walked below but hadn't looked up. Tom repeated the action with a second gargoyle and was soon on the second ledge. By inching along, he made his way to an open window. If he thought he could simply climb into a room, he was wrong. There was a desk in the way that he had to negotiate and scramble over. It was a secretary's desk laden with papers, a dictaphone machine and a typewriter. And sitting at it was the actual, living secretary. Watching him.

"Can I help you?" the secretary asked as if Tom had entered the room the conventional way.

"Window washer," Tom offered, moving off her desk and walking to the door.

"Gee, and I took you for an actor," she said, smiling a full, toothy smile and looking Tom up and down.

"Yeah, well, sure..." Tom answered. This exchange with the secretary was distinctly film noirish, Tom thought, *film noir* being a movie genre just starting to pop up in Hollywood since *The Maltese Falcon* came to the screen the previous year.

"You're probably trying to see a producer, right?" the secretary asked. "And you came in through the window because they wouldn't let you in at the front desk, right?"

"That's right," Tom answered. "I'm just a guy looking for a break in show business."

"Well, good luck," the secretary said, again smiling her inviting smile.

Tom opened the door into the hall and stepped out. There was a sign on the wall with an arrow indicating that the records office was in the same direction he was going. Turning a corner, he stopped. There was an attendant outside the records office reading a novel at her desk. She seemed totally engrossed in her book which was fortunate for Tom.

He took advantage of her preoccupied state, moving slowly and silently past her. He could see the door to the records room was closed. He only hoped it wasn't locked.

It wasn't. Tom carefully turned the doorknob and pushed the door open just wide enough for him to fit through. When he was on the other side, he carefully closed the door so that it didn't make a sound.

No clerk was present inside. Just several dozen rows of filing cabinets which listed, in alphabetical order, the information on thousands of people who were currently working at, or had formerly worked at, Grove Pictures. In the cabinet with all the last names starting with the letter B, he found files on Babson, Bendix, Brolin, no Bradford.

Knowing that this office was set up to keep a record of every employee Grove Pictures ever had, Tom could only surmise that the file on Bradford had been removed. Just as Bradford himself had been removed from his job at the studio. Tom continued his search thinking that maybe Bradford's file had been mixed up with someone else's, but his findings were, again, nil.

Flipping through the files, still in the B area, Tom quite accidentally discovered something he hadn't been looking for, something that interested him. He opened the file on a man called Wolfe Bronchflek, a Hollywood stuntman of an earlier age.

According to the studio bio just inside the folder, Bronchflek had come to the United States from Germany back in 1933, trading a career as a circus acrobat for the rigors of stunt world in the film industry. Apparently he had been engaged in the same kinds of stunts that Tom was currently carrying out, all of them dangerous and calling for someone who really knew what he was doing.

Tom studied the photo of Bronchflek that was attached to the file and couldn't get over the guy's nose. It was probably the largest nose he'd ever seen on a human head. It had a pronounced hook that made the rest of his features look tiny by comparison.

Tom knew most of Hollywood's stuntmen, even the bunch that wasn't active anymore, the guys who were too old to stunt and the ones who'd sustained serious injuries carrying out their jobs. Maybe this Bronchflek had taken a bad fall and had retired. There was no indication from the information in the file and no record of his whereabouts in 1942.

Most likely, Tom decided, Wolfe Bronchflek had returned to

his native Germany at the outset of the war and was now, if still alive, fighting for the Nazis.

Not knowing why, exactly, Tom put the photo in his jacket pocket before returning the file to the drawer. He then got on with the search for Bradford's records, again going from drawer to drawer, determined to find something, anything about Bradford. Absorbed in what he was doing, he didn't hear the door opening behind him.

Chapter 19

To Wanda Belkins, Maggie Graym's look-alike, the Grove Pictures movie lot was one big blur.

The problem was that she couldn't see a thing without her eyeglasses. Emerson Waldie had taken them off her face, telling that under no circumstances was she ever to wear them again. In public, or even in private.

This was Wanda's first day on the lot, and the schedule had been quite rigorous. She'd gone from hairdressing to wardrobe to voice lessons to publicity to the studio of Desmond Slater for a photography session. So when was lunch around here?

Taking her from place to place, she had Emerson's own Chrysler Imperial and chauffeur to escort her. But now the chauffeur had driven off somewhere. Wanda had no idea when, or even if, he'd return for her. Boy, would she complain her head off when she saw Emerson.

And it wouldn't just be the driver she'd complain her head off about, but most of the people she'd come into contact with so far, especially that *Maggie Graym*. She'd demand that Emerson get rid of Maggie right away. Because now she, Wanda Belkins, was going to be the big noise at Grove Studios. Only her name wasn't going to be Wanda Belkins anymore. According to the publicity department, her new name was going to be Aurora Dawn. And that was something else that annoyed her. If she wasn't going to be Wanda Belkins up on the marquee, how would the dumb hicks she left behind in her home town of Boise, Idaho know it was her?

It didn't matter. Once she got this elocution junk down she would take over those parts Maggie was playing and the whole world would applaud, not that she had ever sung or danced in public before.

About the only thing she'd ever done in public before was sling hash at Benny's coffee shop in Burbank where one of Waldie's talent scouts had spotted her less than a week before.

A lot had happened to her since then. For one thing, Emerson Waldie, himself, had been called from the coffee shop phone and had personally, at the suggestion of the excited talent scout, come down there to see her. Waldie didn't normally do this kind of thing; run down to some coffee shop somewhere to look at a promising newcomer. This particular talent scout who'd called him, however, was on special assignment to find another Maggie Graym. And for that, Waldie would have gone to a coffee shop on Mars.

Taking one look at Wanda, Waldie had literally jumped for joy. Both he and the talent scout had come right around the counter without even telling her who they were and had started discussing her as if she was under a microscope.

"The hair will have to go," Waldie had said. "If we bleach it and dye it we should get an identical match..."

"Yeah," the scout had agreed, "but what are we going to do about the Neanderthal hairline? She looks like an ape. We'll have to do a major electrolysis job on her they way they did on Hayworth."

"May as well do the mustache at the same time," Waldie advised.

Wanda hadn't liked any of what was going on, especially the ape business, until Waldie, or "Emerson" as he'd instructed her to call him, had presented her with a hundred dollar bill. Right there in the coffee shop. With all the customers watching, not to mention her boss.

Waldie had declared her to be the perfect replacement. Only she didn't have any idea what he was talking about. Or who it was she was supposed to be replacing.

Until she'd bumped into Maggie Graym that morning. And then it all fell into place. Why, she was going to replace Maggie Graym! The most glamorous star in Hollywood!

No wonder she had been hovered over by a dozen makeover people in white coats. And why they had bleached the black out of her hair and had dyed it red. And had plastered over that recent outbreak of acne. And had fitted her for all those incredible outfits in the wardrobe department.

Well, now that she knew how valuable she was to the studio, she was going to make them pay. And pay good. That old buzzard Waldie thought he was getting some poor sap to take Maggie Graym's place, but he was wrong. She was no poor sap. And she was going to tell him so right to his porky little face the minute she saw him

Not waiting for the chauffeur to return from wherever he'd disappeared to, Wanda left the photographer's studio, and yes, she'd seen the way the photographer, Slater, or whatever his name was, rolled his eyes to heaven so as to say she was hopeless. For that, she'd get him thrown off the lot, too. Along with the voice coach who'd insulted her by saying she could always get a job in sound effects as a screeching tire.

Walking past some of the sound stages, a number of blurs in human form passed her and said "Hi, Maggie," which irritated her no end, but she just ignored them all, the peons.

And then she saw what appeared to be Waldie's office. Only it wasn't. Wanda didn't realize that she was walking into the wrong building. Nor did she realize someone was following her in.

The building she'd entered was an unused soundstage that was dark except for the red exit lights. Wanda didn't yet know she was lost, or that the person following her had also entered the soundstage.

She found the place deserted, but this didn't especially bother her. So many of the places Waldie had taken her to in this last week, including his bedroom, were uninhabited. Wanda pushed a door open and found herself on the unused swimming pool set.

Just at the moment that Wanda was beginning to wonder how she was going to get out of the big darkened room, Emerson Waldie sat in his office anticipating with pleasure the look that would be on Maggie Graym's face when he told her about Wanda. Or perhaps he'd just let her find out for herself.

The first vehicle he was planning for Wanda was a movie originally meant for Maggie: *Fifth Avenue Follies*, a musical about a chorus girl who marries a wealthy socialite and fails in keeping her past from her snobbish Fifth Avenue in-laws.

Waldie was looking forward to the time when the news would leak out that Wanda, and not Maggie, was to be the star of this big-budget extravaganza, Maggie would be certain to get the message that her days at Grove were numbered. In a few months, if not sooner, he'd marry Wanda off to Vance Varley. It wouldn't take much to get Maggie on her knees begging that something be done to build up her flagging popularity. Maybe he'd cast her in a movie as Wanda's sister. Her older sister. Her *much* older sister. In fifth billing.

As for the public, they'd eat Wanda up, the only problem being that before he could put her in a picture, he'd have to make sure those singing and dancing lessons worked out. And he'd have to make sure that she continued with her voice lessons. That high, screechy voice of hers was beginning to drive him nuts. Think what it would do to an audience?

Waldie was still smarting from the Jane Allen affair. The newspapers were making a meal of it, and so was Hollywood society. Going anywhere these days was an ordeal. In restaurants, there was the subdued chatter as he was shown a table. And mingled with the chatter were the snickers. Well, at least the news of his sexual liaison with Jane hadn't been revealed. Yet. He was doing whatever that damned blackmailer of a personal assistant, Lyle Brenner, demanded. He'd, of course, paid him the $10,000. And he'd given him a picture to direct. It was a B picture, but still a picture.

Of course, this whole thing had thrown him into a tizzy. His doctor, upon taking his blood pressure, and finding it dangerously high, advised him to try and relax and not think about business matters and the aggravations of daily life for awhile. The doctor even suggested that Waldie take a vacation. But just as Waldie didn't know how to smile, he had absolutely no idea how to take a vacation. Movies were his life as he pointed out to the doc.

"Yes," the doctor had said, "and if you don't watch it, movies will be your death."

The one thing Waldie had to cling to these days was his newest discovery, Wanda Belkins. He was going to train her the right way. To have respect for him. To be obedient. To do just as he told her. Glancing at the clock on his desk, Waldie suddenly came out of his reverie. He realized that Wanda was supposed to have been back in his office over an hour before.

Waldie pressed the buzzer on his desk, shouting into the intercom. "Where the hell is Wanda Belkins? I told the chauffeur to get her back here by noon."

"I don't know, Mr. Waldie," his secretary, Harriet, answered. "Is there anything you'd like me to do?"

"Yeah," Waldie snapped, "find her!"

Chapter 20

"I have to tell you that I'm totally unprepared for your visit," the somewhat prissy man holding the gun on Tom said. "I mean, it's not as if we weren't expecting you to break in here to get your hands on the files, it's just that I honestly thought you'd do it at night, which is when most normal people break into places."

Tom said nothing, watching the man as he slowly edged his way to a large mahogany desk in the corner where he opened the top drawer and fumbled around for something inside.

"Here it is, exactly the thing I was looking for," he said removing a long, thin silencer and expertly screwing it onto the barrel of his gun. He bore an uncanny resemblance to Clifton Webb, the actor.

"Little did any of us know," he continued, "that you'd be so courageous as to try it in broad daylight. I really do commend you for your bravery, but it does present something of a timing problem. Oh well, I guess we'll just have to kill you a little earlier than originally scheduled."

Tom assumed he was going to let him have it right then and there seeing as he'd attached the silencer. But the man seemed to read Tom's mind and dispelled him of the thought.

"Oh, don't worry about this old thing," he said, referring to the silencer. "I'm just taking a few precautions in case you should become rambunctious."

"Smart," Tom said. "By the way, where's the file on Bradford?"

"Bradford?"

"Yeah, you know, your buddy. Bradford. Or are you going to say you never heard of him?"

"Actually, I wasn't going to say any such thing," the man said casually while picking up the phone and dialing a number. "Excuse me a moment, won't you?"

Tom measured the distance between himself and the man with his eyes and decided not to rush him. In the six or so feet that separated them, there was ample room for this guy to put at least three slugs into him. And he doubted very much he would hesitate.

"Guess whom I've got here?" the man said into the receiver. "The editor's friend, Driscoll. Caught him with his nose in the files." He then lapsed into rapid German. Tom stood patiently waiting for him to get off the line and even though he couldn't really understand what was being said, he could sort of guess that the subject of the conversation was his execution and the disposal of his body.

"Which one were you calling, Himmler or Goebbels?" Tom asked when the conversation finally ended and the man had put down the receiver.

"You'll find out soon enough," the man said, keeping the gun trained on him. "As a matter of fact, the people I just called are on their way over here right now. They're so excited about seeing you. It'll be like a reunion. Seems some of them were dreadfully injured when they tried to detain you recently."

"I guess they were more delicate than they looked," Tom said. "You have to be a lot tougher if you're running a sabotage ring."

"Oh, please," the man replied. "A sabotage ring. That's so

naive and dramatic. You sound just like someone out of those awful spy serials this studio is so fond of producing."

"Well, if it's not sabotage, what is it?" Tom asked.

"I like to think of it as a corrective measure bravely carried out by a small but effective number of dedicated and professional film people in all walks of the industry who feel it is their responsibility to seize, or shall I say, to rescue, the studios from the Semitic faction running them today and to reflect, through the cinematic medium, a purer and truer vision so embodied in the Germanic ideal."

"Does that mean the end of the cowboy picture as we know it?" Tom asked.

The man ignored him and went on. He seemed to be on a soapbox and probably couldn't have stopped even if he had wanted to. His eyes gleamed as he spoke.

"Until our goal is realized," he said, "we shall continue operating as a special arm in the war effort, undermining production whenever possible. Creating wastage in time, money and materials. Exposing highly regarded stars and other Hollywood luminaries for their sexual misconduct and perversions. Dealing with other big stars by other means, usually fatal. Lowering morale and causing general mayhem and confusion in any number of ways. And, oh yes, getting rid of troublesome characters who get in our way such as the talkative Erne Parkin. Of course you knew he had actual evidence, and even photographs, of our operation and was going to the FBI with it?"

"Well, I kinda figured Erne had been up to something like that," Tom said.

"As a matter of fact, he had enough evidence and names to

destroy us," the man commented. "So naturally we had to silence him."

"Yeah, well, Erne always did have a big mouth, that's for sure," Tom replied. "He was always mouthing off about your Uncle Adolph and what a crazy buffoon he was."

As intended, Tom had hit a nerve. He could see it on the man's face. He took advantage of his discomfort. "Somehow, I don't see your goose-stepping clown of a dictator making his way up Hollywood Boulevard, "Tom continued. "Except maybe on his way to be hanged."

"Keep it up and I won't wait for the others to arrive. I'll finish you off myself," the man threatened.

Tom knew very little about psychology, but he was aware that this man, who was so cool at first, had a low boiling point and could be pushed over the edge. That's what he wanted. Without getting killed in the process. If he could goad him to move a few inches closer to him, he had a good chance of overpowering him. Except that he was no high kicker the way Douglas was. Still, it was certainly worth a try.

Remembering the blood-curdling scream Douglas had let out during the ambush on the road, Tom suddenly let out one of his own, not nearly as good as the one Douglas had produced, but effective nevertheless. The man was startled sufficiently enough so that Tom could execute his next move.

This was a well-timed kick which hit the man's gun with perfect precision, knocking the weapon free and causing him to go after it. He never made it. Tom let him have a chop to the back of the head that sent him sprawling.

"Say," the man asked from his prone position, "what do you

call that stuff you just pulled on me?"

"Oh that. It's the ancient art of self-defense known as karate."

"Oh," he said, and seemingly satisfied by Tom's answer, promptly passed out.

"Thanks, Douglas," Tom muttered to himself as he scooped up and pocketed the gun.

Figuring that there could only be a few minutes left before the tough guys would barge in, he decided to take a stab at getting the police involved. He quickly dialed the operator and asked for the Hollywood precinct. Even before the connection was made, Tom knew how stupid he was going to sound. When the desk sergeant got on, Tom pitched right in. "Look," he said, "I don't have a lot of time to talk about this, but there's a group of saboteurs here in Hollywood, and I just knocked one of them out. But there's going to be a bunch more running in here any minute now."

"Yeah, well thanks, buddy," the sergeant on the other end answered predictably. "We get a couple of hundred calls a day from people going on about spies and saboteurs. Why don't you drop in at the station next week and file a complaint?"

It was obvious that arguing with the cop was futile. Life in Los Angeles these days was a paranoid proposition at best with the general population suspicious of just about everything and everyone. He could understand the cop treating him like just another phone crank. Even to his own ears he sounded like just another phone crank. And if he were to trade places with the cop, he would've reacted the same way. Tom put the receiver back on the hook.

He then left the records office and passed the receptionist. Much to his amazement, she was still reading her novel and didn't look up. The book must have been very engrossing for her to have missed his scream.

The secretary into whose office he had entered earlier was busy working at her desk when he returned for his exit from the building.

"Drop in again," she said, flirtatiously.

"Thanks," he said, climbing out the window, "maybe I will."

He had just lowered himself to the ground and was shielded by foliage when he saw the mugs arrive. The same ones that had tried to get him earlier. He was pleased some of them had broken arms and bandaged heads and weren't moving quite as fast as they had last time he'd seen them. In fact, they looked downright funny as they piled into the building.

But to Tom there was nothing funny about this. They'd killed Erne and thinking over the information he'd got from the man with the gun, they'd done a lot more damage besides that. And were continuing to do so.

But who'd believe it?

Chapter 21

At approximately the same time that Tom was leaving the records building, Wanda Belkins, now feeling and acting less than confident, was slowly edging toward Grove Pictures' massive, seventy-five foot deep swimming pool. Backwards.

The specially designed pool was the one and only of its depth and length in the world. It could easily accommodate up to a hundred swimmers at one time as well as a complete underwater film crew. Along with dramatic backdrops such as underwater rock structures and myriad canyons and peaks.

Most recently, it had been temporarily appropriated by the War Department in order to make a training film for the U.S. Navy.

The purpose of this film was to demonstrate the proper procedure for escaping a sinking submarine.

Needless to say, Emerson Waldie hadn't been too happy about having a real submarine lowered into his beautiful pool which had cost a whopping one hundred thousand dollars to build.

"Who the hell do you people think you are, coming in here and trying to take over part of my studio?" he'd hollered when first approached about the use of his pool.

"We're the people who can take over your entire studio for the duration of the war if we so wish," the War Department representative had calmly replied.

But now the training film was made and the U.S. Navy and

their *effing* submarine were gone and the pool was drained of
water. Grove Pictures' swimming sensation, Alexis Lee, for
whom the pool was built, was on leave. She was going to have
a baby and as a result of her absence, no "'water" movies were
being planned for at least six months.

It had been rumored around Hollywood that Emerson Waldie
had given Alexis an additional three months off, not out of gen-
erosity, but so that she could train the newborn infant to swim. It
was his express desire that Alexis and the baby would appear
together in her comeback film. This, according to Waldie, was
something that would certainly get moviegoers excited.

However, that movie wasn't going to be made until well into
1943 and right now, on the darkened soundstage, Wanda was
getting scared. She hadn't yet reached the pool when the man
following her accidentally kicked something.

Wanda turned sharply toward the sound. She couldn't see
anyone, even when she squinted her eyes, but she sensed she
was in danger. She was suddenly gripped by fear.

"Who's there?" she cried out.

The answer came in the form of Marcus Wood. He stepped
out of the shadows and into the eerie reddish light from the exit
sign. He moved purposefully in the direction of the young
woman.

"Stay away from me," she warned. "You come one step closer and I'll scream my head off."

"Be my guest, Maggie," Wood quietly replied, smiling.
"Nobody will hear you."

"What do you mean, Maggie?" Wanda asked. "I'm Wanda
Belkins."

"Sure you are, Maggie," Wood said agreeably. "And I just so happen to be General Douglas MacArthur. By the way, Maggie, where on earth did you pick up that horribly screechy voice? It's absolutely appalling."

"I told you, mister, I'm not Maggie," Wanda insisted. "What do you want?"

"Oh, nothing much," Wood said with an air of nonchalance. "Just your life." With each step he took forward, Wanda took one back. She was now a mere six or eight feet from the edge of the empty pool.

"I swear to you," she said, "I'm not the person you think I am. I'm not Maggie Graym. I'm just made up to look like her. Emerson Waldie wants me to replace her. So he had the make-up people give me the same look. You gotta believe me."

Wood watched the girl's progress. She was just a few feet from the big concrete hole in the floor. This was terrific, he thought. Fortuitous to the extreme. He could kill Maggie Graym without having to as much as touch her. Her death would look like an accident which is exactly the way he wanted it to look.

As had been the case with Dorothy Ennismore, it simply would not "do" for anyone to even suspect that Maggie had been murdered. His aim was that the ordinary soldier, the man on the front line, feel great loss and nothing else. Any hint of foul play was certain to replace a soldier's grief and depression with a need for revenge. Revenge had a strength all its own that made men fight all the more furiously. And that, Wood thought as he strode very quickly towards Wanda, was contrary to the whole point of the exercise.

Wanda, seeing Wood almost upon her, turned to run and then, realizing her mistake, tried to stop in time. Her scream was too brief to be loud.

"So long, Maggie," Wood said as he walked over to the side of the pool and looked down at the look-alike, obviously dead. She'd met the bottom of the pool face first and lay sprawled like a broken doll.

Wood was feeling something very close to euphoria. Ten months earlier, in January of 1942, he'd felt the same thing when the news reached him confirming Dorothy's plane as having crashed just outside of Denver.

In what he'd considered to be a performance of Academy Award calibre, he had wept copious tears and had then insisted on accompanying the bereaved widower, Bax McClain, his squash court and polo pal, along with the rest of the search party to the crash site. He wanted to make sure there was nothing to indicate that this might have been an act of sabotage. And there was nothing. The impact had fairly pulverized the TWA DC-3 so much so that the largest piece of wreckage found was less than a foot long.

But the whole operation had turned out disappointingly. Ennismore had been a great star, although not one who'd as yet established herself as a military favorite. She was laid to rest and, in the face of all that a nation at war had to contend with, pretty well forgotten. Wood had planned that his next victim be a true favorite with soldiers, sailors and marines as well as civilians.

Standing at the side of the pool and looking down at the body, he felt he'd succeeded in doing just that. He was also thrilled this assassination had gone so well, so smoothly, although he was baffled as to why Maggie had protested so strongly that she wasn't Maggie.

Oh, well, he thought. It didn't really matter. All that really mattered when it came right down to it was that Maggie Graym was dead.

Now he could concentrate on some of the *other* projects he'd been neglecting. One of them was the planned derailment of the Hollywood Victory Caravan, a train from which important stars such as Hedy Lamarr, Spencer Tracy, Irene Dunne, Judy Garland, Mickey Rooney, Claudette Colbert, Dorothy Lamour and William Powell sold victory bonds at whistle stops across America. To kill them all in one fell swoop would be a coup greater than Wood could imagine.

He also had his east coast people looking at ways to rig the furnace at the Stage Door Canteen in New York so that an "accidental" explosion would take even more entertainers and a huge number of military to their deaths.

And, of course, there was the need to eliminate the highers-up such as Mayer, Goldwyn and Zanuck. He considered these people the Reich's real enemies.

Lastly, in his position with the MPIB, he'd had access to many of the facts Washington had wanted suppressed. He'd been collecting all these nasty facts about the war and compiling them into a book called *Secrets Washington Doesn't Want You To Know* which he was planning to publish. Anonymously, of course. Then he would publish a sequel called *Secrets Hollywood Doesn't Want You To Know* in which he would dish the dirt on the stars and the studios. Together, these two volumes would most certainly lower morale across the country.

There was a lot of work to be done and so few hours in any given day to do it all.

Chapter 22

Douglas Tanaka thought at first that it was just his imagination working overtime, especially since he was so damned nervous at the possibility of being found out as an impostor on the set of *Behind Japanese Lines*. But now there was no doubting it. The man's eyes were definitely trained on him. More accurately, they were glued.

Not only that, but those small, pig-like eyes had hardly been off him for the past few hours of filming. Starting with the sequence in which he and his fellow "Japanese soldiers" staged an attack on a hospital tent bayoneting wounded U.S. Marines. And continuing with the sequence that almost made him sick when he and a few others were instructed to sink their greatly exaggerated false buck teeth into dinner: freshly caught fish that were still alive and wiggling.

Douglas was doing his best to blend in with the crowd. It seemed like he had succeeded for quite awhile, until the point when he'd noticed this crew member, a lighting technician, looking at him curiously and then menacingly.

As long as a scene was being shot, Douglas felt secure that the man, a short, but muscularly built red-necked kind of guy, wouldn't disrupt the proceedings. As for what he might do later, Douglas wasn't so sure.

Again trying to keep a low profile, Douglas listened intently as to what the director was instructing them to do in the upcoming scene. "Okay, listen up," the director was shouting through a megaphone. "This is the scene in which you guys get yours. The marines are going to swoop down on you and kill you in a number of ways. Some of you will be shot, some bayoneted, some beaten to death with a rifle butt. By the time I call 'cut' you'll all be dead, just lying around on the ground with grotesque expressions on your faces. Okay, got that?"

The sequence took place just as the director had said it would with Douglas falling victim to a bullet in the brain. He lay on the ground, his face twisted in a mask of death until he heard the magic word "cut" being called followed by the equally magic words "lunch break".

Getting up from the ground and dusting off his uniform, he walked over to the refreshments table where coffee, Spam sandwiches and donuts were being served. While wolfing down his first meal that day, Douglas stood talking to a Mexican guy who was made up to look Japanese, a pathetic attempt in his opinion. After a few minutes, he had forgotten about the staring technician. Until he heard a rasping southern drawl that was, for sure, directed at him.

"Boy, that's some great makeup job they done on you," the man said.

Douglas didn't have to guess who was doing the talking. He turned and faced the technician.

"Or maybe it ain't makeup," the technician continued, his eyes glinting as he spoke. "Maybe it's the real thing, maybe you're the escaped Jap kid from the bus they been talking about on the radio, huh?"

Douglas said nothing as the technician ambled over and stood just inches away from him. Silence had fallen over the set leaving Douglas as the focal point.

Suddenly, the man shot out a beefy paw and grabbed Douglas' chin roughly.

"Yeah," he said. "That's a Jap kisser, alright, and there ain't a drop of makeup on it." He barely got the words out when he received a severe blow to the gullet. The action was so fast that it had gone unnoticed by most of the people standing around.

But Douglas' action *was* seen. By the technician's equally squat and red-necked buddy. "Hey, I saw what you did." he said loudly. The next second he, too, found himself painfully incapacitated by Douglas' quick response. The man crumpled onto the floor and onto his pal who was still holding his throat with both hands, his eyes bulging.

By now everyone in the immediate area had seen what had happened. And they were starting to take over from where the two rednecks had left off. They were transformed from a bunch of ordinary film folk into what appeared to Douglas to be raging animals. Both men and women alike. They reminded Douglas of the gangs of hostile whites that had harassed not only his family, but the entire Japanese farming community in which he'd been born and raised.

Memories of those raids reached back into his mind for as long as he could remember. Those men, farmers mostly, had been jealous of the Japanese prosperity. They had accused the Japanese farmers of undercutting their prices on the market, stealing their jobs, their farmlands. There had often been acts of violence against the Japanese people. Their temples had been set ablaze, leaders had been beaten, farmers on the way to the produce market had been ambushed, their lettuces, tomatoes and squash strewn all over the road and trampled under heavy boots. More than a few Japanese farmers had been killed and more than a few of them had been born in the United States which wasn't always the case of the attackers.

It was because of the violence that Douglas' father, a man who'd come to the USA more than thirty years before—and who had continuously been denied citizenship—felt it necessary to teach his sons the art of karate.

"Hey, what are we waiting for," someone shouted. "Let's take care of this Jap. I say we string him up right here and now!"

Scanning the room, Douglas saw there wasn't much clear space for him to escape. And looking the way he did, not to mention being in the uniform of the enemy, there was no telling what dangers he might encounter elsewhere on the studio grounds. As for getting out on the street, he knew it would only be a matter of minutes before he'd be captured.

Even with his extensive knowledge of karate, there was no way he could head off this group of hate-mongers who looked serious about hanging him from one of the beams.

There was only one thing to do and that was to let out his blood-curdling scream. This scream had always had a paralyzing effect on individuals in a small group. Douglas was about to see if it had the same effect on a big one. Opening his mouth and producing the ungodly shriek, the crowd looked stunned long enough for Douglas to karate-chop three men barring his way and leap out the nearest exit door.

The door opened onto a studio street where he found himself suddenly carried along by a stream of several hundred extras just coming off the set of an *Arabian Nights*-type production in full costume.

The *Arabian Nights* extras didn't take much notice of the young man in the Japanese uniform because they knew that, as always, there was a movie being shot with young men who were made up to look like Japanese soldiers.

Douglas found refuge in the crowd, allowing them to serve as a foil until he got to a place where he could either hide or flee the studio grounds altogether.

He was just beginning to feel confident that this plan might work when he heard the shouts. "Stop that guy. He's a Jap. He's a real Jap."

The *Arabian Nights* crowd didn't at first realize the people shouting meant a true, authentic, and perhaps dangerous Japanese soldier, but after a few moments they seemed to catch on. And now most of these people turned on him.

Douglas was a lot faster than they were. He used his feet as well as his hands causing the closest Arabian-garbed guys to fall in a heap. Running then, he turned a corner and made straight for the main gate which was located on Melrose. By now he was way ahead of the mob and was ignoring the guards who were shouting for him to halt. Racing past the gatehouse, he overcame a guard removing his pistol from its holster and leaped over the barrier.

It was only when Douglas had run three blocks that he realized he had unsheathed the bayonet the studio had issued him. He could hear his pursuers behind him as he ran into a busy shopping area.

The place was jammed with people. What they saw was a young guy who looked just like a Japanese soldier carrying in

his hand a sharp bayonet and who, for all they knew, might
have parachuted down upon them. Along with a horde of others, hell-bent on massacring them all.

People started to scream, backing away from Douglas. One
or two women fainted.

"Oh, God, they're invading Los Angeles," somebody
shrilled. "Run for your lives."

The one-man Japanese invasion had effectively terrified the
large crowd of pedestrians who were convinced that the enemy
had finally got through and was going to attack. And who knew,
this could be a large scale find and destroy mission on Los
Angeles with bayonet-wielding parachutists dropping all over
the city looking for men to kill and women to rape.

No one in the crowd appeared to know what to do to stop
Douglas, and they certainly didn't have a clue as for stopping
any of his gang of attackers they knew must be approaching.
Even a cop on his beat that Douglas encountered made no
move except to move away from him.

Stopping for a moment in the shopping plaza to weigh the
severity of the situation from a more rational viewpoint,
Douglas wondered if he would come out of this alive. Up the
street, the studio gang was fast catching up, the red-neck technician and his buddy leading the way and looking totally
deranged.

Douglas didn't know if he saw Tom's Clipper first or if Tom
had happened to spot him as he drove along Melrose. He only
knew the car passed him and had then rounded a corner. There
was no way of telling if this was actually Tom's Packard or if it
belonged to someone else, but it was worth finding out, he

thought. Turning the corner himself, he could see the back of it parked at the end of an alley.

He sprinted into the narrow passage lined with garbage cans and found his pursuers right on his tail. To impede their progress, he knocked over as many garbage cans as he could. This maneuver bought him the time he needed to clear the alley. Then, almost completely out of breath, he jumped into the car without bothering to look first to see if it was Tom or some stranger sitting at the wheel.

It was Tom, and by the time the people chasing after Douglas had reached the end of the alley, he'd exited onto the main road making enough distance so that they couldn't even read his license plate. Some of the crowd wasn't even sure of the make of car.

"It was a Lincoln Continental," one man said.

"No it wasn't, you stupid son of a bitch," another man argued. "Don't you know a Lincoln Continental has a wheel in the back on the trunk? That's what makes a Lincoln Continental a Lincoln Continental. Nah, that car we just saw drive off was a Studebaker."

By the time the first man landed a punch on the second man's jaw for calling him a stupid son of a bitch, Tom and Douglas were a good half mile away.

"'Guess trying to pass you off as an extra didn't work," Tom said. "Feel like taking in a movie?"

Day 6

Chapter 23

Adam Morley, Grove's answer to Robert Taylor, came down the magnificent staircase wearing jodhpurs, tweed jacket, and the air of a pampered young playboy, born to a life of immense wealth and privilege.

Entering the dining room of his ancestral estate, he saw that several family members were already there having breakfast. These included his mother to whom he gave a kiss on her high, aristocratic forehead.

She wasn't pleased with her son this morning. Apparently he'd been seen in the company, of all people, a YWCA swimming instructress! It wasn't as if there weren't a great many girls who were socially *right* for Adam, including Daphne Swade, her own personal choice. But there he was, going out with a *mere* person. The entire episode was just too, too exasperating.

Adam's father, sitting at the head of the table, was a man who liked to keep out of these little family dramas. Instead of joining in the conversation, he concentrated on the financial pages of his newspaper.

But Adam's sister, Eleanora, made no such attempt at reticence. "How could you be seen in public with that...that...mermaid!" she burst out.

"How can you be seen in public with that wet fish of a boyfriend, Wilfred Beeble?" Adam retorted, heading for the long, marble-topped sideboard upon which were the silver salvers containing scrambled eggs, kippers, kidneys, pancakes, bacon, sausages and muffins. He took a dollop of this and a dollop of that, but he wasn't particularly hungry and merely toyed with his food.

In the audience, watching this scene on the big screen, Douglas Tanaka could have climbed right inside the picture and polished off the entire silver salver of scrambled eggs. It was getting on for six a.m. and he'd been in this place since the previous afternoon. Those Spam sandwiches on the set of *Behind Japanese Lines* were the last food he'd had and he was ravenous.

Sitting next to him, Tom was fast asleep. He'd snuck Douglas, disguised in one of his old hunting jackets and caps, into the only place he could think of stashing him: a 24-hour movie house in the seediest part of downtown. And rather than leave the kid there all on his own, Tom had stuck it out with him overnight. Keeping him here would do until he could think of a more permanent solution.

The theatre was a formerly grand movie palace dating back to the 1920s when Los Angeles architecture duplicated the castles of Spain. Today, however, it was a dilapidated habitat for people, mostly derelicts, who stared, glassy-eyed, at the same old feature films being played over and over again. Or slept through them. The sounds of snoring and clattering whisky bottles were constant.

This particular film was called *Swim Queen*. It had been one of Grove's big budget, big box office offerings for 1941. By 1942, with every cent wrung out of it in general release, and every bit of interest in it drained, the film was relegated to fifteenth-rate venues such as this one.

The story on the screen progressed. Adam, having been threatened with disinheritance, had bowed to his family's wishes. He'd broken up with the swimming instructress, played by Alexis Lee, Grove's high-profile swimming star. Accepting her rejection with her head held high, Alexis had gone off to show Adam and that snobbish family of his a thing or two by swimming the English Channel. Not just one way, but *both*.

Now, some time later, Adam, and the debutante to whom he was betrothed, Daphne Swade, were sitting under the stars at an exclusive country club when who should walk in but Alexis Lee. Looking agonizingly beautiful. On the arm of Adam's one-time rival, Dudley Appleworthy.

Sitting several tables from Adam, Alexis was being feted by some country club members who were impressed by her newly-acquired celebrity status. "And when are we going to witness your skills as a swimmer?" one society matron asked.

Alexis, discovering that she was still in love with Adam and wishing there was a way to get him back, realized this might be her opportunity.

"How about right now?" Alexis answered. With Hollywood magic at work, a man in a tuxedo pushed a button and the dance floor disappeared into a wall, revealing a huge swimming pool beneath.

Alexis, who just so *happened* to be wearing a seamless white Jantzen under her gown, climbed to the high board. She knew she couldn't compete with the debutante as far as money and pedigree were concerned, but she also knew she could do something the debutante couldn't. Which, in this case, was a perfect quadruple-gainer that thrilled the crowd.

Afterwards, in the brilliant aquamarine water, made even more brilliant by Technicolor, the cameras captured the lovely Alexis as she performed a series of balletic turns and twists, her stylish upswept hairdo intact.

Meanwhile, Adam, realizing the terrible mistake he'd made giving up Alexis, got up from his table and went to her as she came, dripping wet, out of the pool. Not caring if his tux got sloshed by water, Adam held Alexis in his arms and gazed into her eyes. He was so entranced that he didn't notice as the enraged Daphne turned their table over, kicked a waiter in the shins, dashed her wine glass against a wall, and exited the country club.

With all the male onlookers envying Adam, and all the female onlookers wishing they could look and swim like Alexis, Adam and Alexis delivered their closing words:

"Do me a favor and marry me, willya?" Adam asked.

"I'd like to..." Alexis hesitated, "but what will your family say?"

"Aw, the heck with my family," Adam said in a manly tone.

"In that case," Alexis said, laughing and throwing her arms around Adam's neck, "the favor is granted!"

As the music increased in volume, and as Alexis and Adam kissed on fadeout, Tom seemed to suddenly wake up.

"Hey," he said, getting up from his seat. "That's it. The line about the favor!"

Chapter 24

Maggie Graym, squinted her eyes as she looked through the gunsite of a Browning automatic rifle.

She was lining up on an evilly grinning Yamamoto, architect of the attack on Pearl Harbor and supreme commander of Japan's Imperial Naval Forces. Maggie took careful aim and squeezed the trigger.

Yamamoto, still grinning behind his rimless glasses, fell flat on his back, making the loud, clattering sound of a tin target.

Maggie stood there looking satisfied with her work and then focused her rifle on a leering Adolph Hitler. He, too, fell flat. Lastly, she squeezed off a series of rounds at the menacing Benito Mussolini, plugging him right between the eyes.

The three targets lay in a row as Maggie stepped over each of them.

"Hollywood," Maggie sang, "goes to war. We'll do our bit, we'll settle the score. We'll sell the bonds that buy us the tanks. And Uncle Sam will give us his thanks..."

The camera pulled back to reveal the full figure of Maggie Graym in a gold army uniform with a rhinestone cap and tie as well as rhinestone trim and a slit that rode up the side of a very short skirt.

Behind her, on an enormous soundstage, a hundred beautiful girls, also in uniform, echoed Maggie's song.

The choreography, which called for the girls to be in formation and for Maggie to call cadence, was based on authentic military drill.

"At-ten-HUT," Maggie ordered, followed by "shoulder arms." This was followed by "inspect-shun arms" but instead of rifle bolts being opened, each girl's madly tapping shoes made the sound.

She moved from girl to girl to girl until she'd tapped past them all, leaving them tapping in perfect unison along with her.

"Shoulder arms," Maggie shouted as she danced to the front of the formation. "Forrrwarrrd march.!"

The girls moved in one precise unit—singing loudly as the cameras slowly panned them from above: "Hollywood goes to war. We'll do our bit, we'll settle the score. We'll pack our bags for the USO and give the boys one heck of a show."

At this point, the director shouted "cut" and said it would all have to be done over again from scratch.

"What?" Maggie asked. "This is the fifth time we've gone through this routine. What's the big problem anyway?" They'd started shooting this scene the day before and she was getting tired of doing the same thing repeatedly for no apparent reason.

"You," the director said emphatically. "You are the big problem."

"Come again?" Maggie said.

"You are continuously out of step and out of tune and just plain out of it. It's easy to see you haven't even taken the time to rehearse this number."

"Now listen..." Maggie started.

But the director wasn't listening. He whispered something in the ear of his assistant director and walked away.

"Take a break everybody," the assistant director announced. "Back in 30."

Maggie was pretty annoyed at the director's remarks, but Buddy Branston, the choreographer, went up to her and told her that she wasn't out of step at all during any of the routines and that this new director was crazy.

"You know, you could pull rank and get him dumped off the picture."

"Why bother? They'd just replace him with some other creep," Maggie replied.

"Well, as soon as he comes back from the break I'm going to tell him to stick to his so-called directing of this picture and to leave the dancing to me."

"Thanks," Maggie said, "but I don't think he'll hear you."

"Who is this guy, anyway?" Buddy asked. "I've never even heard of him before."

"Oh, he's been around," Maggie said. "His specialty is horse-operas. Waldie probably assigned him to this production just to needle me."

"Needle you?" Buddy asked, surprised. "Why would Waldie want to needle his top star? His bread and butter? The very person who's keeping this studio in business?"

"It's a long story," Maggie said. She removed her sequined military cap and decided to spend the rest of her rest period doing just that: resting.

"I'm gonna head back to my dressing room for a few minutes," she said. "I have to get away from all this nuttiness for a little while."

On the way back to her private trailer, she spotted her dear old friend, Marcus Wood, way over on the other side of the set. She waved, but he had turned his head just at that moment and didn't see her.

This was, ostensibly, an official studio visit for Wood. But his real mission was to find out why there had been no news released regarding Maggie's death. It occurred to him that perhaps her body hadn't yet been discovered. An anonymous call would fix that, but no, that would give the authorities reason to believe that Maggie's death was the result of foul play. And he didn't want that idea floating around.

Just a few hours before, he'd driven to a non-descript store front off Franklin, a location as yet undetected by the FBI. It was here that he'd arranged, through an intricate network, the sending of an important communiqué.

The message, addressed to the German High Command in Berlin, was carefully coded and re-coded so as to elude American cryptographers. And in it, Wood proudly announced the fact that he'd eliminated the American movie star, morale booster, and Victory Bond fund raiser, Maggie Graym.

Wood, still riding high on the achievement he felt sure der Fuhrer would duly appreciate and reward, now saw Maggie walking toward him. For a moment he thought his heart would stop. He couldn't believe that Maggie was alive and healthy and standing right there in front of him. He leaned heavily against a wall as everything went around and around.

"Marcus," Maggie said, rushing to him, "what's the matter? You look like you've just seen a ghost."

"So that...wasn't you...after all," Wood said, hardly able to speak.

"Wasn't who?" Maggie asked. "Marcus, what in the world are you talking about?" But Wood wouldn't answer. He just pushed himself away from the wall and rushed past Maggie.

Not far from this set, Emerson Waldie's secretary informed her boss that there were several studio police officers outside his office wishing to see him.

"Studio police," Waldie exclaimed, sitting at his desk and puffing on a cigar. "Well, show them in."

The cops entered Waldie's office with their hats in their hands. It was obvious that they weren't there to tell him something that would overwhelm him with joy.

He just hoped that it didn't have anything to do with any of his stars and the stunts they pulled all too often, such as drunk driving. There had been enough dirt about Frances Farmer and all her citations recently. He didn't want this kind of thing happening around his studio.

"Mr. Waldie," one of the cops said, respectfully, "we've found a body in the swimming pool..."

"A dead body?" Waldie asked.

"Yes sir," the cop said. "Very dead."

It was Grove policy for the studio police to inform Emerson Waldie personally of all accidents and other such problems before calling in the regular L.A. police, just in case the situation was going to cause the studio any embarrassment. And to provide the time to create a suitable cover-up.

"The swimming pool," Waldie said, " doesn't have any water in it."

"That's right, Mr. Waldie," the guard said. "The person didn't die from drowning. The person died of a broken neck from the fall and has been dead for awhile. We estimate the time to have been sometime yesterday."

"Wonderful," Waldie said sarcastically. "Just what I need. A person with a broken neck in the swimming pool. Whose body is it, anyway?"

"I'm afraid I have to inform you, Mr. Waldie, that the body in the pool is that of Maggie Graym."

"Maggie Graym!" Waldie yelped. Momentarily stunned, he didn't know how to feel about this. He'd been trying to do her in professionally for so long and here she was. Dead. And then he remembered. Maggie was on soundstage 3, doing the military musical number. He knew that for a fact because he'd just peeked in on her a few minutes before to see how she was dealing with the horse-opera director he'd purposely stuck on her picture. He thought the look of anger on her face was so funny that he had laughed himself all the way back to his office.

So the cops had to be wrong. It couldn't be Maggie who was dead, but somebody else. Sitting now at his desk, he suddenly realized who that somebody in the pool was.

He allowed himself to be escorted over to the swimming pool set in order to view, and possibly identify, the body.

It was Wanda's, just as he thought. No wonder she hadn't returned to his office last night. No wonder he couldn't locate her today. He thought she'd chickened out and run away. "Dammit, dammit, dammit," he shouted. "Dammit, dammit, dammit."

Only after Waldie identified Wanda, did the studio cops call in the L.A. cops. They, in turn, made Waldie answer a lot of questions. "I hardly knew the girl," he told them. "One of our talent scouts discovered her, that's all I know."

Waldie looked sad, however, almost close to tears. To the

people who'd accompanied Waldie to the swimming pool set to identify Wanda's body, it looked like he was genuinely upset. Despite his statement about hardly knowing the deceased.

But then, due to the remarks he made enroute back to his offices having to do with the time and money he'd poured into Wanda's "development", it became obvious that he wasn't so much affected that a young girl's life had been snuffed out as the fact that he was grieving a lost business opportunity.

Meanwhile, in her dressing room and totally unaware of Wanda Belkin's death, Maggie was experiencing a somewhat delayed, creepy sensation. And, along with that, a feeling of fear.

It had to do with the way Marcus Wood had looked at her in the hall. She had never seen him look at her in such a way. It was as if he wanted to harm her, to hurt her.

But she knew she had to be wrong about all this. She had to be reading Marcus wrong.

As far as she was concerned, Marcus was the gentlest, kindest, warmest, sweetest, and most thoughtful man in Hollywood. Probably the last of his breed in the business.

She decided that she was, in reality, reacting to the strain of repeating the musical number for that weird director so many times. Thinking it over, though, this didn't ring true, either. Aside from an initial annoyance, she couldn't take that guy seriously. She'd been hoofing for so many years that she wasn't bothered for long by these movietown Mussolinis.

Of course, as a star, she really could have pulled her weight to get things her way. But Maggie had long ago decided that it was easier to just go along with things than to fight them. Not that she was a pushover. She drew a line when they started fooling with her private life.

An indication of that was just recently when Waldie tried to marry her off to Vance Varley.

Maggie sat down at her makeup table and tried to relax. This was interrupted by a knock on the door, probably Johnny coming to touch up her hair and face.

Maggie opened the door and found Tom Driscoll standing there. It might have been that her toleration for Hollywood ego types went as far as the obnoxious director of this current picture, but it didn't go as far as this obnoxious stuntman.

Before Maggie had a chance to say anything, Tom spoke. "Remember that favor?"

Chapter 25

"You'd like me to *what?*" Maggie asked.

Tom Driscoll stepped into Maggie's dressing room without waiting to be asked and had then closed the door firmly behind him. He didn't want anyone but Maggie within hearing distance when he repeated his request.

"I'd like you to hide someone at the house you own over in Malibu," Tom said again. "He's the young kid you've been hearing about on the radio, the one who jumped off the bus taking him and all those other folks to the internment camp out in the desert. I've got him lying low in a 24-hour movie house and I need a permanent place for him to stay."

Maggie looked at Tom with a look of incredulity on her face. "I don't believe I'm hearing this," she said.

"Look at it this way," Tom said confidently, "you're the one who said you wouldn't be happy until you paid your debt to me. So all I'm doing is giving you your chance."

Despite Tom's apparent cockiness, which irritated Maggie no end, she detected a certain seriousness in his manner.

"Let me get this straight," she said. "You're asking me to harbor an escaped evacuee at my house in Malibu, someone every cop in L.A. is on the lookout for, right?"

"Right."

This had to be one of the craziest ideas Maggie had ever heard, even crazier than some of the things Emerson Waldie had dreamed up for her when it came to promoting Grove

Pictures and the movies she was making there.

"How did you know that I had a house in Malibu?" she asked suspiciously.

"I saw it on the Movietone News. There was that short with you driving through the studio gates and the announcer saying: Miss Graym likes to get away to her Malibu hideaway every possible chance she can." Tom recited this in the same manner as the announcer. "And there are a few other things I know about you," he continued.

"Such as?" Maggie lit a Lucky and exhaled the smoke through her nostrils.

"Such as the fact that you're one hundred percent against the internment camps," Tom said.

"Oh, really?"

"And that you personally went to your boss, Emerson Waldie, and asked him to use whatever influence he had on Roosevelt and the government in order to stop these evacuations."

"Don't tell me that you saw that on the Movietone News, too," Maggie said.

"No, my friend Erne was waiting outside Waldie's office late one night to see him about something or other and he overheard the entire conversation. And he told me about it. Said you did a tremendous job trying to get Waldie's help but that Waldie wouldn't budge."

"Your friend Erne has a big mouth."

"Had," Tom corrected her.

"Had?"

Tom changed the subject. "Look, are you going to help this

guy or not?"

Maggie thought about what it was Tom was asking her to do. She felt that by granting him the favor, it would free her of any debt she might owe him.

After all, he did save her from the Hollywood Canteen rapist. And he did save her from being splattered all over the set during the Ferris wheel incident.

Of course, doing this presented an enormous risk for her and she knew what would happen regarding her career and her future and her life, in general, if she were caught. But all this was a small price to pay when measured against what she would personally achieve if she was able to pull off what was being asked of her.

For one thing, it would be her way of helping to right a terrible wrong in terms of what this country was forcing upon so many of its loyal citizens.

Maggie had, indeed, been one of the very few in the Hollywood community who'd made a statement in defense of the people who'd done nothing, absolutely nothing, to receive such harsh and unreasonable treatment at the hands of the government.

Down near San Diego where Maggie had come from and where she'd grown up, many of the people she'd come into contact with were of Japanese descent.

At least a quarter of her classmates all through grade school and high school, and quite a few of her close friends, had been Neisi—born in her sleepy little American hometown.

It was incredible to think that they had all been rounded up and shipped to unheard-of places in the Californian desert as well as to northern California and Utah and Nevada, even Arkansas. Packed onto buses and trains, onto the back of trucks in some cases, with not much more than a suitcase or two and leaving everything else behind.

Maggie mashed out her cigarette and lit another one. She knew she'd have to give this irritating stuntman some sort of an answer. It kind of surprised her that Tom was so concerned with the problem. She had no idea that a guy like him could really care about these people and what they were going through. But apparently he did care, and this made Maggie curious as to what other virtues he might be hiding. She was even beginning to forget how rude he'd been to her.

"Okay," Tom said impatiently, shattering Maggie's softening thoughts toward him. "Are you gonna put your money where your mouth is or are you just another empty-headed Hollywood dame who likes to shoot her mouth off?"

"I don't go back on my word," Maggie said, annoyed all over again. "Just tell me when you're planning to bring the boy to Mailbu and I'll be there."

"That's easy. I can have him at your place just after mid-night."

"Fine," Maggie said. "And after that, I hope I won't have to see any more of you. "

"You can be sure of that," Tom said.

"Fine," Maggie replied.

"Yeah, fine," Tom agreed and after going over the details of their plan, left.

Shortly after, Maggie informed the producer of the film she was working on that she wasn't feeling well. And while changing out of her costume into a pink angora sweater, a neck scarf with tiny red hearts on it, slacks, and a pair of ankle-strap wedgies, she remembered she was supposed to pose for a publicity shot later that afternoon that called for her to stand on the wing of a B-17.

Postponing that, Maggie got into her powder-blue Lincoln Continental convertible for the drive to Malibu.

She had made a decision. Without discussing it with Tom, she planned to hide Douglas Tanaka at her house for the duration of the war if need be. Tom was going to collect Douglas from the movie house and deliver him to her by midnight.

She realized that if news of her actions ever got out, she'd be considered a traitor by everybody, and that her career in Hollywood would be forever over.

Not only that, but she knew she would be arrested by the FBI and probably sent to prison. No doubt they'd compare her to Tokyo Rose and Axis Sally.

But Maggie wasn't dwelling on those possibilities. They were minor penalties in comparison with all the good she would be doing in helping to safeguard the freedom of these wronged American citizens and their families.

If she could only help one person, it would be worth it. Driving past the swimming pool soundstage, she saw the studio police wave her to a standstill. It occurred to her they'd been tipped off about Douglas Tanaka.

"Miss Graym," one of the cops said falteringly. "We thought you were...that you were..."

"Were what?" Maggie asked, not knowing what to expect from these policemen who, by their expressions and actions, seemed not only surprised, but shocked to see her.

"We thought you were...well...you know...dead," the cop finally explained.

"If you mean as far as the box office, yeah, that last picture was a stinker," Maggie joked.

The cop didn't laugh. Obviously this was no laughing matter. "We found a body on the swimming pool set and we thought it was yours."

"A body?"

"Yeah. A young woman. Looks just like you. I mean, you'd have a hard time telling the difference. At least we did."

Maggie opened the door of her car and got out. "May I see it, the body?"

"Are you sure you want to do that, Miss Graym?" the cop asked.

"I'm sure," Maggie said.

"It's right over there," the cop said. He escorted Maggie across the street to where an ambulance was parked. Several men were carrying a stretcher to the vehicle.

"Has Mr. Waldie been informed about this?" Maggie asked.

"Yes," the cop said. "In fact, he was just here. Left a few minutes before you arrived."

"Did he identify the body?"

"Well, not officially," the cop said. "He just sort of stomped his foot a whole lot of times and let out with a few curse words. That was about it."

The stretcher with the covered body was now being held before Maggie by the two attendants. The cop lifted the white sheet covering the girl's battered face.

"Oh, the poor kid," Maggie said. She recognized the dead girl as the look-alike she'd bumped into in the makeup department earlier that day.

She also recognized the fact that Emerson Waldie was probably going nuts right this minute seeing as how his plot to replace her had been prematurely terminated by this terrible accident.

But that, she thought, was Emerson Waldie's problem, not hers. Maggie took one last look at the young, misguided girl on the stretcher.

"Does anyone know how it happened?"

"We don't know anything yet," the cop said. "Looks like she just walked into the empty pool in the dark. But one thing's for sure, and that's how glad we are that it wasn't you who fell in, Miss Graym."

"Thanks," Maggie said, walking back to her car. While getting in, she recalled something that had happened about an hour earlier. When she had run into Marcus Wood. He had acted in such a strange way when he saw her.

She remembered what he'd said to her. Something like: "So that wasn't you." And the look on his face, the way he just seemed to glare at her. There had been no doubt about it. Maggie had definitely felt threatened.

And yet, there couldn't be any real reason for her feeling this way. Marcus had always been so nice to her. Going back to the very start of her career. Whenever she'd had a problem she couldn't work out for herself, and there had been many, she would always go to Marcus. And he had always been there for her, giving her the benefit of his wonderful wisdom and strength.

She decided to drop the whole issue about Marcus for the moment. There was no telling why he'd acted that way. Who knows, she thought, maybe he had indigestion from the Spam which Waldie had so patriotically ordered everyone to eat in the commissary.

She started the Continental's powerful V-12 engine and passed the ambulance carrying the young woman to the morgue. She could see it in her rear view mirror as she drove toward the main gate. What she couldn't see was the car that was directly behind the ambulance, the car that would soon be directly behind her own, following her as she drove along Melrose to Sunset Boulevard, the latter being a circuitous and somewhat dangerous road.

Friends thought she was mad buying a house all the way out near Malibu Point. The journey, they said, was enough to put anyone off. But to Maggie, getting out of Los Angeles, when she had enough ration tickets for gas, kept her sane. She wasn't the only movie star who felt this way. A small community of movie people was springing up in the "colony" as it was called. But on the whole, Malibu was peaceful and quiet, two things Maggie loved most about the place.

The trip was arduous. It always took about two hours, at times on unpaved, one lane roads, but she would have driven twice as long just to have that peace and quiet.

Chapter 26

It had been too late to stop the wire. Marcus Wood's sources had informed him that the transmission had been extremely smooth.

And now, as he drove a safe distance behind Maggie, Marcus knew only one thing and one thing only: he had to make good on the wire he'd sent.

The nausea in the pit of his stomach hadn't abated since seeing Maggie alive. It had been a physical shock to his system that had the force of a massive blow to the solar plexus. How had it happened? Who on earth, if it hadn't been Maggie Graym, was the woman he'd murdered? It didn't matter. The main thing was to remedy whatever mistake he'd made back there on the swimming pool set.

His hands on the steering wheel shook almost uncontrollably and he realized how irrational he was being by attempting to take care of matters this way. Clearly, he was panicking. A wiser choice would have been to select someone else to deal with Maggie. There were several people he could have called to do the job including Bradford who'd been pulled out of the studio after the Parkin killing and was now doing nothing but sitting around in some damned hotel room.

Yes, he could have had Bradford remove Maggie, but there were reasons he'd decided against it. For one thing, he wanted total credit for this kill. In the wire he'd sent he'd made sure the Fuhrer knew this was his undertaking, his alone. And there was no way he was going to share the glory with anyone else.

If Wood had even the slightest inkling as to the reaction the wire would bring about in Berlin, he wouldn't have been so anxious to claim credit for killing Maggie. And little could he know that by signing his name to the wire, he had also signed his own death warrant.

At that moment the very same communiqué sat in the 'out' tray awaiting delivery to der Fuhrer who would be, as the office joker had said "Fuhrious when he saw it," which was true. And which was also the reason why no one at Hitler's headquarters was willing to take it to him.

They knew that it would be upon that poor soul's head that all of Hitler's venomous rage would fall.

The message had come through a very complicated coding system via Seattle, Vancouver and Nova Scotia. It had then been signaled by way of secret radio conveyance to agents in Lisbon for immediate dispatch to Berlin.

The whole operation had taken a total of 25 minutes and 17 seconds.

When the trembling aide, selected from the lowest of the low on the Gestapo administration totem pole, brought the communiqué into der Fuhrer's offices, he was hoping and praying that Hitler's personal secretary would be kind enough to deliver it for him.

He had, as an extra safeguard, buried it in a pile of other, far less important communiqués so that she wouldn't notice.

But she did notice.

And when she read what it said, she dropped it back into the aide's hands as if it was a live grenade. Taking absolutely no pity on the scared aide, she threatened to inform his superior if the communiqué wasn't delivered to der Fuhrer without further delay.

Taking a deep breath, the aide entered der Fuhrer's office. Hitler was dressed in a burgundy smoking jacket and had been in a jovial mood all morning. He was still reveling in the news that his troops had recently annihilated an entire village in France where the occupants had been giving him so much aggravation.

He took the communiqué from the aide's hand and read it, the smile on his face disappearing rapidly only to be replaced by one of violent wrath.

He became inconsolable. This was lucky for the aide because der Fuhrer was now isolated in his own grief and couldn't focus on anyone else. He could, however, focus on things and objects and having wiped his desk of everything on it in one crashing heap, he proceeded to smash every piece of priceless crystal to be found on his shelves.

As the aide snuck out of the office he left behind a madly muttering Adolph Hitler. In the outer office, Gestapo staff felt quite safe from Hitler's lashing out while he was so occupied with ranting and raving.

But they were but all too aware how highly dangerous it would be for them once the ranting stopped. And it was.

It was at this time that der Fuhrer paced back and forth across the room demanding explanations as to why his little nightingale, his little dancing bluebird, hadn't been protected in Hollywood, why she hadn't been accorded the same security as others valuable to the Reich.

To this, not one of the officers present had anything to say. What did they know of this episode? Nothing. They remained silent and hoped to blend in with the wallpaper.

"I want only one thing," der Fuhrer shrieked. "And that's the animal responsible for this!"

He grabbed the communiqué that he'd crumpled and smoothed it out. "It appears that this criminal swinehunt has even signed his name to this heinous act." Obviously, Hitler hadn't recognized Wood's name or remembered their brief meeting seven years before. Addressing his chief aide, he said: "You will go to Hollywood. You will locate this Marcus Wood who took it upon himself to snuff out the life of my beautiful flower. Then, you will personally transport this vicious beast back to me in Berlin. You will embark upon this mission immediately."

The chief aide considered the task before him and after a few moments, spoke up.

"Mien Fuhrer, we have agents in the Los Angeles area who will be more than willing to cooperate in the capture of Marcus Wood for us. Upon contacting these agents in Los Angeles, they will get right on with the assignment. They will track this man down and they will even execute him for us. That way, we won't have to go all the way to the United States ourselves..."

Hitler, his face turning the burgundy red of his smoking jacket, walked over to the man who had just spoken and in one swift movement, ripped off the insignia of Oberstumbandfuhrer off the man's chest.

"Traitor!" der Fuhrer spat. "You've had the opportunity to serve me and you have refused. Now, instead of Hollywood, you will visit the rock quarries of outer Bulgaria where you will spend the rest of your pitiful life!"

The man was led away wishing Hitler had ordered him shot. Anything was better than this sentence of slow, harrowing death in the rock quarries of outer Bulgaria.

"Now," Hitler continued, turning his attention to the remaining men in the room, "whom amongst you is willing to serve his Fuhrer in the pursuit and capture of his beloved Maggie's murderer?"

Before any of the others could raise their hands, one of the young officers, Lieutenant Gerhardt Vanderschloffer, was wildly waving his.

Lieutenant Vanderschloffer was the very same young man whose execution by firing squad had recently been ordered. The words of the officer who'd spared his life came flooding back: "Just stay out of der Fuhrer's way for a few days and he'll forget he ever had you killed."

What he'd said had proved to be the absolute truth. Hitler had indeed forgotten all about it.

Gerhardt, after keeping a low profile for three days and becoming totally bored with just hanging around his room listening to the radio and reading movie magazines, had reported back to Hitler's headquarters as if nothing had happened.

He'd even picked up his old job as the coordinator of Maggie Graym's movies. And here he was, waving his hand frantically in der Fuhrer's face, wanting so much to be chosen for this assignment.

He'd been hoping and hoping that he might be able to go on a mission such as this one, not because he wanted to serve der

Fuhrer or because he wanted to do something for the glorious Reich, but when it came right down to it, because he wanted to take in some sightseeing in Hollywood, the film capital of the world.

Gerhardt had heard so much about Grauman's Chinese Theatre and the La Brea Tar Pits and the Santa Anita Racetrack and the Brown Derby and the Hollywood Hills and the Hollywood Bowl and Hollywood and Vine and the Mocambo and the Trocadero, he'd always wanted to see them for himself.

And he wanted to see the homes of the stars. Perhaps he could take one of those tours around Beverly Hills to see where Lana Turner and Alan Ladd and John Wayne lived. He especially wanted to see where John Wayne lived. He'd virtually learned to speak English through watching Wayne's undubbed films, and could do an uncanny imitation of the star. Maybe he would even see Wayne, speak to him, get his autograph...

Gerhardt was so lost in this fantasy that he only awoke out of it to the sound of Hitler's raspy voice commending him for responding so quickly and fervently to this request.

"Splendid, splendid," der Fuhrer cooed, smiling a bizarre yellow-toothed grin and exuding a stale smell on his breath. "You know how to serve your master and the Reich and I can guarantee that your bravery and patriotic spirit will not go unrewarded."

Gerhardt stood at attention as der Fuhrer spoke. He had absolutely no idea as to how he would get through the net protecting the west coast of America, but it didn't matter. Hitler knew exactly how he would do it.

"Your assignment comes at a most opportune moment,"

Hitler announced. "We are now developing a plane that will fly three times as fast as an ordinary plane. You will be one of the first people to fly aboard our new, secret, experimental, jet-propelled prototype Messerschmitt-262 that travels at 540 miles per hour. It's still years before we will be able to mass-produce this plane and there's a chance this prototype, like all the prototypes before it, will malfunction and disintegrate in mid-air, but should it not malfunction and disintegrate, you will transfer in Iceland to a confiscated American dive-bomber which will drop you, if this plane isn't shot out of the sky by enemy fire, by parachute, at a point over Canada's Pacific coast where you will travel, by submarine, if the submarine isn't blown up by the United States Navy, to the Los Angeles area. You will leave immediately and the entire journey should take no more than a day."

Hearing the words "jet propelled" and "malfunction" and "disintegrate" and "shot out of the sky" and "parachute" and "blown up", Gerhardt suddenly felt ill, but rather than tell der Fuhrer that he didn't feel qualified after all, and knowing what had happened to the last man who'd refused, he instead said: "I will deliver the criminal's corpse to you personally, Mien Fuhrer."

"Who said anything about a corpse?" Hitler asked, agitated. "I intend for you to bring this monster...this...Marcus Wood... back alive."

"Alive?" Gerhardt asked, astonished.

Chapter 27

If the death of his protégé, Wanda Belkins, represented a big headache to Emerson Waldie, he was about to get a visit from someone who represented an even bigger headache.

He hadn't been back in his office more than a few hours after identifying Wanda's body when who should barge in like he owned the place but Morrie Goldstrohm, returning to Grove after two months sick leave.

As Waldie's studio manager, Morrie was the unsung hero of Grove Pictures. That was because for all the years that the studio had been in business, it had been Morrie who'd kept the place together. Latterly, with the box office receipts of a dozen Maggie Graym flicks.

Emerson Waldie and Morrie Goldstrohm had come from the same New York tenements and had started their careers in the same way via the early one-reelers.

Morrie had hired Waldie to run some picture houses south of 23rd Street in Manhattan back in 1919. These were the days when you could make a lot of money on one-reelers and the good times were to last until talkies.

It was around 1929 that Morrie's little empire came crashing to the ground and he had to sell off everything he had in order to cover his sizeable debts.

Waldie had worked for Morrie for seven years and had saved his money. He'd also, being the extremely sharp wheeler-dealer that he was, managed to buy some prime properties in

Manhattan which had escalated in value.

These he sold to Fred Trump, and getting a good price for them, set his sights on something that would be his and his alone: a film studio. Waldie combined the money from his sale with his savings and bought a hundred acres out in California. These he transformed into a studio and named it, after the orange groves that had formerly occupied the land, Grove Pictures.

The first thing he did after founding Grove was to hire Morrie.

"I want you to work for me," Waldie had told the man who'd worked him ruthlessly 18 hours a day for seven years, the man who taught him everything he knew.

"Work for *you?*" Morrie had said, as if he was hearing things.

"That's right. I want you to manage the studio for me. If you can get my other employees slaving away the way you had me slaving away all these years, the place is bound to be an enormous success."

"I'll do it on one condition," Morrie had said.

"What's that?" Waldie had responded.

"That I'm my own boss. You don't get in my hair. I run things my way or I walk."

"Agreed," Waldie had answered immediately. And in truth, nothing much had changed in terms of their relationship. Morrie still acted like the boss and Waldie let him. After all, it was to his benefit. Morrie did all the work, Waldie got all the credit.

And now, back from two months in the hospital with bleeding ulcers, Morrie Goldstrohm sat in Waldie's office looking grim.

"Morrie," Waldie said, greeting him, "you're back!"

"Yeah," Morrie said, "I'm back and I was feeling like brand new until I walked back into this place and found what I found."

Morrie had always been a *kvetcher*, Waldie knew that. That's why he had bleeding ulcers in the first place.

"So what is it, Morrie? What did you find? We didn't do a good job for you while you were away? We let things slip?"

"Slip isn't the word for it. Try suicide. That's maybe a better way to describe what this studio has done to itself."

"I don't get you, Morrie," Waldie said. "We hired the best people we could find to take your place when you had to go into the hospital. We hired three people in your place. Three people to do what you usually do on your own."

"That's all very fine and good," Morrie said as if he was talking to a child, "but where, may I ask, are they?"

"What do you mean where are they?" Waldie said. "They're where they usually are—in their offices—and I'm keeping them on at the studio to help you until you're on your feet again and are used to things."

"I've got news for you," Morrie interrupted. "They've flown the coop. There's no sign of them. They did such a lousy job, I'm not surprised they took off."

"Took off? Don't be ridiculous," Waldie said, lighting up a Havana, "As far as I'm concerned, things are running very smoothly."

"Oh sure, sure," Morrie said sarcastically. "Things are running *very smoothly* with crews working all night and film stock being used up like there's no tomorrow and productions not only going over schedule but their budgets looking like something out of *Gone With The Wind*. I tell you I never saw such a mess."

Waldie took an expansive drag on his cigar, still under the impression that Morrie was exaggerating as usual.

"Morrie," Waldie said, "maybe you're not ready to come back to work yet. Maybe you've come back too soon. Take another two weeks. Take a month."

"Emerson," Morrie said, "remove the cigar from your mouth. I don't want you swallowing it when I show you what I have to show you."

"You want to show me something?" Waldie asked. He didn't know what Morrie was getting at.

Morrie took a sheaf of papers out of a file and shoved them on the desk.

"Read them," Morrie said.

Waldie looked down at the papers and then took them in his hands and started to leaf through them. They were the financial records of all the productions that had been completed during Morrie's sick-leave.

It didn't take long for Waldie to gasp.

The first budget, for a B movie that wasn't supposed to exceed $90,000, cost $126,950.

The second budget, for a western for which $200,000 was allotted came in at twice that figure.

By the time Waldie was looking over the third budget, he was also looking very ill.

"How could this have happened?" he asked, his voice hardly audible.

"How the hell would I know?" Morrie replied. "I was busy bleeding internally at the time, remember?"

"Look at this," Waldie said, searching through the expenses for *Dive-Bomber Rendezvous* and not believing his eyes. "They did 12 takes on one faraway shot, 12 fucking takes on one fucking faraway shot, a nothing shot, how in the fucking hell did they get away with it?"

"All expenses were approved by that bunch of monkeys you put in my place," Morrie said. "You know, the guys who took a powder that I was just telling you about?" He regarded Waldie in the same way one regards a child.

"Well, find them," Waldie suddenly exploded. "I want them here in this office to explain how they did this to me and then I want them arrested and put in jail."

"I gotta tell you something, Emerson," Morrie said, interrupting Waldie again. "I've been trying to track down those bums ever since I got back today. The crooks have just disappeared into thin air. It's like they were purposely trying to ruin you and ruin the studio and to tell you the truth, Emerson, I'm not sure they haven't succeeded.

Morrie Goldstrohm's speech was cut short by an urgent buzzing on Waldie's intercom.

"There are two gentlemen waiting here to see you who say they're from the FBI, Mr. Waldie," Harriet said. "Do you want me to show them in?"

"What? The FBI?" Waldie stormed. "Who the fuck sent for the FBI?"

"I sent for them," Morrie said. "Too much funny stuff has been going on in my absence. All this financial waste and mismanagement, plus the murder of Erne Parkin, and then, this morning, the young girl that everybody thought was Maggie Graym, found dead in the pool. We're still trying to find out who she was and what she was doing wandering around the Grove lot."

"Her name was Wanda Belkins although I was going to change that to Aurora Dawn," Waldie said. "I brought her in to take over from Maggie and I had big, big plans for her."

"Oh, the old feud between you and Maggie, huh?" Morrie asked. "No wonder this studio has gone to hell what with you concentrating on getting rid of the only asset you ever had."

"I was just trying to bring new blood into the studio," Waldie said, defensively.

"Gimme a break, willya?" Morrie retorted. "Here you've got the biggest, most popular, number one box office goldmine of a star locked in a seven year contract and you become obsessed with replacing her. And in the meanwhile, everything around here is totally neglected. I come back from the hospital to find a major disaster. I tell you, Emerson, you and your damned ego."

Waldie reached over and pushed the intercom button. "Tell those FBI guys to come in," he said. Anything had to be better than listening to Morrie kvetch, kvetch, kvetch.

The door opened and Waldie's secretary showed the two FBI agents in. One was short and paunchy and the other one was tall and talkative.

"Looks like you called us to come down here just in the nick of time," the talkative one said right away.

"Huh?" Waldie responded, completely confused.

"The fact is," the agent continued, "we were going to do a raid on your studio today."

"A raid?" Waldie yelled, his face turning beet red. "A raid on my studio? What for?"

"Spies, Mr. Waldie, Nazi spies," the agent said. "This place is riddled with them. According to our sources, your studio has been the center of an espionage ring operating in Hollywood for the past two years."

"It's all lies, all lies," Waldie gasped.

"No, Mr. Waldie, it's all spies, all spies," the agent answered, laughing at his own play on words.

"So anyway," the short, paunchy agent inserted, "just as we're about to pounce on the whole gang of them, what do all these rats do? They disappear."

Waldie was no longer listening to what the FBI agents were saying. He was too busy trying to loosen his necktie. He couldn't breathe. All he saw was a blur of people standing around him as he struggled for air.

And then there was the excruciating pain in his arm and in his chest. His head dropped suddenly and heavily onto his desktop making a loud crashing sound. His open eyes stared at nothing.

"Emerson?" Morrie said, going over to the motionless figure. "Emerson?"

Chapter 28

Just as Morrie Goldstrohm was trying to tell if there was any life left in his boss, Emerson Waldie, Giuseppe Lambozza stood on the side of a hot, dusty road trying to tell if there was any life left in Izelda, his 1912 Model T Pickup. The ancient vehicle had stalled on him near the Rancho San Vincente Y Santa Monica which covered everything from Hollywood on the east to Topanga Canyon on the West.

Pounding the old car's hood with a huge, meaty fist, Giuseppe heard the engine suddenly cough and turn over. Without waiting to see how long this would continue, he jumped into the car and got it rolling again.

The car backfired like crazy but didn't stall, and then moved slowly along Sunset Boulevard going northeast away from Santa Monica Bay. On Giuseppe's lips were the words to one of his favorite Italian songs, the one he sang as a small boy in Naples where he was born, some 62 years before.

The Model T was doing better now that the road was leveling off. Giuseppe waved at the attendant of a one-pump gas station whose sign advertised last chance gas for people traveling along the sea toward Malibu Judicial Township as it was called. He maneuvered a rickety turn into the station and pulled Izelda up to the lone pump that was attended by Doc. Doc owned the place as well as the diner next to it.

"Howdy, Gus," Doc said. "Ain't seen you down here in a long time."

"That's because I ain't been down here in a long time," Giuseppe explained with more than a noticeable trace of irritation in his accent. "Hey, Fill her up, eh?"

After collecting a few monosyllabic answers to his questions, Doc collected a dollar and seven cents and the corresponding amount in gas-rationing stamps from Giuseppe. The Model T rattled back onto the road again. It painfully climbed a hill and then, reaching the top, coasted down the other side.

Doc watched the Model T's progress and wondered just how much longer old Giuseppe would be able to hold onto it before it gave out forever. The car had to be at least thirty years old. That was almost as long as Doc had known Giuseppe.

He, in fact, remembered when Giuseppe and his young, Neapolitan bride, Rosa, arrived here in sunny California, straight from Italy. It had been in 1910 or 1911 or sometime around then.

The young couple had at first labored on the Rancho Topanga, Malibu Y Sequit, known simply as Rancho Malibu, living in a house owned by the rancho. In those days everything as far as the eye could see was owned by the rancho. But the rancho was no longer intact, having been forced by the government to parcel out its land. And as everybody knew, once this war was over, the place would be overrun with architects and contractors transforming everything they touched.

Doc had also been a field worker at the rancho. Twenty-seven years. But he'd saved to buy the gas station and, later on, to add the little diner. He felt a certain kinship with Giuseppe in terms of something they both shared: an unbreakable will to survive in this still-undeveloped terrain of endless gullies and canyons

The Model T disappeared over the hill and Doc went back to his little sun shelter where he would wait for the next car to come along. These days there weren't too many civilians out on the road. Mostly, it was the military and the like.

Meanwhile, Giuseppe drove along and saw, or thought he saw, someone in the distance walking toward him. Another twenty yards and Giuseppe saw that the person was female. A beautiful female at that. Her clothes were torn and she was bruised.

He slowed down the Model T and brought it to a noisy halt just a few yards from the woman. But even with all the racket the car was making, she didn't seem to hear.

"Hey you, Miss," he called to her. "You in trouble or something?"

"Boy, am I glad to see you," Maggie Graym said, suddenly coming out of her daze. "Some nut ran me off the road..."

"No!" Giuseppe said, his expression one of shocked disbelief. "You mean somebody came along and ran you off the road and then he just kept going?"

"That's exactly what I mean," Maggie said, rubbing her bruised shoulder. "I was driving along not far from here and this guy pulled up right next to me. The sun was in my eyes so I couldn't really see his face or anything but I could tell he was looking over at me and I thought he was just a wolf, you know, a guy getting fresh, but then he started edging me closer and closer to the side of the road. And then I found I was going straight over the edge. The whole thing happened so fast that I honestly didn't know what was happening, except that somebody was trying to kill me."

"You're lucky you're alive," Giuseppe said in a warm, fatherly tone.

"You're telling me," Maggie replied. "My car was completely destroyed and I was thrown clear, into a clump of bushes. I've been climbing out of them ever since. Say, do you think you could drive me to the nearest telephone?"

Giuseppe answered that he could do much better than that. "I'm gonna take you back to the house where my wife, Rosa, can take good care of you, put some iodine and bandages on those cuts you got. She's a good woman, my Rosa; you'll like her."

"No, really, that's very kind of you, but what I need is a telephone," Maggie said, protesting this man's obvious concern for her. The thing she wanted most right now was to get in touch with Tom before he left the studio. Otherwise, he'd get to her place in Malibu and, not finding her, think that she'd chickened out.

Not only did she want to avoid him thinking this, but far more importantly, she didn't want to leave this young kid, Douglas Tanaka, stranded.

"I'll get you to a telephone," Giuseppe said, "and some hot minestrone soup, Rosa's special minestrone. People come from miles around for Rosa's minestrone."

"I don't want to put you or your wife to any trouble," Maggie said, climbing into the Model T. "I can make all the arrangements for help with just a call or two. Honest..."

"No trouble, no trouble," Giuseppe insisted, turning the car around heading south. "You rest a little while and let Rosa take care of you.

"Okay," Maggie said. "Maybe that would be the best idea. But on the other hand, I wouldn't mind making the phone call first. Look, there's a gas station over there. Maybe they have a phone."

But Giuseppe drove past Doc's without stopping. In fact, it seemed to Maggie that he sped up as they passed the place.

"You come back to the house," Giuseppe said. "Rosa, she'll fix you up good."

Chapter 29

As the evening hour approached, a shocked Hollywood learned of Emerson Waldie's death.

And while there were certain people in the film capital who had commented upon how untimely Waldie's demise had been, there were many others, the vast legion of people he'd fired, banished, ruined, stabbed in the back, fleeced, or injured in an infinite variety of other ways who considered his demise timely. Very timely.

But this was Hollywood and the glittery show of grief had to go on. After all, when a figure of Waldie's stature went the way of all flesh (or, as Time Magazine would put it, 'The Way of All Flash'), the surviving family, stars, directors, producers, and studio brains were expected to put on a command performance for the rest of the world.

"We're all going to miss him terribly," Hedda Hopper sobbed during a special radio broadcast, her voice breaking with the same brand of believability that had forced her out of an acting career half a decade earlier.

Her rival, the imperious Louella Parsons, on a competing radio station, labeled Waldie a compassionate man, a magnanimous man, a forgiving man, forgetting, for the moment, the fact that she and Waldie had been arch enemies intent upon destroying one another by whatever means possible.

Waldie's body, which had been removed from the pink and yellow palace on the Grove Pictures lot several hours before, now lay on a cold marble mortuary table, stripped of all clothing, awaiting preparation for the funeral which was scheduled to take place the following day.

Waldie, born Ezra Shlomo Waldenbaum, had often bragged to various friends, family members and business associates that even though he had never followed the Jewish faith in life, he was going to be a good Jew in death. Should that very unlikely occurrence ever take place.

Therefore, under Waldie's instructions as stipulated in a memo to his attorneys dictated back in 1931, there was to be absolutely no embalming performed on the body, and the burial ceremony would take place before sunset on the day following his death. These were Jewish Orthodox tenets that were, without fail, to be carried out to the letter.

Having been informed of the embalming embargo, the morticians were very disappointed that they couldn't drain a real studio mogul corpse of its blood. But at least they could run the body through makeup, hairdressing and wardrobe.

The chief makeup mortician, who'd actually had experience in the makeup department at 20th Century Fox, decided that he and his staff would work overtime to get Waldie ready for his big day. He was aware that his artistic endeavors would soon be buried under six feet of earth, but that was okay with him. As long as he could do a perfect job that he would be proud of.

For him, there was no thrill quite like the one when a relative of a deceased subject would comment on how "good" the corpse looked. It was at times like these that a makeup mortician could look back upon with real pleasure.

To start the "makeover," a base of white foundation was

applied in liberal amounts to the dead face. Letting that set for a few minutes, the chief then doused Waldie with an avalanche of white powder. Wiping away the residue, he then produced a bright red lipstick, similar to the one used on Alice Faye for *Tin Pan Alley* and created cupid lips on an otherwise straight slash of a mouth.

Given Waldie's obsession with the cupid figure, a fact known all over Hollywood, the cute little mouth was just the touch to make the chief makeup mortician giggle as he worked.

Black pencil, number 36, was used to bring out the eyebrows, false eyelashes to cover the sparse ones. Finally, a coating of rouge to give the illusion of cheekbones finished the job. Standing back, the chief makeup mortician surveyed the transformation and was instantly gratified.

The fun of doing corpses, in his estimation, was that they never argued with you the way live subjects were apt to do. He was so sick of those temperamental stars and was glad not to have to put up with them anymore. Having a dead star to work on was, to him, the ultimate in fulfillment.

But turning to the subject at hand, he examined the quality of its hair. "I can't do a thing with it," he complained. "I was thinking of putting him in a wig."

The wig, a sleek matinee-idol-type rug, met with the chief's approval and was placed on Waldie's head completing the picture. All that was needed now was the clothing.

"It's the clothing that makes the corpse," the chief was fond of saying.

Waldie's widow had arranged for him to be buried in black tie and tails, but there was no way in hell that the chief could accommodate the top hat. Not if the lid to the coffin were to close properly.

Having had to bury the recently deceased cowboy star, Montana Jones, in his six-gallon Stetson had been a nightmare.

When the body of Emerson Waldie had been completely dressed, it was lifted by four assistants and placed in the bronze coffin that Mrs. Waldie had ordered.

"Loverly, just lov-er-ly," the chief makeup mortician said, looking back admiringly over his handiwork. "Let's just leave him with the lid up. Mrs. Waldie has ordered there be a last viewing before the funeral."

It was now after ten in the evening and time to call it a day. The men working on Waldie wheeled the coffin into the viewing room and dimmed the lights. One major beam played upon the coffin and upon Waldie's upturned face.

"It's a shame we can't keep you around here for a few days," the chief makeup mortician said, addressing Waldie. "But that's the way it goes, I guess."

A few minutes later, the men were gone and the mortuary was extremely quiet, even for a mortuary. But then, in the extreme quietude, there was a very low moan coming from the bronze coffin of Emerson Waldie.

And a very slight movement of his right hand.

Chapter 30

Back at the pink and yellow Waldie compound at Grove Pictures, it seemed that Morrie Goldstrohm would never stop crying real tears and calling out the name "Emerson" over and over again. The place was packed, even at this late hour, with newsmen who had arrived at the studio for a chance to interview the man who was last to see Emerson Waldie alive.

As for the two FBI agents, they had disappeared hours before, and there was no evidence that they had ever been there. When Waldie's secretary, Harriet, had asked Morrie if she should mention the visit of these two agents, Morrie had blown his top.

"Of course not," he'd said loudly. "Isn't it bad enough that we've had this great tragedy today? Do we want to drag in a whole other thing?"

Harriet had felt the sting of Morrie's words, and realized it wouldn't be wise mentioning the FBI. The last thing she wanted to do was cause her own termination at Grove. Not when, at last, that tyrant Waldie, that Hitler, was gone. Who could tell but maybe now she'd get a boss who was a human being. And she might get something else she'd been denied through the years: a raise.

"Okay, Mr. Goldstrohm. I get your point," she said, "I won't mention a thing."

"Make sure you don't," Morrie said, dismissing her for the evening and considering dismissing her for good. The only reason he didn't fire her was because he knew that she'd probably talk to the press for revenge.

Now, hours later, Morrie was relating to the news-hungry newsmen and women what a great man Emerson Waldie had been. He was telling them how the film industry owed Emerson Waldie an enormous debt of gratitude for so many years of selfless dedication.

"But isn't it true that Mr. Waldie was a vicious dictator who was generally hated here at Grove Pictures as well in the rest of Hollywood?" one of the newspaper men asked.

"Mr. Waldie had to be firm at times," Morrie said. "But he was always fair and always loving and it would hurt him when he had to fire or chastise someone. As the head of Grove, he was responsible for so many, many people. So many, many livelihoods. To answer your question regarding Mr. Waldie being a vicious dictator who was greatly hated here at Grove Pictures as well as the rest of Hollywood, the answer is no. He was a magnanimous leader who was highly respected."

Emotionally unable to finish the sentence, Morrie fell back into a crying jag. "Emerson, oh, Emerson," he wailed.

"I think that has to be enough of the questions for tonight," a Grove Pictures spokesman informed the sea of reporters. "As you can see, Mr. Goldstrohm is greatly broken up, as are we all regarding the death of our beloved founder, mentor, and friend, Emerson Waldie."

After the reporters started filing out of the compound, the spokesman asked Morrie if he would like to be driven home.

"No thanks, Jim," Morrie answered, the crying having suddenly ceased, "I need some time alone. I'll drive myself."

It was after ten in the evening by the time he drove through the studio gates enroute home to Brentwood. But he wasn't going home to Brentwood.

He was going to visit his brother-in-law, Bernie, in Encino. Bernie would be waiting for him, along with his cousin, Jake. And just to be on the safe side, he checked his rearview mirror every few seconds to make sure that he wasn't being followed by anyone. He wasn't.

Exactly ninety-nine minutes later, he pulled up in front of a shabby 30s Spanish-style bungalow in a working-class neighborhood. Most of the residents of the area were employed in the numerous war plants that had sprung up in and around the Los Angeles area in the months since Pearl Harbor.

This was where Morrie's sister, Marj, and his brother-in-law, Bernie, had been living for as long as he could remember. But they wouldn't be living there much longer because as of the following Monday morning, Bernie would be heading up production at Grove Pictures. His title would be executive vice president and he would have his offices in the execs building.

And then Marj and Bernie would be moving to Beverly Hills where they had the house already picked out. A mock Tudor mansion near Rodeo Drive.

Not bad for a man who was currently employed as a stevedore on the San Pedro docks.

Morrie got out of his car and walked up the path to the front door and gave a short rap on what was mostly badly peeling paint.

The man who greeted him before he had a chance to give a second rap was the short, squat FBI agent who had appeared at Waldie's office that afternoon. Only he was no FBI agent. He was Morrie's brother-in-law, Bernie.

Upon seeing each other, the two men fell into each other's arms and started laughing loudly and slapping each other on the back. Standing nearby with a big grin on his face was Morrie's cousin, Jake, who was drinking a beer in his undershirt. He joined in with the other two men and the three of them laughed loudly and slapped each other on the back for another couple of minutes.

Jake, who had appeared as the second FBI agent that afternoon was, in truth, a dogcatcher from Burbank. A soon-to-be ex-dogcatcher from Burbank.

In a few days, he would be joining Bernie in the exec building as VP/Head of Accounts.

"I can't believe we pulled it off," Jake said, laughing so hard that he had to hold onto Morrie's shoulder for support.

"I can't believe it, either," Morrie said, flushed with the mood of celebration which this surely was.

"There I was," Morrie said, "lying in that hospital bed for two months trying to figure a way to get control of the studio and then it came to me. Out of the blue. Just make up a story about spies at the studio. But for him to believe us and then to drop dead, my God! I thought he'd just agree to my taking over as studio head in order to save himself a ton of embarrassment. His *plotzing* was a bonus, a gift from heaven."

"It worked out poifect," Bernie said, removing his fake FBI identification from his wallet and lighting a match to it. "And it gave me a chance to show off my acting abilities. What did you think of me, Morrie, I was good, eh? Good enough for the lead in a movie?"

"You gave an academy award-winning performance. You both did," Morrie said. "Every time I think about it I can't stop laughing. All the time people thought I was crying over that *momser* tonight, I was laughing so hard tears were sprouting out of my eyes like fountains. It was priceless, unbelievable."

With that, Morrie started laughing again, along with the two impostors.

"And to think," he said, hardly able to catch his breath, "to think that anyone would actually believe that there could be such a thing in Hollywood as a spy ring, I mean, I tell you."

Chapter 31

Tom was making good time. He expected to be at Maggie's on schedule. About the only thing he worried about his rapidly diminishing fuel supply. The Packard did about nine miles to the gallon on the open road and the needle on his gas gauge was moving dangerously close to empty.

He was out of gas-rationing stamps. It would be necessary to use some of the contraband gasoline Erne had got for him somewhere which he carried in a canister in his trunk.

He'd been saving the gas for an emergency. Well, this was an emergency.

Tom glanced over at Douglas Tanaka, slumped down in the passenger seat. In the hat and coat Tom he'd worn in the movie house, plus a pair of sunglasses, Douglas looked more like a Mexican tourist than a teenage Japanese/ American runaway evacuee.

"How far is it to Akron, Ohio?" he asked suddenly.

"I don't know," Tom said, "but I can tell you we're not going there on my supply of gas, why?"

"Akron's the place I'll be heading just as soon as the heat is off me and I can move."

"What's in Akron?" Tom asked.

"I've got an aunt and uncle there. I heard the authorities back east weren't putting people in camps and I figure if I can make it to Akron, maybe I can spring my family out of Manzanar."

Tom didn't see what Douglas getting to Akron, Ohio had to do with getting his folks out of the camp.

"In Ohio, I can arrange to have them brought east," Douglas said.

"Are you sure about that?" Tom asked.

"No," Douglas admitted. "But it's worth a try, don't you think? And besides anything else, I can't stay hidden for the rest of the of the war. It could last till 1960."

"Well," Tom said, "the first thing we have to do is get you safely to Maggie Graym's. And then you'll have plenty of time to figure out how to get to Ohio."

"You're right," Douglas said. "And I'm certainly grateful to you and Miss..."

Douglas stopped talking in mid-sentence. Up ahead about a half mile or so there were some glaring lights and a crowd. "Uh oh," Douglas resumed. "Looks like a roadblock."

Tom drove a little closer and spotted cops and saw that in addition to the crowd there were also about ten black and white police cars lined up on the narrow, two-lane section of road that would one day have three lanes on either side replacing canyons and bush.

"Stay calm," Tom said.

"They're probably after me," Douglas said. Tom stepped on the brakes and considered attempting to turn around even though he was certain he'd be seen. And he didn't want to draw any suspicion to the car. Then he noticed the ambulance that was parked alongside all the police cars, its red siren light revolving, making the scene even more eerie than it already was.

"I've got a hunch that this doesn't have anything to do with you, Doug," Tom said. "But just wait here. I'll walk over there and find out what's happening. If it looks like I'm being detained or if the cops start walking toward the car, pile out and hide yourself off the road, in the gorge."

Getting out of the car, Tom approached a group of cops, rescue workers and onlookers who were standing on the side of the road, looking down into the canyon below.

"Accident?" Tom asked one of the cops.

"Looks that way," the cop said. "We got a call just before sunset. Some hikers apparently sighted a car that went off the side here. That's a twenty-foot plunge down there. We've located the car. Found it standing on its grill right at the bottom. We've got guys down there right now hauling her up. Next thing's to find out what happened to the person or persons who were in it."

"Any idea who they are?" Tom asked.

"No idea, but whoever they are, they're not hurting for money. I'm told the car's a fancy Continental convertible. Light blue from what we can see in this light."

Tom left the officer and walked back to his car to let Douglas know what the fuss was all about.

"We gotta hang around here until they get the car up and clear the road," Tom informed Douglas. "Best thing is to sit tight until they get the job done."

It didn't occur to Tom that the wrecked car might belong to Maggie Graym. A Lincoln Continental convertible might be a rarer car than most, but he'd seen them around from time to time in Hollywood, and there was no reason to think they wouldn't be fairly common amongst the rich folk with houses in the Malibu area.

But upon returning to the scene of the accident, Tom noticed a rescue worker making his way back onto the road holding something that glittered in the revolving red light.

It was a beaded handbag that was found in the car. And, as Tom, got closer, he could see monogrammed in the beadwork the initials MG.

Day 7

Chapter 32

It way nearing two in the morning as Giuseppe Lambozza spoke on the phone.

His demeanor had turned from warm, friendly and fatherly to mean. snarling and frightening

"Listen," Giuseppe said angrily into the receiver, "I've been trying to get ahold of you people all night. Where the hell you been, eh? You think all I gotta do is spend my time trying to get ahold of you or something? You told me you wanted me to call you if anything got screwed up, and that's just what the hell I been trying to do. Only you don't have nobody there who knows how to answer the frigging phone."

Giuseppe paused and took a long swig from the whisky bottle he'd been drinking from all evening. And then he started talking again. "I don't know who you put on the job to finish her off, but whoever the guy was, I gotta tell you he fucked up royal."

The room, like the sky outside the window, was dark and gloomy. Only one dim light coming from a small lamp prevented the room from being almost totally immersed in blackness.

Giuseppe let the person on the other end get a few words into the conversation and then he cut him off. "Lemme tell you it's just a good thing I went out to check everything yesterday after you called me. I took the truck out and I'm riding along towards Santa Monica and who do I find? Maggie Graym. And not just her dead body, either. I find her walkin' along with just a few little scratches. Yeah, that's right, she's alive."

Giuseppe took another swig on the bottle and listened for instructions.

"Sure, sure, I can take care of her, that's notta problem, but I sure as hell would like to know what happened to the son of a bitch you told me bumped her off in the first place. He starts something and then he don't finish it..."

Across the room, Maggie Graym sat on a wooden chair bound and gagged. Struggling with the ropes around her wrists and ankles, she made the muffled sounds of someone helpless.

She was still reeling from the shock of finding the nice, helpful man who'd given her the ride to be, in reality, anything but nice and helpful.

As soon as they'd arrived at his farmhouse, he'd pushed her onto this horribly uncomfortable chair under a framed photograph of Benito Mussolini, He had then tied her up and wrapped a dirty old handkerchief around her mouth. Well, one thing she could be grateful for was the fact that he hadn't tried to rape her.

Watching the old man on the phone and straining her ears to hear what he was saying, Maggie was still trying to figure out what this was all about. Were they going to hold her for ransom? It would come as no surprise to her if Emerson Waldie failed to cough up the money, considering how he felt about her.

It occurred to Maggie that maybe Waldie was behind all this, and that he was the person the old man was talking to. But would Waldie go to all the trouble of doing this just because she had refused to marry Vance Varley?

Then it occurred to Maggie that perhaps this was just some dumb publicity stunt Waldie had dreamed up. But that thought quickly diminished.

She heard the man on the phone say something about them taking care of her that night. Somebody or other would be coming up to see the job was done. And then he hanged up. Turning toward her, he wore the unmistakable expression of an executioner.

And then, once again, she remembered the look Marcus Wood wore on his face when she'd bumped into him; was that only yesterday? That look had also been murderous.

Wood's words from the day before came filtering back to her as in a bad dream. "So that wasn't you," he'd muttered.

That seemed a strange thing to say. What had he meant? And then she knew.

It had to do with the young woman who'd fallen into the empty pool. Only she hadn't fallen. She'd been pushed. By somebody who thought she was Maggie Graym.

Maggie strained against the ropes as she realized that *the young woman had been murdered by Marcus and that Marcus later discovered that he'd killed the wrong person.*

And it was Marcus who'd followed her down the narrow inclines of Sunset Boulevard where he could run her off the road. Maggie had seen the man in the other car, although just for an instant. And yes, it could have been Marcus Wood.

Maggie couldn't think of a reason why Marcus would want her dead, but she knew one thing: this was no time to solve it. She realized that unless she took some action, and fast, the people who were so intent on rubbing her out would succeed.

Tugging at her ropes for the thousandth time since her abduction, she found that she still couldn't budge them. Nor was there a sharp surface nearby that she could rub the ropes against until they broke. Not that she had the strength, even if there had been a sharp edge. She'd been given just a little food and liquid during the past twelve hours, or however long it had been since Giuseppe had tied her up.

The only relief from this terrible situation were the times when she would lapse into a kind of semi-conscious state.

To her, this whole scene reminded her of one of those Hollywood B productions in which the villain was always trying to inflict some horrible injury on the helpless heroine.

Thinking about that for a moment, Maggie also knew that the poor heroine was always saved in the end, and she was now praying that real life would imitate those story lines.

Corny as they were, Maggie felt that she'd be grateful for a little corn right now.

Meanwhile, many hundreds of miles away in the skies over north-western Canada, a German lieutenant sat directly behind the pilot of an American-made long-range dive bomber.

He was Gerhardt Vanderschloffer who had been ordered by Adolph Hitler, not even twenty hours before, to capture and remove to Germany, that *swinehunt*, Marcus Wood.

The plane was a Brewster Buccaneer with U.S. Navy markings, manufactured in Long Island City, New York. Scheduled for a routine check, it had been flown right out of the hangar at LaGuardia Airport. Never to be seen again. When it hadn't returned, the authorities thought it must have crashed into the Atlantic. The truth was, it had been flown to a secret airfield in

Nova Scotia's wilderness. There, it had then been made ready for der Fuhrer's special missions.

Such as the one that Gerhardt Vanderschloffer was on at this very moment.

Looking down into the darkness of the Canadian terrain, Gerhardt was feeling sick. This was the part of the journey he'd been dreading. The part when he'd have to parachute into that void. He was just waiting for the pilot to signal him and then he was actually supposed to stand up on his seat, climb onto the side of the plane and jump. Hard as he tried, he could not picture himself doing this.

In fact, he wouldn't do it. He simply would not do it. He was frozen with fear. He would refuse the order to jump and then return to the airfield from which they'd taken off. The realization that he wouldn't be alive by the time they landed, that the pilot would shoot him for refusing to jump, didn't seem nearly as bad a fate as jumping.

Then Gerhardt began to think about what he would be giving up, besides his life, if he didn't jump. He'd probably never get a photograph signed by Maggie Graym. He'd never get to watch a premiere at the Pantages Theatre. He'd never have a hot dog at the *Pig 'n Whistle*. This was enough to make him reconsider the parachute jump. If he could only put aside this stupid fear of heights, all of Hollywood would be his.

The plan called for him to rendezvous with ground agents once he descended onto Canadian terra firma. From there, he would be taken aboard a submarine. This submarine, of American manufacture like the plane, had been sunk by German forces off Greenland the year before. After two months in the frigid waters, it had been resurfaced by the Germans. Its United States Navy markings had been restored and its newly appointed German crew thoroughly schooled to appear as American gobs so that, in theory if not in practice, it could even dock for liberty in any port without fear of detection.

For this assignment, the sub would, as it had done a half dozen times previously, pass through the numerous nets set up along the west coast by identifying itself as an American vessel.

In approximately twelve hours, Gerhardt would be put ashore near Los Angeles. He'd be wearing the uniform of an American naval officer and he'd have papers showing that he was on leave. If asked to speak on any occasion, he could do John Wayne better than John Wayne, having seen his films numerous times. Once ashore, he'd find a car waiting for him in an isolated wooded area not far from the ocean. With his instructions firmly imbedded in his brain, he would then drive to Los Angeles.

That part of it would be easy. Gerhardt may never have been to L.A. before, but he knew it intimately from years if studying maps. Not only did he know where everything was, but where everyone lived. Finding Wood's mansion wouldn't be hard. From the address, he knew it was right up the street from Norma Shearer's. No, the tricky part would be getting into the mansion. How would he manage it? Would there be guards? He'd cross that bridge when he came to it.

Nestling as best he could in the cockpit, Gerhardt looked straight ahead. It was several hours before dawn over western Canada.

It was also, as the pilot indicated, time for Gerhardt to bail out.

Chapter 33

The Valley of Heavenly Dreams Chapel and Mortuary, with its meticulously landscaped gardens and myriad fountains, nestled sedately in the Holmby Hills.

And within its whitewashed walls, Emerson Waldie lay at peace in his bronze coffin.

The chapel bell had just chimed eight times on this sunny morning, but even at this early hour a record number of people had already filed past the open casket.

For most of the people attending Emerson Waldie's funeral, it wasn't so much a case of paying their last respects as it was to make certain that Emerson Waldie was, indeed, dead.

"The minute I heard over the radio that Waldie had bought it, I chartered a private plane and flew all the way from New York," commented a prominent producer.

"But you detested Waldie," a friend of his replied.

"Exactly," the producer said, smiling and moving on.

Emerson's widow, Enid, stood in the doorway greeting people as if at a garden party. She'd arranged the funeral so that it would be over early in the morning. She didn't want it interfering with anyone's schedule for the day.

As for herself, she didn't want her day interrupted, either. She was not about to miss her usual Tuesday Bridge game or her wash and set afterwards. And, of course, she would be opening her home that evening for a gathering of intimate friends. About seven hundred and fifty intimate friends.

Enid was resigned to the fact that she'd have to spend some part of the day dealing with the caterers and making sure they got everything right. She'd also have to look into getting the right band. At such late notice, most of the good bands were already booked.

What she had in mind was some fabulous South American rhythm so that the conga line would be truly memorable. She wondered if Xavier Cugat might be available.

By eleven in the morning, people were still pouring through the mortuary to view the body. Enid had given the attendants strict instructions that the coffin was to be closed by eleven-fifteen so that the procession of cars and limousines out to Forest Lawn Cemetery could begin soon afterwards.

"It's eleven-fifteen, Mrs. Waldie," one of the attendants mentioned to Enid just as she was getting into a deep conversation about winter fashions with Mrs. Gary Cooper and Mrs. James Cagney and Mrs. Louis B. Mayer.

"Oh, yes," Enid said, and then in a louder, almost singsongy voice: "we're closing the coffin everybody, we're closing the coffin. If you want to say one final bye-bye to our dear departed Emerson, this is the time to do it."

When everyone had had their fill of Waldie and were satisfied his death wasn't just a rumor, Enid approached the bier and allowed out of tightened jawbones, a "bye-bye Emerson," before lowering the top of the coffin herself.

"Okay, everyone," she said cheerfully. "You all know the way to Forest Lawn. And if you don't, just follow Emerson."

Emerson Waldie, his countenance never again to be viewed, was wheeled out of the chapel and down a series of halls to what was known as the "waiting room" from where he would be wheeled into the back of a waiting hearse.

Only the hearse wasn't waiting. Apparently it had a flat tire that was now being fixed in the mortuary garage.

The two attendants whose job it was to load the deceased for the final journey were told that it would only be a matter of five or ten minutes before the hearse would be ready. Which was roughly the amount of time it usually took the mourners to reach their cars and get ready for the trip.

"Time for a smoke," one of the attendants said, heading for the staff room with the other attendant following.

There had been a period in the mid-thirties when Emerson Waldie had made a dozen or so horror films such as *The Coffin Creaks* and *The Zombies of Zanzibar* and *The Creeper*. But none of them had a story line or visual shock element that could compare with the moment when the dead man in the coffin in the "waiting room" at the Valley of Heavenly Dreams Chapel and Mortuary lifted the lid of his own coffin and sat up.

"Where the fuck am I?" grumbled Emerson Waldie who, although he'd been pronounced dead once at his offices and once again at the hospital, was anything but.

Climbing out of the coffin, Waldie let the lid drop and went sliding across the highly polished floor in his stocking feet. It was the policy of this mortuary never to bury the dead in shoes as the corpse's feet weren't visible to viewers, hidden as they were under quilted padding.

In his garish white makeup and formal tails, and obviously mis- diagnosed as dead, Waldie opened a door leading to the hall and went through it.

The hall was deserted as was this part of the building. The mortuary staff was busily attending to the many guests who'd come here to be part of the Waldie funeral, the largest, and in the words of one guest, the most "awaited" funeral in Hollywood.

Waldie was extremely groggy from his ordeal which had been caused by a cataleptic seizure. Although rare, this malady was a known medical condition, characterized by a heart rate and pulse that seemed nil. A person suffering from certain forms of catalepsy almost always appeared to be dead. He or she might not stir again for days, often when six feet under.

But Waldie had awakened from his trance-state earlier than usual and was, at this very moment, shuffling toward the side exit of this mortuary, instinctively wishing to be away from the building.

Once outside, Waldie made straight for the road and was walking along when a pickup truck screeched to a halt.

"Hey, old timer," called the driver of the truck, a young gardener, "can I give you a lift?"

Waldie, not yet functioning, climbed into the truck and let himself be removed from the grounds of the Valley of Heavenly Dreams Chapel and Mortuary.

A few minutes later, his coffin was loaded onto the hearse by the attendants who commented on how "light" this particular body was.

"Damn near got a hernia carrying that Fatty Arbuckle onto the wagon that time," one of them said.

"Know what you mean," the other replied.

The funeral possession began shortly after, the Cadillac hearse leading at least one hundred cars to Forest Lawn Cemetery where the empty coffin was duly buried.

Chapter 34

By eleven in the morning, a glaringly bright white sun was beating unmercifully down upon the multitude of search teams, rescue workers, state police, studio officials, and local gawkers at the Maggie Graym crash site.

The beaded handbag which had been found just a few hours earlier had now been positively identified due to the contents inside as having belonged to Margaret Mary Winifred Graym whose principal address was stated as Beverly Hills. Or so the information read on the California driver's license and Grove Pictures gate pass.

And it was precisely because this identification had been authenticated that members of the press were arriving by the dozens from Los Angeles and elsewhere.

All over America, people were stationed by their radios listening for news of Maggie Graym and to the many tributes that were already being made to this beloved Hollywood star whose body had not been found and whose death had not yet been established.

And while Louella Parsons and Hedda Hopper, each having arrived at the site by separate chauffeur-driven limousines, were arguing as to who got there first, it was the king of the journalists, Walter Winchell, broadcasting from New York's Rockefeller Center, who was keeping the nation abreast of the progress being made in California.

Praising Maggie as the most luminous actress ever to shine

before a camera, Winchell stressed what a great morale booster she'd been for all the men in uniform.

"We're all praying that Maggie will be found soon and that she will be found safe and sound and as lovely as ever," Winchell said during this specially arranged emergency broadcast. "And we know that the entire country is praying for Maggie Graym during this very trying time."

At the USO on Hollywood and Vine, the day shift hostesses were finding that they had a bunch of glum, worried looking GIs on their hands. Concerned about Maggie, the servicemen congregated around the radio waiting for news of her.

Even George Burns and Gracie Allen, regulars at the USO, were having trouble cheering the men up.

"We know just how you feel, fellas, but don't worry," George said. "They'll find Maggie any minute now and she'll be fine, absolutely fine. Tell them, Gracie."

"Maggie will be fine, absolutely fine," Gracie said.

Only their audience didn't look so sure.

At the crash scene, Tom had been working for the past eight hours with the rescue workers in order to help locate Maggie. Because of his skills as a top stuntman, he was able to search areas that were too treacherous for the others.

Climbing down the steep ravine, he discovered the spot where the sleek Continental had originally come to a halt.

The car, having been lifted out of the ravine by crane hours earlier, had left its imprint on the large jutting rock with which it had come into contact. Parts of the car now lay scattered everywhere, along with a sea of broken glass.

Observing all this wreckage, it was apparent to Tom that

such an impact couldn't have left any survivors. Climbing to the relative safety of an upper perch, Tom met with some of the rescue party and reported that there was no sign of Maggie Graym down below.

"She must've been thrown clear out of the car," one of the men said. "The question is: where did she land?"

As the day wore on, it was becoming more and more obvious that wherever Maggie Graym happened to be at this moment, whether dead or alive, she wasn't in this ravine.

By six in the evening, the search was called off for the day and the rescue authorities began debating amongst themselves as to whether or not there was any point in resuming the search the following day.

"We don't even have any real evidence that Miss Graym was in the car at the time of the crash," the head of the search team said. "I mean, there isn't any trace of blood to show that she was injured, and there aren't any clothes or personal articles found at the scene, aside from her handbag."

With the rumor going around that the search might be called off altogether, a tremendous uproar in the ranks of Hollywood's powerful was heard, led by Hedda Hopper and Louella Parsons.

"We're not going to just return to Hollywood and leave Maggie down there to be devoured by wolves and scorpions and God knows what else," Hedda stormed. "You'll just have to go back down there tomorrow and find her. We have to have positive evidence that Maggie is either alive or, God forbid, dead."

"That's right," Louella chimed in, hating to be in a position that called for her to agree with *that woman*, but having no real choice in the matter.

"This isn't the same situation that we had with poor Amelia Earhart when she was lost at sea," Hedda droned on, ignoring Louella completely. "Maggie Graym is lost in a mere ravine and it's your job to go down there and find her for us and for all Americans."

Tom left the besieged rescue workers trying to ward off the likes of Hedda and Louella and headed back to the car where he hoped Douglas hadn't perished from the heat while waiting for him.

Only Douglas wasn't there.

Chapter 35

On the back seat of his car lay the hat and sunglasses Douglas had been wearing in disguise. They'd been discarded. Along with the oversized jacket that Tom had lent him.

Tom considered what might have happened in the time he'd left Douglas sitting in his car. First of all, there was the possibility of Douglas heading for the midwest where he had relatives, and where there would be a certain amount of safety. But he certainly wouldn't have gone without the disguise of the hat, glasses, and jacket.

What was more probable, as Tom saw it, was that Douglas had been spotted by some authorities approaching Tom's car and rather than get Tom into trouble, had made a run for it. There was even the chance that he hadn't got too far before he'd been captured and returned to the camps.

Feeling certain that he'd badly failed Douglas, for whose cause Tom had become so involved, he now leaned against the fender of his car and envisioned the young man being delivered, probably at gunpoint, back to the authorities in Los Angeles. For Tom, there was no other way of looking at what had happened except as his fault. And besides, he'd really taken a liking to the kid.

So deeply entrenched in this feeling of self-recrimination was Tom that he didn't realize that somebody had come up from behind him.

"Hi," Douglas said.

"Jeez, Douglas, where were you?" Tom said, relieved at seeing him, and hustling him into the car.

"Out looking for Maggie," Douglas said. "I felt useless just sitting here, so a couple of hours ago, I went way down into the ravine. There wasn't any sign of Maggie and I would know. I used to go rabbit hunting with my dad. I'd know if an animal or a person was in the vicinity. There's nothing down there except snakes. The place is loaded with them."

"I don't get it," Tom said, puzzled. "Nobody walks from an accident like that,"

"If it was an accident," Douglas ventured, sounding to himself like his favorite movie serial character, *Richie O'Rourke, Boy Detective.* "Maybe somebody knew she was on her way to harbor an escaped evacuee. Maybe she was captured by some gang or other. Like that bunch of hoods that attacked you the other day."

"There's no one that could have known what she was going to do," Tom replied. "Unless she blabbed it to somebody."

"Or," Douglas conjectured, "unless she was followed here, forced off the road and abducted. With her car being shoved off the road to make it look like an accident."

Tom remembered what the man at the records office had bragged to him about. *Dealing with other big stars by other means, usually fatal.*

"Let's get out of here," Tom said, realizing Douglas could be right. A few minutes later he parked the Packard near Doc's brightly lit diner. He found it full of police, rescue workers, press photographers and reporters. In one corner of the diner, Hedda Hopper had set up her headquarters from where she transmitted an hourly bulletin to her large radio audience.

Louella Parsons, with a similar set-up, ran her empire from the opposite corner of the restaurant. She made it quite clear on the air waves that hers was the very latest news regarding Maggie. The disappearance and search for Maggie Graym was proving to be one of the biggest news stories since the attack on Pearl Harbor.

"I ain't never done business like this, I can tell you," Doc said happily while tending the constantly ringing cash register.

Tom used up most of his food rations on a couple of ham sandwiches to go, and was waiting for his order when he overheard someone ask Doc if he'd seen somebody called Giuseppe Lambozza recently.

"Come to think of it, I saw Gus yesterday. Looks like he's got a woman friend. Saw him driving past the station with a woman in that beat-up old Ford of his. I waved at him, but he speeded up, as much as that old rattlebox could take."

"A woman, huh?" the customer replied. "Well, maybe that's what Giuseppe needs. He's been up there on his farm alone ever since his wife, Rosa, died, when would you say that was, about eighteen or twenty years ago?"

"More like twenty-five," Doc answered. "And of course some people around these parts say Gus was a son of a bitch who worked poor Rosa to death. Renting her out to work as a rancho field hand from morning to night and at the same time making her keep up on all her other duties. So I feel sorry for any woman who gets in his path."

"What did she look like anyway?" The customer asked.

"What are you talking about?" Doc asked. "You seen her

around town just like me. She had black hair and had a face fulla moles and by the time Giuseppe got through with her she weighed about eighty pounds."

"Not Rosa," the customer replied impatiently, "I'm talking about the woman in the car. The woman who was in Giuseppe's car. What did she look like?"

"Oh, her," Doc said. "I couldn't rightly see. I only know she was a woman."

Tom had only been half listening to this conversation while waiting, but something about what they were saying made a connection for him. A longshot connection, to be sure, but still, something to go on.

He rushed Doc, momentarily startling the old man.

"Where does this guy live?" Tom demanded.

"Hold on, young fella, hold on," Doc said, "where does who live?"

"This guy you two were just talking about." Tom said, "This Giuseppe guy!"

Chapter 36

Marcus Wood sat in the mahogany paneled library of his Bel-Air mansion and sipped a glass of Salon Mesnil Champagne, possibly the best champagne in the world.

Everything that Marcus drank, ate, wore, and owned was the best in the world. In the display cases that spanned all but one of the walls was the famous Marcus Wood collection, including an original manuscript of "A Midsummer Night's Dream" signed by the author.

On the remaining wall, set out in resplendent frames atop the sixteenth century harpsichord, were the many photographs. There were Wood and FDR strolling in Hyde Park, deep in conversation, Wood with "Winnie" Churchill playing snooker in Great Windsor Castle, Wood with General MacArthur trooping the colors in Manila, Wood with Albert Einstein playing chess in Switzerland.

The only well-known person missing from this roster was his idol, Adolph Hitler. Not that he would have been able to display a photograph of himself and Hitler for others to see, but he certainly would have liked to have *at least* had a photo of himself and the Fuhrer to commemorate their three-minute chat. Oh well, there would be plenty of photos later, when Hitler would be sure to honor him for his work in helping to secure Hollywood for the Reich.

Wood had been honored many times before. Hanging in a small room off the library, there were dozens of plaques, all of them praising the vast achievements of Marcus Wood, philanthropist.

In one year alone, 1941, Wood had proposed the building of a hospital for lepers in Tanganyika, a school for retarded children on an Indian reservation near Cheyenne, and a facility to train seeing-eye dogs in Rangoon.

So far in 1942 he'd been on the boards of a scholarship program for impoverished but brilliant students in Brazil (his contribution to the Good Neighbor Policy), a home for orphaned hemophiliacs in war-torn China, and half a dozen shelters for the elderly.

The big advantage to all his international connections, even in wartime, was that he had access to enemy territory, which was how he had been able to send the wire relating to Maggie. But now he was in an absolute rage that she'd been able to cheat death three times in a row. There had been the Ferris wheel attempt on her life and that had been bungled. And then there was the swimming pool incident with that look-alike he had mistaken for Maggie. And finally, there was attempt number three in which he had forced her off the road down into a deep ravine.

Damn that woman, Wood thought. She had nine lives, or so it seemed. But now her luck had run out because a spotter had picked her up walking along the road. Any minute now yet another man would be on his way to finish her off—and all the best of luck to him as far as Wood was concerned.

That man was Bradford who'd apparently worked it all out with the spotter who'd found Maggie on the road. He would have liked nothing better than to have gone himself.

Unfortunately, he was already scheduled to appear that evening at a relief-fund dinner for Czechoslovakian war refugees. This event wasn't one from which he could easily absent himself because he had set up the relief fund himself and his appearance was sure to guarantee an extra generous contribution from the Hollywood crowd of patrons.

Of course, the money raised for this worthwhile cause would never get to the Czech refugees because Wood was simply using their tragic plight as a front, the way he used many of the other charitable organizations he'd created.

While under a halo of magnanimity and public praise for the excellent work he was doing in the name of humanity, Wood would coolly deposit 80% of the hundred thousand dollars or so brought in from the evening's efforts into a secret bank account. And there it would remain until such a time as it could safely be snuck out of the country. It would only take a few weeks after that to reach the hands of the "money lender to the world", Switzerland.

In exchange for its neutrality being observed, Switzerland had been financing wars since long before Napoleon's time. Once Wood's money reached Zurich, it would automatically transfer to Berlin where it would help maintain the Nazi war machine. This was the same procedure for most monies collected from Wood's charitable fronts throughout America. Every once in a while, however, Wood did actually build the odd hospital here or there or create a home for boys in some backward country, but these enterprises were only for show. They were evidence that he was really doing something to help mankind.

It never failed to make Wood chuckle with delight at the way patriotic Americans thought they were supporting the Allied cause. Never did they suspect that much of the money they contributed was being used in the manufacture of the very planes, ships and munitions that would, as far as Wood was concerned, one day help to annihilate them.

The whole thing was just too funny for words. A real scream. About the only complaint Wood could conjure up was that there were so few people with whom to share the joke at the present time.

The "Head" as he was often referred to, would have been the ideal person, but because of this latest mishap with Maggie Graym, he had become highly critical of Wood's handling of the matter. This had caused Wood no end of sorrow.

But not to worry, Wood now thought. After tonight, he'd be out of the doghouse. Because tonight, Maggie would be transported from where she was currently being held and taken to a place a mile or so from the car crash location. There, the death of Maggie Graym would be re-enacted. It would be made to look as if she'd somehow survived the crash, had wandered away although injured, and had eventually succumbed to those injuries.

To expedite the discovery of her body, one of Wood's "workers" would infiltrate the rescue team and lead everyone right to the body. Of course there was bound to be an investigation as to why the body hadn't been found earlier. But Wood was too elated with the prospect of Maggie's death to worry about such things as investigations.

He was gratified to think that within the next 24 hours, confirmation of Maggie's death would be all over the news. Equally important, it would be channeled to America's fighting forces, wherever they might be scattered around the world. The main hope was that the effectiveness of the GI in battle would be reduced considerably due to depression.

Draining the last few drops of champagne, he placed the glass on the beautifully shined India-wood end table that reflected in its patina the glowing embers of the fireplace.

In the main hall, with the Venetian handblown crystal chandeliers hanging from an authentic, hand-painted twelfth century Florentine ceiling, he climbed the grand stairway to his bedroom suite so that he could have a long, relaxing soak in the marble bathtub and then leisurely change into the clothes he would wear that evening.

Wood's imported French manservant had been given strict orders to have his bath drawn by six-fifteen sharp and to have his "uniform" laid out. This was an impeccably tailored military-style suit made of the finest silk with buttons of pure gold. Added to this, Wood had the audacity to have five gold stars woven on each shoulder. This suit was one of a dozen that Wood had ordered in different shades.

When dressed as a self-appointed five-star general in all his finery, he tended to make any high-ranking military officer in his presence look positively shabby by comparison, something that Wood enjoyed to the extreme.

What Wood found when he entered his bedroom were his clothes neatly laid out on the bed with its Louis the Fourteenth stead, and his French manservant neatly laid out on the bed next to them. Bound and gagged.

Sitting on a chair upon which Marie Antoinette had once sat, Gerhardt Vanderschloffer was calmly reading a movie magazine.

In his left hand, dangling casually by his side, was a long-barreled pistol.

"Greetings from Uncle Adolph," Gerhardt said, looking up and smiling at Wood.

Chapter 37

Nothing seemed to be going right for Emerson Waldie. Having awakened in a coffin was bad enough, but trying to get home again had proved to be a nightmare.

After his ride off the grounds in the workman's truck, he'd picked up another ride, this time in an old, beat-up Dodge driven by an old, beat-up looking guy.

"You going to a Halloween party?" the man asked, Halloween being just a few days away.

Having no idea what the man was talking about, Waldie hadn't answered. And since he hadn't seen himself in a mirror, he didn't know that he strongly resembled Count Dracula.

The fact was, Emerson Waldie had clearly been out of it. Whatever caused his deadly state, it left him feeling weak and frail. There was only one thing he wanted, and that was to get home.

'Listen, fella," Waldie said, addressing the man in a slurring way that suggested intoxication. "Would you drive me to my house in Beverly Hills? I'll give you a hundred dollars. I'll give you two hundred dollars."

"Beverly Hills, huh?" the driver replied, playing Waldie along. "You probably live in one of those great big houses with all the cars and all the servants, right?"

"109777 Roxbury Drive," Waldie said.

"You wouldn't mean the Waldie place, now would you?" the man said, winking broadly at Waldie.

"That's right," Waldie said. "And I'm the Waldie who owns the Waldie place."

"Gee," the man said teasingly, "I thought you were dead."

"Dead?" Waldie asked. "What do you mean, dead? Just get me to my house and I'll give you the money."

The man, coming to a main intersection, decided that perhaps it was time to let the shoeless old drunk out of the car before he became a problem.

"Here you are, old-timer," the driver said. "I'm dropping you off near a bus stop. You can get a bus to your place in Beverly Hills."

It was only when Waldie was watching the car departing that he realized that he had no money. He didn't have a wallet. And he didn't have any identification. He didn't even have a pair of shoes.

His most current need had been to sit down, which he did on a park bench, his heart pounding. People passing by seemed to pity him, but no one came over to ask if he was okay.

Finally a cop came along on his beat, and spotting Waldie, chased him off the bench. "Now get along with you," the cop said with a distinct Irish accent. "Or I'll run you in."

"Don't you understand?" Waldie asked, his parched tongue sticking to the roof of his mouth as he spoke, "I'm Emerson Waldie, the head of Grove Pictures."

"Keep it up and I'll run you in for making fun of the dead that way," the cop said. "Now move!"

Waldie walked along, not knowing where. He hadn't actually walked anywhere in years and he didn't recognize this neighborhood. But he kept walking because now there were some smart-aleck kids on his trail heckling him.

In the distance were a bunch of stores. Waldie decided his best bet would be to get into one of them. Where it would be safe and where he might find a phone.

The kids were closing in on him so rapidly, he began to run. Making a mad dash across a busy road, he barely missed being knocked down by an army convoy truck. By the time he reached the other side of the street, he was completely out of breath and wheezing loudly. Rushing into a drug store, he found a pay phone. He had no money so he'd have to reverse charges in order to reach anyone at his home. How happy they'd be to hear that he was alive and well.

"Will you accept a call from Mr. Emerson Waldie?" the operator asked as soon as the phone was picked up at the other end. Waldie recognized the voice of his butler.

"Operator," the butler said, "this is a crank caller. Mr. Waldie has done us all a favor and has dropped dead. Tell your caller that and good day!"

"Philip, Philip," Waldie yelled into the phone, but both the butler and the operator had clicked off.

Waldie tried the number again and the new operator informed him that he couldn't be Emerson Waldie because everyone knew that Emerson Waldie had died of a heart attack the day before and that what he was doing masquerading as Waldie was very mean and hurtful to the grieving family.

"But I am Emerson Waldie," Waldie insisted. "And I don't know anything about dying. I'm just as alive as you are. Please, you've got to help me."

"Disgraceful," the operator snorted and hung up.

Leaving the phone booth, Waldie quickly walked over to the newspaper stand. On the front page of the Los Angeles Times were two photographs. One was his and the other's was Maggie Graym's. Hers was a lot larger which made Waldie angry. He wanted to know why he and Maggie were on the front page of the L.A. Times and why her picture was larger than his.

Without his glasses, there was no way he could read the copy surrounding each photo, and it was only with extreme difficulty that he was able to make out the headline above his own. What he read shocked him.

"EMERSON WALDIE DEAD," the headline announced.

"But I'm not dead," Waldie said loudly, not bothering to read Maggie's headline. "I'm not dead, I'm not dead, I'm not dead, I'm not dead."

It was then that a store clerk grabbed him roughly by the back of his collar.

"Yeah," the clerk said, *but you will be* if you don't get the hell out of my store, Mac. He then propelled Waldie rapidly to the door and pitched him out onto the street.

The push sent him flying into some garbage cans which was both a bad thing and a good thing. A bad thing because he grazed himself on the elbow and knee. And a good thing because he knocked over one of the garbage cars out of which fell, amongst a ton of onion skins and rotting fish innards, a decrepit-looking pair of workman's boots.

True, the boots were at least two sizes too large for Waldie and had flapping soles with enormous holes in them and were scuzzy and smelly, but for Waldie, they represented a way for him to be mobile.

Waldie fought the impulse to throw up at the horrible odor coming from the laceless boots, as well as the feeling of hopeless humiliation as he gingerly put his feet into them and started walking toward what he hoped was the direction of home. Several hours later, after endless trudging, Waldie seemed to recognize the area he was in and weakly forged ahead toward Beverly Hills. He was incredibly hungry and thirsty, but more than that, he was extremely fatigued. He could have happily laid down on the side of the road and dropped off to sleep. But still he trudged on and entered, by evening, Beverly Hills. He was determined, if he never did another thing, to reach his home and his bed.

It occurred to him as he dragged himself along that he couldn't walk through Beverly Hills without being seen by the police that patrolled the area on a regular basis. Any person walking in the vicinity of residential Beverly Hills was subject to bodily removal from the area, as well as harassment and, possibly, jail.

Waldie felt that if he was picked up by the police, the very police that he and other prominent Beverly Hills residents had insisted comb the streets for undesirables, he would never reach home again. He knew that no one would believe that he was Emerson Waldie, but rather, a raving old man. He'd probably wind up in the state mental hospital and never be heard of again.

For that reason, he moved along with extreme caution, stealing across lawns and hiding behind trees and hedges from the black and white patrol cars that moved slowly from street to street.

Nearly dead now from exhaustion, Waldie finally approached the cul-de-sac that wound around in an upward spiral until it reached the gates of his twenty-five acre estate. Only there were no gates.

Waldie thanked providence that he'd recently ordered the massive steel gates taken down and donated to the steel drive in aid of the war effort. It had merely been a publicity stunt to show himself off to the world as a concerned, self-sacrificing patriot.

The lack of gates meant that Waldie, ever on the lookout for the security police he'd hired, was able to make his way past the twelve room guest house with its own pool and tennis courts and down along the private lake with its long pier that was situated about a thousand yards from the big house.

An asphalt drive led to the house. Waldie, thinking it would never end, eventually reached the highly ornate structure, a replica of the Taj Mahal.

He moved around to the side of the house where there was a great deal of activity going on. There were a number of trucks up there, several of which belonged to a Hollywood caterer. What in the hell was a caterer doing up there, Waldie wondered.

And then he remembered: this was the day he'd been buried and, of course, Enid would be obliged to put on some sort of open house for the mourners. After all, that was the custom, to feed friends and relatives after such an ordeal. But this was ridiculous; there was enough food being unloaded to feed Patton's army.

From where Waldie stood, behind a clump of bushes, he could see right into the brightly lit windows of the kitchen and main dining room. Enid was going from room to room issuing orders to the many people rushing around her. It was as if she were directing an epic movie. Her voice cracked out instructions regarding the banquet table, the bandstand, the balloons...the balloons???

It had now occurred to Waldie that this was not going to be just a gathering of people coming together to honor him for the great and generous and loving and warm man that he had been, a man who would be sorely missed for years to come. This was going to be some kind of fantastic celebration!

It was like...like people were really happy that he was dead. He winced at the sight of a South American rhumba band assembling on the patio near the pool. its members wore sombreros, ruffle-sleeved shirts and colorful vests. And when they began to rehearse, Enid could be seen in the window swaying to and fro, this way and that, to the hot rhythm. For a few moments she just danced around by herself, her hips moving with the beat.

And then she accosted a waiter carrying a heavy tray of dishes and began interrupting his work so that he would dance with her. She was laughing like Waldie had never seen her laugh, and she was teasing the waiter, making him lose his balance so that he had to put the tray down on the table rather than drop it on the floor.

Waldie watched fascinatedly as his wife, the staid Enid, flirted and danced with the waiter who was stiff and uncomfortable-looking at first, but who was now really getting into it.

Enid, laughing wildly, clicked her fingers over her head just as the sultry Rita Hayworth had done while dancing with

Anthony Quinn in *Blood and Sand*. She took little flamenco-type steps in front of, and then around, the waiter who was busy clapping his hands and shouting "ole" all over the place.

Waldie couldn't get over this scene taking place with his own wife, in his own dining room, in his own house, and with his own body supposedly not even cold yet.

Stepping angrily out of the bushes, Waldie walked past a few female workers busy setting up outdoor tables and chairs. They couldn't help but notice the funny little man in the oversized army boots that caused him to walk like Charlie Chaplin in "The Gold Rush."

"She must have hired a clown for the party," one of them commented as Waldie walked by.

"Yeah," another agreed. "This is a big occasion for her what with the old tyrant dead. This is going to be the party to end all parties."

"What I don't get," still another worker said, "is how she rates all this food, considering there's a war on and everything. Guess with her money she can pull strings and get anything she wants. And from what I hear, with the husband out of the picture, she's in for millions more."

"Over my dead body," Waldie muttered to himself as he entered the house. He shuffled through the enormous kitchen as fast as his big boots would carry him. A legion of chefs and their assistants worked feverishly preparing the food for the party. There were roasts, turkeys and ducks cooking away, and on the long butcher-block tables were the salads, soups, pastries, breads, desserts.

On one such table was a gigantic layer cake. It had to be

about six feet by six feet. A chef, working on it, artistically captured the likeness of four faces. Waldie recognized Hitler's, Hirohito's, Mussolini's...and *his*.

Watching the cake being created as if in a trance, Waldie saw the chef then bring the frosting case down upon his own cakeface, laying over it a red, creamy line. A moment later a second line was applied crossing the first one so that there was a big X over his likeness.

As a final touch, the chef scrawled in huge strokes across the top of the cake the words: *One Down, Three To Go.*

This was too much! Waldie angrily pushed open the dining room door planning to surprise the merry widow in the middle of her dance. Only she'd disappeared.

Just then Waldie caught sight of her as she walked through the wide archway on the other side of the dining room. She'd removed her shoes and was moving slowly and sensually toward the staircase. With the excited waiter trailing behind her.

It was obvious what Enid had in mind. A "quickie" before the celebration.

"Well, we'll just see about that," Waldie said aloud. He started across the dining room but hadn't walked five paces when he felt a heavy hand on his shoulder. Turning, he saw the hand belonged to an unsmiling security officer.

"And where, may I ask, are you off to, old timer?" the officer asked.

"Take your hands off me," Waldie growled. "I'll have you thrown off my property."

"Oh, so this is your property, is it?" the officer said as if weighing up whether or not this guy was going to be any trouble.

"That's right," Waldie said and started walking across the room again. Obviously, this guy was going to be trouble. He'd only got another step before he found his arms pinned behind him.

"Now we're just going to turn around and march right out of here," the security officer said.

Which is when Waldie started bellowing and twisting his body and kicking at the officer.

His rebellion didn't last long, however. The officer, used to this kind of disturbance, removed the nightstick from his belt and let Waldie have one swift taste of it over the top of his head.

Chapter 38

It had been 30 amazing hours since Gerhardt's departure from Germany. First there had been the ride in the Messerschmitt. If he lived to be one hundred, he knew he could never duplicate that thrill. And then there was the leap from the American long-range bomber. plane. It had turned out to be nothing short of exhilarating. He'd wished that he could have done it all over again. But there had been work to do. And now that work was done. He had come to Los Angeles as ordered, apprehended Marcus Wood as ordered, and had delivered Wood to the very hatch of the submarine. As ordered.

But get on that ship himself? Forget it. As far as he was concerned, he'd done his duty by the Reich and there was no way in hell that he was going back to Germany, to Hitler, to hardship, to deprivation.

At roughly ten in the evening, he dutifully rowed Wood via dinghy to the waiting sub. He remained in the dinghy while Wood was taken aboard. Then, when it was his own turn to get into the claustrophobic chamber, he pushed off, rowing for all his worth toward the shore. The beautiful Californian shore.

The submarine commander, taken by surprise at Gerhardt's actions had, in as loud a voice as he dared, ordered Gerhardt's immediate return. Gerhardt, knowing there was no chance the sub commander would attempt to capture him, and no chance he'd fire on him for fear of attracting the United States Coast Guard, just laughed and rowed, rowed and laughed.

He was free and it felt great. Of course, he would have to be on his guard for those in Los Angeles who might have helped in the abduction of Marcus Wood. For example, they had a car waiting for him at the sub rendezvous location so that he could transport Wood. He'd been instructed to dump the vehicle off a cliff into the ocean before reboarding the submarine, but he hadn't done it. Why destroy a perfectly good car? He'd need it to get around. But could these people trace him through the license plate? No big deal. He'd simply trade license plates with another black, 1942 Ford sedan. There had to be thousands of them in L.A. alone. As for his appearance, he would shave off his mustache. And start parting his hair on the side instead of in the middle. And maybe wear sunglasses all the time like the movie stars did.

It was a moonless night which was good for the submarine's departure. It occurred to him that Hitler might send someone to capture him the same way he'd been sent to capture Wood. Although would Hitler bother with such an insignificant person as himself? Gerhardt thought not.

The main thing was that he was now in the land where movies were made, where movie stars lived, and where he, himself, with his not bad looks and his strong if not perfect command of American English (he could recite whole movie scripts with a Kansas accent), would make his fortune. Maybe even become a movie star himself. Take Deanna Durbin on a date. Change his name to something movie-starrish. Kirk Sinclair? Deanna Durbin was sure to go out with a guy called Kirk Sinclair. Gerhardt decided to give it some more thought. After all, what was the rush? He had the rest of his life to live in this fabulous paradise called Hollywood, this incredible wonderland.

"Hollywood," he repeated to himself several times, as if he couldn't really believe he had it in the palm of his hand. This was the place he'd waited all his life to visit. He just stood above the crashing waves for awhile, perfectly happy to breathe in the delicious California sea air and to contemplate all the wonderful things he had to look forward to. He couldn't recall a time when he'd known such excitement.

Gerhardt thought about how easy it had been to complete this mission. Of course, Marcus Wood had put up a terrific struggle when it was revealed to him just why it was that Adolph Hitler, some ten thousand miles away, wanted to see him. And just what it was that Hitler had in mind for him.

"But I was just getting rid of Maggie because I thought he'd be pleased," Wood had raved just before Gerhardt had gagged him. "I was doing it for the Reich."

The sub with Wood aboard would now take a longer route back to Germany, down around South America, stopping in Argentina to refuel. In two weeks and a few days from now, a rabid Hitler would be presiding over Wood's trial himself, if, indeed, there was to be a trial. One thing was a certainty, what the verdict would be. There was no question but that it would be guilty. Following that, there would be a slow, agonizing death, probably by hanging from the neck by piano wire. "The Hitler Special," as it was often referred to by Hitler's staff in Berlin.

And all because Wood had murdered the woman that Hitler loved and adored above all women. *Well, Adolph Hitler wasn't the only one who felt this way about Maggie Graym.* Gerhardt thought. He'd loved her himself and had even envisioned meeting her one day in this fabled Hollywood. It was a fantasy he'd enjoyed since first setting eyes on her beauteous film persona.

But due to Marcus Wood, that meeting would never take place, Gerhardt thought, bitterly. The only satisfaction he would ever get out of this tragedy was the knowledge that justice would be carried out and that Maggie would be avenged. And that he, Gerhardt Vanderschloffer, would have played a prominent role in making all this happen.

And now he could start his new life although he really had no idea what his next move would be. The only things he had were the car, the U.S. Naval officer's uniform he was wearing and the falsified papers.

The uniform had originally been intended as a kind of passport around Los Angeles. In uniform, he'd hardly be noticed, but out of it he might be regarded with suspicion. If there was any trouble with the authorities, there was always the little capsule fastened in the lining of his jacket pocket to be used without hesitation in case of capture and interrogation.

Gerhardt was aware of how, the previous June, a Nazi sub deposited eight saboteurs on the east coast of America. Their mission had been to blow up munitions factories, but before they could strike the first blow, they were nabbed, put on trial, and immediately put to death in the electric chair. Gerhardt shuddered at the thought.

He reached into his pocket, found the capsule, and threw it into the darkness. Also in his pocket was the hand-written note he'd seen on a table in Wood's bedroom before Wood had come up to change.

Not knowing why, Gerhardt had quickly read the note and although he couldn't understand all the words, he got the main idea. Apparently there was to be a gathering at the home of Emerson Waldie, the late Emerson Waldie, that is. Gerhardt had heard about Waldie's death on the car radio and about his funeral which had taken place earlier.

The note, written in what was a generous hand complete with flourishes and hoops, asked that Wood join the mourners (there was a 'ha-ha' next to the word 'mourners') at the Waldie estate in Beverly Hills that evening. The message related that *everybody* was going to be there and was signed *Your adoring Enid.*

Gerhardt considered showing up at the Waldie place. This was the start of his new life, wasn't it? And he needed to make some new friends, didn't he?

The Waldie party would be as good as anywhere to begin with. There were bound to be important people present, people that might aid him in getting established. The only problem Gerhardt could see facing him was that of actually getting in the front door.

He started driving toward Beverly Hills and even though he'd only been there once before, to scoop up Marcus Wood, he had no trouble finding his way. He'd studied the city map many, many times since the age of sixteen in preparation for the time when he would be lucky enough to travel there. He probably knew Los Angeles better than the people who actually lived there.

By the time he arrived at the big mansion on the hill, he

knew exactly how he would present himself. It would be as Emerson Waldie's nephew, just back from the war in the Pacific.

His acquired limp would lend credence to his story that he had received a serious leg wound from which he was recovering as best possible. Who was going to turn away a limping war hero nephew from New Jersey?

He just had to remember to keep talking like John Wayne. And, for God's sake, not to lapse into German. Or lose the limp on the conga line.

Chapter 39

As Gerhardt was heading toward Beverly Hills, Tom was heading toward Giuseppe Lambozza's place. There were a dozen or more cars following him in the far distance, their headlights just a glimmer in his rearview mirror. He'd raced out of Doc's fast, once he'd got the directions from the old man, and was now trying to remember them. Obviously, due to the cars following, Doc had told others of Tom's hunch, that Giuseppe might be holding Maggie. And they were just as determined to find Maggie as was Tom.

The directions given Tom by Doc had him first following Mailbu Road and then up into Topanga Canyon. He wondered if Doc had sent him on a wild goose chase. But he stayed with it. What choice did he have? Eventually, after four or so miles of twists and turns Tom saw two jutting rocks Doc had pointed out as a landmark. So perhaps Doc had been on the level, after all. And then there was the mile or more of unpaved road, full of potholes and foot-deep craters that Tom expertly avoided.

The Lambozza place was a grim and desolate wasteland with a field behind it that was barren and untended. It appeared not to have been farmed for at least a dozen years. At the entrance of the house was a sign warning visitors that they were not welcome.

Fifteen minutes before Tom's arrival, another car had approached the rickety looking farmhouse, the driver having ignored the warning sign. He stopped the car and blasted the horn, though he needn't have bothered.

Giuseppe Lambozza had been pacing back and forth on the ramshackle verandah for quite awhile and had seen the car's lights as they grew brighter and nearer.

Bundling a still bound and gagged Maggie over his shoulder, he left the house and headed toward the car, a pre-war fastback.

He placed Maggie on the back seat of the car with as much care as he would a sack of potatoes.

Maggie lay there in terror. She didn't know what was going to happen to her but she had no illusions that it would be pleasant.

Giuseppe got into the front seat of the car and for the first time spoke to the driver.

"Gotta get her near where her car went off the road. Throw her down a ravine. If that don't kill her, the wolves down there will. Let the search party discover what's left of her in a day or two," Giuseppe said.

Bradford, who'd been ordered out of the public eye by the "Head" for fear that Erne might have spilled some incriminating information linking him to the organization, drove wildly along the treacherous road, disregarding the holes.

Maggie, trying to stay on the seat during the bumpy ride, could hold on no longer and was thrown painfully onto the floor of the car. With the noise of the engine, she was at least spared having to hear the two men planning her murder.

As Bradford was turning onto the main road, he and Giuseppe sighted a car coming toward them. Giuseppe removed his gun from an inner pocket of his coat. He was prepared to use it if necessary. It wasn't necessary. The car driven by Tom passed in front of them and sped along.

Finding the house, Tom and Douglas entered the front door. It was wide open as if someone had left in haste. There was a musty smell inside coming from the furnishings and lack of cleaning. Tom lit a match and looked around.

On the floor in front of him woman's scarf with little red hearts on it. It was obvious it had been worn by someone glamorous and that someone was, no doubt, Maggie Graym.

With Douglas right behind him, Tom jumped back in the car and went in pursuit of the car they'd passed about ten minutes before. He avoided the holes in the road as best he could, and was glad to be back on the paved roadway.

"I hope we haven't lost them," Douglas said, suddenly getting down in his seat as dozens of cars came from the opposite direction. These were the people on their way to Giuseppe Lambozza's. If there had been time, Tom would have stopped them and told them that Maggie was possibly in the car he was chasing. But there was no time.

The road was nothing but curves, but Tom had the gas pedal to the floor. There was no sign of the fastback for at least a mile. Then Tom spotted the twinkle of red tail lights and just hoped that they were those of the right car.

He kept his foot on the accelerator and noticed that the other car had suddenly put on speed, also.

The fact that the driver ahead was trying to put distance between them told Tom that Maggie was in that car. Or, at least, there was somebody in that car who could tell him where she was.

The road now changed character so that both cars were moving amongst high boulders. Any driver, misjudging the curves on the road, might smash into one of those rocks like an insect onto a moving windshield. Soon, both cars were traveling at a high speed through an area where the houses were built on rocky terrain, still in Topanga Canyon..

The strata of the rock was piled high like shelves atop one another, and due to erosion, each terrace ended abruptly with a drop of some thirty feet, usually into the garden of a house that might be situated below.

The two cars were intermittently visible to one another as they traveled on different plateaus. Tom didn't realize at first that Giuseppe was firing a gun out of his window until his windshield cracked, spraying glass over him and Douglas.

The next moment, Giuseppe managed to put a bullet into Tom's front right tire. The Packard went out of control and out of commission. Tom practically swerved off the road several times but was able to bring the car to a halt before it plowed into a tree.

Jumping out of the car along with Douglas, Tom tried to figure out what to do. He felt totally powerless in the situation. There won't be any saving Maggie Graym this time, he thought. It hit him with a powerful force that he'd ultimately failed in keeping this woman, whom he hadn't any real regard for, out of the jaws of death.

No real regard for, he thought. Just another Hollywood redhead who'd been lucky. Very lucky. Until now.

"We've got to save her," Douglas yelled. "look..."

Leaning against a wall not twenty feet away were two bicycles.

"Let's go," Tom shouted in response.

He and Douglas ran to where the bikes were leaning and jumped on them, pedaling as fast as they could down several levels of terrace. But there was no sign of the fastback which had to be traveling at an extremely slow rate due to the many curves in the road.

Continuing to pedal, they entered the open drive of a terraced residence. Neither Tom nor Douglas had any definite plan, just a shared instinct as they rode furiously on the paved path to the side of the house. In back of it, facing west, people in evening dress sat on the patio having drinks. The area was ringed with colorful paper lanterns and in the distance, Tom could hear the tinkle of a piano.

"Hey," someone yelled. "You can't come in here." But Tom, with Douglas following, whizzed past the people and headed for the abrupt edge of the garden and over.

Douglas, who some time earlier had taken off the heavy overcoat he'd been wearing now appeared in the Imperial Japanese Army uniform.

"Banzai," he shouted as he flew past this distinguished group.

"I knew there were enemy soldiers on this coast," an elderly woman said softly and seemed to faint. For a moment no one moved and then all at once they began running, some toward the house, some toward their cars. "Let's get out of here," a man yelled. "There's bound to be more of them following. We'll all be killed."

Meanwhile, both Tom and Douglas seemed to hang in space, twenty feet above the next terrace. The drop was then rapid and the landing watery as they found themselves in a swimming pool directly below, having barely missed a late-evening swimming party. One of the bikes landed smack onto a buffet table.

Tom and Douglas were out of the pool in an instant and running fast. The car possibly carrying Maggie was on its way down this terrace.

Tom saw it from where he was running and was considering leaping onto it as it passed. He'd just about be able to do it with the time he had.

He was no stranger to leaping. He'd had his share of horses to leap upon as well as the backs of cars and trains, and even from one plane to another. Sprinting across a vast lawn, he now felt that all this training he'd had was something that would really serve its purpose. And he had to do it now if he was going to do it at all.

By virtue of the curving road. Bradford had been forced to slow to a crawl, but he was able to speed up when the road straightened as it did now. It would soon be past the estate gates and gone.

It was at this time that Tom found a second and far more effective way to stop the car.

Parked in the crescent-shaped drive was a Pierce Arrow limousine. Tom raced to the car with Douglas just a few feet behind. As they reached the car, Tom yanked open the driver's-side door and released the emergency brake.

"Let's get this baby on the road," he shouted to Douglas who now understood what Tom had in mind.

Together, they pushed the car from the drive onto the road where it would block Giuseppe and any accomplices he might have with him.

The fastback Bradford was driving came along the road at high speed tearing up gravel in its path.

Tom assumed that whomever was driving the fastback would be forced to slow down and come to a halt. He and Douglas stood on the side of the road and watched the driver attempt to do just that.

But he didn't slow down in time.

The sound of the crash was deafening. The fastback collided with the Pierce Arrow, and immediately two heads, those belonging to Giuseppe and Bradford, emerged through the windshield followed by their upper torsos. Both men, streaming blood, appeared to be dead.

It then occurred to Tom that by his actions, he might have caused the deaths of two innocent men. After all, he had never had any definite proof that they'd abducted Maggie. It had all been a hunch.

And then came the thought that if she was in the car, she, too, would be dead. Or badly injured. The collision, which Tom had never intended to happen, had been pretty fierce.

Running to the crashed fastback, Tom gripped the handle to the trunk and twisted it so that the trunk opened. Aside from a spare tire and some tools, the space was empty.

There was only one other place Maggie could be, Tom opened the passenger side door. Giuseppe's lower torso and legs hung grotesquely off the dashboard. Pulling the seat forward, Tom found Maggie on the floor. She didn't move. He didn't know if she was dead or alive.

Until he heard her groan. Her body had been cushioned between the front and back seats during the collision. While Douglas held the front seat forward, Tom gently removed Maggie from the floor of the car. Neither Tom nor Douglas seemed to notice the group of people, including the irate owner of the house and the Pierce Arrow, running toward them.

Someone shone a light on Maggie as Tom untied her hands and feet and removed the gag that was around her mouth. It was precisely at that moment that two things happened.

First of all, Maggie opened her eyes and saw Tom's face.

And secondly, a horrible moan of pain came from Giuseppe Lambozza showing that he, like Maggie, was still alive.

Day 8

Chapter 40

The Hollywood Canteen had never been so crowded. It seemed that every sailor from every ship in the area and every soldier and marine from every base was jamming into the place to get a good look at the lady they loved the most: the warm and smiling Maggie Graym.

Less than 24 hours had passed since Tom had rescued her from the clutches of her abductors and although she was still shaken by her harrowing experience, plus the news of Emerson Waldie's death, she felt it was her duty to make an appearance for the sake of the boys in uniform. And to show Tom that she was, at last, grateful, for all he'd done for her.

Tom, much to his discomfort, was getting his full share of accolades and attention, not just from Maggie, but from everyone else in Hollywood.

He might not have been a member of America's fighting forces, but in light of how he'd saved Maggie's life a total of three times, he'd earned the admiration and respect of servicemen and civilians alike.

And for this particular evening of celebration, he'd been relieved of his duties as dishwasher by Fred MacMurray so that he could stand on stage with Maggie in the deafening applause.

There was even talk of awarding him a special medal. As an admiral of the U.S. Navy, addressing the audience, stated: "This young man, while not on active duty in the armed forces, has accomplished something just as vital as capturing a Japanese garrison or destroying a Nazi ship. He has preserved one of America's true treasures, the beautiful Miss Graym who, in her shining way, represents American womanhood."

Tom, now feeling extremely uncomfortable, wished it had been because of capturing a Japanese garrison or destroying a Nazi ship that this praise was being heaped upon him. He still desperately wanted to be part of America's fighting machine.

Instead of that, here he was, being honored for saving the life of a movie star.

He had tried to play down his part in Maggie's rescue, but thanks to Hedda and Louella, that hadn't been possible. They, along with journalists from all over, had plastered his photo all over the newspapers, and had mentioned his name continuously over the airwaves.

They had also made it known that the attempt on Maggie's life had been part of a conspiracy carried out by Axis sympathizers working in the Los Angeles area.

This information had been gleaned from one Giuseppe Lambozza in the none too gentle care of the Federal Bureau of Investigation with J. Edgar Hoover personally taking charge.

Appearing to have been killed in the car he was riding, it later turned out that Lambozza was merely stunned, although his accomplice, one Dennis Bradford, had indeed died of serious wounds including a massive brain concussion.

Lambozza, succumbing to J. Edgar Hoover's ferocious bulldog manner and threat of summary execution, had broken down and had pleaded for his life.

J. Edgar, while not guaranteeing that he could prevent a grand jury from condemning Lambozza to death in San

Quentin's gas chamber, did, however, impress upon the scared farmer/saboteur that a grand jury was more likely to show him mercy were he to cooperate and describe exactly what he had in mind by abducting Miss Graym.

Lambozza had eagerly agreed and it was then that the whole story came out. How there had been a small, but well-organized ring of Axis sympathizers in L.A. and how they'd worked diligently to undermine that powerful organ of entertainment, information and propaganda: the American movie industry.

And with his confession came the names, as many names as Lambozza knew or could remember, including that of Hollywood's most prominent citizen, Marcus Wood.

Wood, as it was later discovered, had apparently disappeared without taking so much as a toothbrush. His trussed-up manservant had been found in Wood's bedroom, but the man could only relate to the police that he'd been knocked on the back of the head from behind by an assailant or assailants unknown and, therefore, as he was unconscious for quite some time, was unable to provide any useful information.

Upon checking Wood's many bank accounts around Los Angeles, it appeared that these were intact. Wood, according to the Federal Bureau of Investigation, was now the subject of a national manhunt.

"To think that one of the most trusted leaders in our little community has turned out to be one of *them* chills me to the bone." Louella Parsons had commented upon entering the canteen that evening. "It makes me wonder just whom else in our midst may be in league with the enemy," she added, glancing significantly in the direction of Hedda Hopper who had coincidentally arrived at the same time.

As for the name of the ring's leader, Lambozza denied knowing anything about him. "I never knew who he was, I swear to God, may a crucifix come crashing down on my head if I'm lying."

He could, however, identify Erne's killer: "It was Bradford. He told me himself. He waited for the guy to come out of his house in Silver Lake and gave it to him with a hunting knife." This last bit of news, conveyed to Tom by the authorities, had been especially hard to take. Tonight, however, standing on the stage at the Hollywood Canteen with Maggie, Tom felt that Erne was also there, looking down from some cloud or whatever, on the ceremony.

On the left of Maggie stood Vance Varley, seemingly miffed at having to, on studio orders, appear at the canteen to lend support to his almost constant co-star. Various other studio personnel, such as Morrie Goldstrohm, stood behind Maggie wearing a wide smile. With the death of Emerson Waldie, Morrie was going to do everything possible to protect his most viable property, Maggie Graym. At least as long as she brought in the kinds of profits the studio had become accustomed to.

Tom, seeing Vance nearby, seemed to stare at the pampered star. There was something about Vance's face that bothered him and he couldn't figure it out. And then he realized what it was that had suddenly caught his attention. The thought jolted him as would a jolt of electricity.

Before he could say or do anything, the master comedian, Jack Benny, walked out onto the stage to thundering applause. Embracing Maggie, he then turned to the audience.

"As many of you know," Benny began in a somber tone, "Maggie Graym was recently in the clutches of enemy saboteurs, men and women who were out to kill her and deprive us all of one of our most loyal, hard-working and beloved entertainers, someone who boosts our morale here on the homefront and those of you on the battlefield.

"But due to the gallant efforts of one young man," Benny continued after a deafening roar of clapping and cheers from the audience, both for Maggie and for Tom, "the traitor's plan didn't work out so well. Maggie Graym is with us safe and sound, and all of those people who were so intent upon weakening Hollywood and weakening America are tonight behind bars."

"All but one," Tom interrupted, taking a photograph out of his jacket pocket. It was the same one he'd removed from the Grove Pictures Records Office several days before. He'd forgotten he even had it on him.

The people in the audience who'd been hanging onto every word being spoken waited, along with Jack Benny, Maggie Graym, the Grove Pictures executives, the Army and Navy brass, and all the others onstage and off, to hear what Tom was going to say.

"How long were you a stuntman here in Hollywood, Vance?" Tom asked. "And just when was it that you had that big German nose of yours fixed so that you could become a leading man in motion pictures?"

Vance, looking at Tom in total disbelief, paled at the questions that had so suddenly been put before him.

"I have absolutely no idea what you are talking about,"

Vance said, outraged. "I was never a stuntman in Hollywood. I've only been a star in Hollywood. A big star. Big enough to see to it you'll never work in this town again after tonight. And as for my nose, I'll have you know it's the one I was born with."

"Something else I'd like to know," Tom said, ignoring Vance's monologue and the fact that Morrie Goldstrohm was now trying to silence him, "has to do with the changing of your name. When did you drop Wolfe Bronchflek and adopt Vance Varley?"

"This," Vance said, searching the ceiling dramatically as if an answer were to suddenly drop from there, "is just too much."

"Isn't it true," Tom said, "that you were not only fully aware of the faulty Ferris wheel the night you went up with Maggie, but that it had been your idea to have it rigged in the first place? And that with a little shaking and stomping up there in the car it would detach and fall to the ground, instantly killing Maggie in the process?"

"I know no such thing," Vance argued. "I didn't even want to go up there in that contraption. I begged and pleaded with the director not to send me up there."

If Morrie was trying to stop Tom from attacking one of Grove's biggest stars, he stopped. Vance was now doing a good job at destroying his own public image.

"But you knew you *would* get into that car with Maggie as planned and that you would exert enough force so that the car would detach and fall with Maggie trapped inside while you, with your talent as a very capable stuntman, would somehow manage to land yourself in another car. Only it didn't exactly work out as planned, did it, Wolfe? Maggie didn't die."

"Stop calling me Wolfe," Vance said loudly. "My name is Vance. Vance Varley."

"Perhaps to millions of movie fans out there and to most of the people here in Hollywood you're known as Vance Varley, the boy next door, but to a select few, you're not only known as Wolfe Bronchflek, but as the top man in a sabotage ring that's been operating out of Hollywood for the past few years."

It was as if everyone in the big, barn-like canteen decided to gasp in unison at what Tom was saying.

Vance just stood silently for a moment, his blond hair falling slightly over his forehead the way the bobby-soxers loved it. And then, without warning, he produced a gun from out of his jacket.

And, just as suddenly, he grabbed Maggie close to him and placed the gun barrel against her head.

"Keep your distance," Vance said, "or this time Maggie gets it for sure. And don't think I wouldn't enjoy blowing her brains out all over the Hollywood Canteen."

"We've got to do something," Jack Benny said. "We can't just let this bastard get away. We've got to stop him."

Tom took a tentative step toward Vance and Maggie but stopped short when he heard the distinctive click as Vance cocked the trigger.

He'd rescued Maggie three times in the last few weeks, but the way things looked, he wouldn't be able to manage a fourth. As long as Vance held the gun to Maggie's head, the show was all his.

Meanwhile, a bunch of men in the audience, soldiers, sailors and marines, started to rush the stage. Some of them had been in combat and looked it. It was apparent that if they got their hands on Vance, they'd rip him from limb to limb. Vance's eyes widened as he tightened his grip on Maggie and half dragged her with him. He moved to the stage door which was directly behind him. He was almost to the door and was clearly beginning to panic.

"I'll kill her," he screamed, his free hand fumbling for the door knob and finally getting the door open. "Stand back or I swear I'll pull the trigger."

The voice that came from behind Vance was both calm and direct, carrying with it an air of authority.

"You won't kill anybody, Vance," Emerson Waldie said. "Now put down that gun."

Okay, some Waldie impersonator trying to trick him, Vance thought, but when he turned his head for that split second, he knew it was no trick. It was really him. Really Waldie. Back from the dead.

Waldie had just been released from jail after spending twenty-four hours there for disturbing the peace. Leaving the station house in Hollywood where he'd been incarcerated, Waldie had been walking past the canteen and thought there would be some people there who might know him and help him prove that he really was Emerson Waldie.

The attendants at the front of the canteen had denied him entry and so he'd gone around to the stage door, a door he'd often gone through as one of the directors of the organization. Which is when he came into contact with, of all people, Vance Varley, backing out of the canteen with a gun aimed at the head of Maggie Graym. It must have been Vance's jealousy of

Maggie's popularity that had driven him over the edge, Waldie thought.

Dressed as he was in the ghoulish tux and with the white powder still clinging to his face in spots, Waldie looked as if he had, indeed, just returned from the dead. He put a hand out toward Vance for the gun.

"Stay away from me," Vance shrieked, seemingly unhinged at the sight of Waldie. He let go of Maggie and also of the gun which went clattering on the floor.

The servicemen who'd been advancing toward Vance now grabbed him as Waldie stepped through the door. Spotting Morrie Goldstrohm, he started to walk toward him as Morrie started inching away.

"Morrie," Waldie said.

"No...no," Morrie said, cringing at the sight of Waldie, the man whose heart attack he'd purposely caused.

It now appeared as if he was having one of his own. He collapsed in a heap as Waldie reached him.

"Oh, dear God," Jack Benny said as Emerson Waldie stood amongst them on the stage. "The guy's been thrown out of hell. They didn't want him, either."

Part II

Chapter 1

Jimmy's Tropical Bar and Grill had miraculously missed the wrecker's ball that had shattered almost every other building near it.

Only Jimmy's wasn't Jimmy's anymore. The little Greek had died in 1955, and there was no one to take over the running of this eating and drinking establishment that had become legendary amongst Hollywood's behind-the-scenes workers. Since the demise of Jimmy's, the premises had become a French restaurant which failed, a Laundromat which failed, a record store which failed, a beauty salon, bakery, hardware store, dry-cleaner, all of which had failed, and finally a cocktail bar which had somehow succeeded. Entering the dimly lit interior of the lounge, appropriately called La Nuite, the Japanese/American gentleman was shown a table off to the side.

He looked about 70 or 75, but was very well groomed with graying hair swept back off a high forehead. He wore an extremely well-tailored blue suit with a pearl-gray tie.

The bar waitress came over to take his order, but he told her he was waiting for someone and would order when his friend arrived which, he thought, would be any minute now.

Douglas Tanaka had aged very well. And he'd done very well in his business as a building contractor. Over the years he'd built up such a big company in the construction trade that he'd retired at fifty to his Toluca Lake estate, just down the road from Bob Hope's. That had been twenty-three years before, and as for his so-called retirement, his devoted wife, Minnie, often laughed at the word when used in reference to Douglas. He'd done the Japanese/American community a great service by heading various committees dealing with such issues as reparation for Americans incarcerated by their own countrymen during the war.

He now sat at the table thinking back to those days so many years before when he'd escaped from the evacuation bus heading him to Manzanar.

He recalled how the friend he'd made, Tom Driscoll, had helped him in the early days and weeks of his escape and afterwards, how he'd helped him reach the midwest where there wasn't a movement to put all people of Japanese ancestry into concentration camps.

The war had changed Douglas forever. Embittered at the beginning of it due to the loss of his and his family's way of life, he eventually reconciled himself to the way things had turned out. He had even entered the army, the famed 442, back in 1944, and had not only served his country with distinction, but had been decorated with the silver star.

After his discharge from the army in '46, Douglas had returned home to Los Angeles to reclaim what he could for himself and his parents. There hadn't been very much to reclaim. The house had been lost. There were now people living in it who'd bought it from the bank. And nobody in those days was investigating how banks had appropriated such property. Realizing it was futile to try and retrieve anything from their old life, Douglas helped his parents and brothers and sisters settle into a new one. They'd rented a rundown farm outside the city where they at first grew carnations and, later, a variety of flowers. In time, the family was on its feet again. With the profits from the business, they bought large tracts of forest land and built up what turned out to be one of the largest housing developments in the county.

It would have been nice had Tom Driscoll been able to see the results of all the hard work Douglas and his family had put into the business. He wished he could see Tom again and talk to him, like in the old times. But, of course, that was impossible.

Douglas looked at his watch and realized he'd arrived at this place more than twenty minutes early, so excited was he by the prospect of this appointment.

His life and world had been so far removed from his experiences of those long-ago years, that when the call came, he was greatly surprised. He couldn't wait for his reunion with this wonderful old friend: Maggie Graym.

She had been just as helpful to Douglas as Tom had been, willing always to assist him in any way she could. But what had always stood out in Douglas' memory was the way she'd been so concerned for, and supportive of, Japanese/Americans in their darkest hours. Douglas could still remember the strong public statement she'd made, right at the height of the war, in the interests of those that had been incarcerated. This act had definitely tarnished her career in pictures. And now she was entering the room, being shown to his table by a waiter who, judging by his youth, probably had no idea that this lady had once been the most famous in the country.

"Douglas," Maggie Graym said, rushing forth and giving him a big hug.

"I've waited more than half a century for this," she continued. "It's been on my mind all these years to give you a call and I finally couldn't wait any longer."

"I'm very glad to see you again," Douglas replied. The woman who stood before him had aged, that was for sure. No longer was there the long red hair and the perfect figure. She was now handsomely gray and wore a flowing dress to hide the shape that had filled out.

But the legs were just the same. Maggie sat down opposite Douglas and crossed her knees. They were still as shapely and beautiful as they had ever been. Some things never changed, and Douglas was glad this symbol of her beauty remained.

He also noticed some of the men drinking at the bar. They were mostly from an older generation and who could tell? Perhaps they'd come here, during World War II, when the place belonged to Jimmy the Greek.

Douglas wondered what they'd say if they knew Maggie Graym was sitting just a few feet away from them.

Maggie had been retired from movies since early '45 when Emerson Waldie, another Hollywood legend, had finally found a replacement for her. Or so he thought. The new actress had lasted only a year or two. Maggie, on leaving Grove, had been offered work by other studios, but by then the silly, contrived musicals she'd become famous for had ceased to make money and so had her brand of good-looking redhead. Instead of trying to push herself onto a movie-going public that preferred Ava Gardner, she graciously retired from movies to marry and have kids.

Emerson Waldie had tried to get her back for a picture in 1947 in order to revive a failing studio. She couldn't do it, however, because she was now totally involved in raising the twins and was still trying to accept the death of her husband, two years prior, just before the end of the war.

"It's funny," she said to Douglas, "but I still miss Tom. It's been so many years since he was killed and I still think of him every day."

Tom, who'd been kept out of the war for the first three years of it, had finally persuaded the Navy to let him join. He couldn't believe it when they'd said yes. This had been one of the happiest moments in his life. And one of the hardest because he was leaving Maggie.

"Maybe if he'd known I was pregnant, he wouldn't have joined up," Maggie said. "But I didn't even know until he was away for a month." It was off Iwo Jima that Tom's ship came under constant Kamikaze attack. Tom, a seaman first class, had displayed incredible courage, first manning the guns and downing three suicide planes, and then when the ship was badly crippled risking his life by carrying or dragging injured shipmates to comparative safety. It was during one of the rescue attempts that the section Tom was working in received a direct hit killing everybody outright.

"We weren't married very long before he went overseas," Maggie said. "Just about two and a half years. I never thought that I'd wind up marrying this guy. Couldn't even stand him at first, but fate kept throwing us together. Well, I don't have to tell you about that because you were there to witness all that stuff about the sabotage ring here in Hollywood."

Douglas sat listening to Maggie, letting her tell her story about Tom. And it was true that she didn't have to go into the sabotage ring stuff. He remembered very clearly that night back in 1942 when Tom and he had saved Maggie's life on that winding road by rolling the big limo into the path of the abductor's car. And how, after Maggie had been saved, Tom had pushed him away into the darkness of the night before the crowd of angry residents had descended upon them. There, Douglas waited until Tom could return for him. Which he did just hours later, picking him up and delivering him to Maggie's house in Malibu as originally planned. And it was there that both Tom and Maggie had kept him safe until Tom could find a way to get him to the midwest.

This he did through an organization called the 'Underground Group'. These were men and women who operated very quietly, helping various people, many times Japanese/Americans who'd been victimized by the United States Government.

With the help of this group, Douglas was relocated to Akron, Ohio where he had relatives.

He hadn't seen Maggie since. He'd contacted her by phone after the war when he'd learned of Tom's death. And they'd kept in touch very sporadically, always planning to meet.

"I guess you could say I miss Tom, too," Douglas said, taking a sip from his glass. "He was the best friend I ever had. But I firmly believe he did what he had to do, getting into the fighting. He wanted to be part of it."

"That's the kind of thing people did back then," Maggie agreed. "But then again, it was that kind of war, wasn't it? We all did our bit."

For a few moments, neither Maggie nor Douglas spoke,

each thinking back to that time.

"I'd remarried a few times since Tom died," Maggie said. "The first guy after Tom was a disaster. You probably read in the newspaper how he embezzled most of my money. It was awful. But my next husband was a wonderful man. His name was Kirk Sinclair, a producer. Made quite a name for himself in the film business. And speaking of names, do you know what he told me on our wedding night? That his real name was Gerhardt Vanderschloffer. Isn't that amazing? Anyway, we had a beautiful marriage until he died four years ago. Now I just enjoy living at the house in Malibu doing my own thing, gardening, reading a little. It's a far cry from the hectic studio routine at Grove. The head of it, Emerson Waldie had me making one picture after another. Good old Emerson. Did you know he went on to live until he was one hundred and four! Only died last year!"

Maggie and Douglas reminisced for another few minutes and then Douglas noticed a young man enter the bar. He couldn't actually see the man very well as he stood silhouetted in the semi-darkness of the place, but it was obvious that he was looking for someone.

"Over here, Tom," Maggie suddenly waved.

For a moment Douglas felt as if his heart was stopping. The young man walking toward him was Tom Driscoll. It couldn't be but it was. Douglas thought he might be hallucinating.

"Douglas," Maggie said, "I want you to meet my grandson, Tom Street, my daughter Rosemary's boy. He's delivered me here in his pride and joy, a '65 Mustang, and now he's ready to take his old granny home. I just hate driving these days in all this crazy Los Angeles traffic."

Douglas stood slowly and shook hands with the young man, this duplicate Tom Driscoll. He was of the same height and build as his late grandfather and had the same black hair and blue eyes.

"I've heard all about you, Mr. Tanaka," Tom Street said. He was about twenty or twenty-one and wore a UCLA T-shirt which indicated that he might be a student there.

Douglas watched as Tom wrapped an arm around his grandmother's shoulders and planted a kiss on her cheek. "No doubt my pinup girl here's been talking your ear off," he continued with a huge grin. Tom Driscoll's grin.

"Just going over old times," Douglas said, wanting suddenly to know young Tom Street, the grandson of Tom Driscoll. He couldn't help but feel that Tom Driscoll himself had somehow managed to join Maggie and him through the young Tom, and it seemed very appropriate that their reunion had been at this location which had once been Tom's favorite hangout.

"Those days must have been something else," Tom Street said, extending a hand for Douglas to shake goodbye. "I'm always hearing stories from Granny about old Hollywood and the way things were. Ready to go, Granny? I've got football practice in a few hours."

"I'm ready," Maggie said in a way that elderly people sometimes speak when a person from a younger generation has done them a favor which they don't want to abuse.

Getting up, she took a few steps over to Douglas and gave him a warm hug and kiss.

"Don't be a stranger," she said to him. "I'm only down the road, you know where. Come and have lunch with me and bring your family. I'd love to meet them."

"I'd like that," Douglas said, knowing, as did she, that they would never meet again. That having this drink today was just a way of completing something. A trust or bond that was just there. Permanently. Forever. And then he watched her as she and her grandson maneuvered their way around the tables, already engaged in a conversation about Tom's classes and someone called Alison, probably Tom's girl.

Douglas sat back down at the table and, while finishing his drink, thought about the beautiful young woman who'd come into his life many years before with the red hair piled high on top of her head and her winning smile.

Her smile was still the same. And as she was escorted by young Tom past the bar toward the exit she, for some reason, flashed that smile at a guy sitting there, a guy about her own vintage, and then she was out the door and gone from sight.

Douglas watched the old codger for a moment. He seemed to be deep in thought regarding the fabulous smile he'd just received and the person delivering it.

And then he said to the bartender: "Hey, that was Maggie Graym you just had in here!"

The End

About
the author

Charles Rubin, author of the hilarious novel, *Hard Sell*, has always wanted to write about Hollywood as well as the Second World War. With his novel, *4-F Blues*, he was able to combine both subjects.

Born and raised in New York City, Charles attended an arts and drama high school. After a stint in the U.S. Marine Corps, he attended Columbia University, worked as a stevedore on the New York docks, and as a gofer at CBS. He then chose a career in advertising, becoming a top, Clio Award-winning writer/producer and creative director in New York, Boston, London, and San Francisco.

Charles has also written for TV sitcoms in the U.S. and England. A venture into the world of nonfiction produced a book that has greatly helped parents, the controversial: *Don't Let Your kids Kill You: A Guide For Parents of Drug and Alcohol Addicted Children*.

Still involved in the ad business, as the head of Rubin Advertising, some of Charles' clients include Apple Computers and Levi Strauss. His headlines include *For people who can't stand self-indulgence in others, but often forgive it in themselves* for Piper Heidseick Champagne, and *Reserve The Edge of Your Seats* for San Francisco Opera.

Charles and his wife, Betty Bethards, author of the internationally acclaimed bestseller, *The Dream Book*, live in Sonoma County, just north of San Francisco. Between them, they have four sons and one daughter.

Currently, Charles is working on a mystery novel that takes place in London, and involves the late Princess Diana.

About
the designer

Often, a book designer is relegated to the shadows after a book is published. But this is not the case during the time when the book is in production. It is then that an enormous amount of work goes into the actual design and layout of both the cover and the pages.

Those of us at NewCentury Publishers feel very fortunate that *4-F Blues* was in the very capable hands of designer Estera Alvarez.

Estera is not only an expert in the field of typography, but she is addicted to it. Her instinctive talent for creating the readable page is something appreciated by her many clients in the publishing and advertising worlds.

A native of Poland, her quality style and quick eye stem from ten years as an art director in both Europe and America. This experience has now expanded into the area of book design. Her list of awards is long and impressive.

Estera lives in Berkeley, California with her Emmy Award-winning, musician husband, Dan, and their daughter, Debora.

Not wishing to keep Estera a secret, her email address is: danseq@slip.net.

About the heros and heroines

Alfred S. Los Banos, U.S. Army. Alfred fought bravely in the Philippines during WWII. But it was in the Korean War that he received injuries that led to the loss of both his legs. Never one to let a handicap pull him down, Alfred, a native of Honolulu, spent his last years campaigning for veterans' rights. A project close to his heart was the construction of the WWII Memorial in Washington, D.C. His wife, Carol Los Banos, carries on his work.

Kenny Ruth, U.S. Navy. Originally from Ohio, Kenny was stationed at the Brooklyn Navy Yard in the early part of the war. It was in the New York City area that the fun-loving, gregarious Kenny was "adopted" by the author's family. Many a Sunday would find him at their house, but there came a Sunday in 1943 when he didn't arrive. After a few weeks of not seeing Kenny, the family investigated and discovered that Kenny had been shipped out without warning. It wasn't long after that Kenny's name was listed as a casualty in the Pacific.

Don Schneider, U.S. Army. Don had just graduated from Columbia University in New York City when he was drafted and sent to fight in Europe. He was a very popular young man who planned on going to law school after the war. But at barely twenty-two years old, he was killed in action. Among those he left behind was his fiancee, Babette. Many of his friends learned of Don's death in a painful way: the letters they had sent him in Europe were returned and stamped "Deceased." Don is buried in the American Cemetery in Normandy.

Frances Langford, singer, actress and entertainer. Frances, a regular with the USO during the war years, traveled to various battle zones in the Pacific and in Europe, almost always with Bob Hope. And while Hope has been lauded for his great genius and ability to bring a bit of America to the boys, Frances has yet to be fully recognized for her equally selfless and courageous efforts. Having sung her famous ballads in areas where, on more than a few occasions she almost became a casualty herself, this is a good opportunity to applaud Frances now.

Doris Miller, U.S. Navy. As a black man, Doris couldn't attain rank higher than that of mess attendant. But that didn't stop him from becoming a hero. Aboard the U.S. S. West Virginia during the raid on Pearl Harbor, Doris helped carry the injured to safety before grabbing an idle machine gun and blasting away at enemy planes. For this he was awarded the Navy Cross. Doris Miller was killed in action in 1944 when his ship was torpedoed in the South Pacific.

Jerry Blank, U.S. Marine Corp. Jerry joined the Marines in October, 1943. After training in the Hawai'ian Islands, he fought in Okinawa. Following this, he participated in disarming the enemy in North China. Recently, an American flag honoring Jerry was flown over Washington, D.C. in recognition of his war record. Today, Jerry operates, with his wife, Pearl, Paragon Sporting Goods in Manhattan, an establishment begun by his father in 1908.

Hattie M. Stone, Norma Edwards, and Rita Jacobsen, WAVES. All young women at the time of WWII, they joined the WAVES where they took on a variety of duties, from radio operator to warehouse superintendent. Today, Hattie proudly marches in local Veterans Day parades while Rita flashes her WAVE '42 license plate around town. Norma, equally proud of her WAVE days splits the year between Montana and Arizona. All three still fit into their WAVE uniforms.

Howard K. Petschel, U.S. Army Air Corps. Howard, a second lieutenant, helped evacuate endangered citizens of Java to Australia. On March 3, 1942, while ferrying the injured to hospitals near Broome, Australia, his plane was shot down. Just 23 years old at the time of his death, Howard has never been forgotten by his wife, Kathleen, his son, Howard, Jr., or his sisters and brother.

Cheryl Walker, actress. Originally a stuntwoman for such stars as Veronica Lake, Cheryl was making a sagebrush western on location when she was summoned to United Artists for the part of Eileen in *Stage Door Canteen*. Excited, she got back to Hollywood as fast as she could, the only available seat being on the back of a truck. As Eileen, Cheryl's performance spoke volumes for the many wives and sweethearts left behind during WWII. She died in 1971.

Earl Holger Sorensen, U.S. Navy. Earl was one of the 1,002 naval personnel who lost their lives on the U.S.S. Arizona, December 7, 1941. Little is known about Earl. It appears his family in Nebraska is gone also. On the 50th anniversary of the attack on Pearl Harbor, the names of those killed on the Arizona were attached to leis to be thrown into the waters off Pearl. Earl's name was attached to the lei chosen by the author of this book.

The U.S.S. Arizona Navy Band. Too many names to mention, the entire band was lost on the Arizona, December 7, 1941. Just the night before the attack, these musicians participated in the Battle of the Bands. The U.S.S. Pennsylvania won the contest, but because the musicians of the Arizona played so well, they were given permission to "sleep in" on the morning of December 7th. It was a sleep from which they would never awaken.